I0676616

This is a work of fiction. The author has invented the characters solely for the reader's entertainment.

Copyright © 2012 by Brenda Frances.

Publishing Company a G.R. Carl and Brenda Hardson Company
8306 Wilshire Blvd, Suite 202
Beverly Hills California 90211

inhouseprods@yahoo.com
Consulting: G.R. Carl

Published by IN-House Productions March 2012

Printed in the United States.

Chapter 1

Like so many millions of Americans, I was born on the welfare rolls, and raised a low-income recipient. We lived so far beneath the poverty line that the Census Takers never so much as gave a passing glance at my mother's apartment door, let alone stopped to count the family inside.

My mother, Teresa Barber was known as Yorkie (a simple nickname that came out of her New Yorker state of mind). Early on, Yorkie fell into a bad habit of settling for "no account men". Handicapped by those choices, resulted in five baby daddies and six children. They were four girls and two boys-- all born stair-steps behind each other. It's a wonder if Yorkie's poor pussy ever had time to mend.

Most late nights, I would often worry about Yorkie. I'd worry about her making it home before dawn, because I knew that that's when the dope fiends and the crack monsters plagued the streets in search of their next hit. Not even the Devil was safe being amongst them!

I worried because I knew that my mother would be making her way back home, pussy packed tight with earnings from having checked the traps of those who were her regular tricks. Yorkie could have minimized her risk of being jacked if she'd had a pimp or ho'ed for one of the madams; but the outlaw hoe and independent bitch that she was, just wouldn't allow her to break herself to no pimp, nor cut up her bread with some boss-bitch in the name of protection especially when she could just as soon cut a trick, kill another hoe and post her own bail if she got busted. What made the most sense to Yorkie was that she had cubs to feed that needed clothes and a roof over their heads, so fuck breaking bread with anyone but her own.

As Yorkie's first born most of the house work and looking after the kids fell on me; but I never once complained about doing my part, nor gave thought to knocking my mom's hustle in the name of survival. I was even sympathetic to Yorkie for all the nickel slick, fast talking busters she brought home thinking she'd finally found the one. I felt that my mother honestly believed that out those losers she'd crown her king, and the tricks she tossed up would be the family's ticket out of the ghetto, and onto the good life.

Yorkie only learned the hard way; while ho' money, was fa sho' money, it was slow money, and never enough money. So with that, the family's ticket out the ghetto would never come flat on her back, or down on her knees, because every time Yorkie would get ahead, some bill would come along and set her back further than where she'd started.

Yorkie had reached an all-time low. She just couldn't do it anymore. She felt that there was just no future in New York for her family.

One evening, Yorkie received a call from Mac Anthony, a true friend. Mac had grown up with Yorkie in the same Brooklyn borough, just a rock's throw from the Brooklyn Bridge.

Mac had long broke wide from Brooklyn over to the West Coast, where he went into business for himself.

He invited us to move out to Los Angeles he told Yorkie that he would help her find a job, and how California's welfare system paid more than any other state. Yorkie's spirit seemed to lift overnight. Shortly thereafter; Mac wired her some money through Western Union to cover the cost of moving. By the week's end, movers had picked up the few possessions we owned and off we went on a Greyhound bus bound for South Central Los Angeles.

That was 1993; I was just an eleven year old, skinny,dusty-hair-color girl. My brown eyes, light skin, and disarming charm came with a sharp tongue. I was fearless, and even as a kid, I viewed life with a "nothing to lose and everything to gain" mind-set. My siblings were everything to me, and there was nothing in the world that I wouldn't do to keep them all together. They were well fed and their old second-hand, hand-me-downs cleaned and pressed. Yorkie would often say to me about her kids, "I brought em' into the world Sessie girl, but you been mo' momma to 'em, than I ever had time to be, and I love you fo' that".

No sooner than my family was settled in California, I got a job at Mac & Hughes Liquor Store on the corner of 24th Street and Central Avenue, stocking the shelves, sweeping and dusting. Mac was very kind to me. The first father figure I'd ever known that really wanted me to do something positive with my life.

Mac would encourage from behind the register while I was standing several aisles away dusting canned goods. "Hey Sessie-Gal, I want you to be better to Ya'self than those ho's you see out there on the corner up and down Central Avenue. You're very beautiful, and naturally smart. Of course now just simply put, why you can go plenty far in this big old world with them book smarts you got going baby girl, if only you stick to applying em." Mac was always lacing me in a "straight shot, no chaser" kind of way. Like a father would his son. And he'd always kill game with, "whatever you do with ya'self in this life, never ever let no man abuse and misuse you or take away what God blessed you with."

I had nothing but praise for Mac's raw brute honesty as a man, while I held nothing but contempt for his business partner Mario Hughes. I found no earthly good in him, and thought of him as a rotten jerk and a cock-hound pervert. That sleazy bastard's mind was always looking to lure the bird-brain hoe's on Central Avenue out of their panties before they realized that he had played them, laid them, and never intended on paying them for their services. But a broad didn't have to be a bird brained hoe to fall victim to Hughes. Hell his motto was, "fourteen to eighty, cockeyed, blind, cripple or crazy, sloppy fat and outright nasty, as long as the pussy got warm and wet, the female was a candidate for getting it ran to the nuts."

One day while sweeping the store floor, Hughes came up behind me and grabbed one side of my butt cheek with his fingers gripping in the crack of my ass. "What the fuck is wrong with you, you damn asshole" I shouted at him.

"What the fuck is wrong with yo' tight-ass? You know you like that," Hughes replied with a shit-eating grin smeared across his face. He sucked his teeth while staring at me as if I was a steak dinner.

"I'ma tell Mac what you did and he's gonna fuck you up you punk ass nigga."

Hughes turned and looked at me raising his eye-brows saying, "Tell him! Mac don't give a flyin' fuck about yo' hot ass. Hell he's just savin' you fo' himself. Shit he don't run nothing round here but his mouth any damn way." He stated as a matter of fact.

The fact that Hughes would dare say something like this about Mac, only served to piss me off more. My love for Mac gave me courage to stand up to this scandalous loser. "You's a damn liar and you ain't got a drop a truth in ya' black ass. Mac ain't a dog like you!" I said it with so much rage that I could hardly hear my own voice through its sudden hoarseness.

I visualized just where and how I would whack Hughes with the broom stick if he touched me again. I pictured myself in slow motion, taking a step back and catching him across his nose with the first blow of the broom, and then ramming its handle tip into his nuts with all my might and running like hell was after me.

Hughes was no fool, he could feel that my little ass might be dangerous and I wasn't about to be hooked or crooked out my panties. Naw, he figured he'd just lie back in the cut on busting a nut, till he figured out a better way to play it.

He folded his arms across his chest and leaned back against one of the aisle shelves. "Tell that chump-ass Mac if you want to. If he got an issue with me hittin before he get it, I'll shoot his ass and then yo' lil foul mouth you damn rodent," Hughes said with anger in his voice.

Chapter 2

Mac opened the store the following morning to no sign of me and that alone was unusual because I was never late or absent.

He then called Yorkie, who found me in my room seated on the bed painting my toenails, with the sound of my Walkman turned up so loud she could clearly hear the force of Janet Jackson's *"Rhythm Nation"* spilling out of the headphones.

"Mac just called, and wanted to know why you ain't showed for work Sessie?" Yorkie ask.

I never so much as glanced up at her, who in turn pulled the headphones from my head. "You heard what I said girl?"

"Fuck that store." I said in a sassy disrespectful way.

"Hey now! you better watch yo' mouth!" Yorkie snapped in a commanding tone of respect, that only a mother could muster in her child when demanding as much without saying.
No stranger to the tone, I took that cue and checked myself and gave Yorkie my full attention.

"Now you wanna tell me what the hell is going on? am I gonna have to put two and two together myself before shit starts addin' up?"

I told Yorkie what Hughes had done to me and what he said about Mac and me.

"Is that so?" Yorkie said as she folded her arms across her chest, momentarily gazing off.

I knew that look all too well and knew Yorkie was planning to get in somebody's ass. She turned back to me after a moment, "I got this. You chill-out till I get back."

It was noonday when Yorkie returned home high spirited with bags of groceries in her arms. I prepared a lunch of canned pork and beans with wieners cut in them. That was a favorite in our house for lunch or dinner. Yorkie told me how she blew Hughes foul shit by Mac. As soon as Hughes came into work late that morning, Mac threw the closed sign on the door and commenced to kicking off in Hughes's ass with both feet.

She described how Mac had sucker punched Hughes "Girl his jaw breaking made me think back when I was a little girl, and my mother would be snapping fresh stringed beans for dinner." Then she went on telling me how Hughes howled for forgiveness like a dog does when he hears a fire-truck with its sirens on. Both of us laughed till we cried.

Being that it was the last day of summer, Mac had me take that whole day off to just prepare myself for school. That next day, I brought my new after school schedule into work with me.

I had saved enough money over the summer session to buy new clothes for myself and a few things for my brothers and sisters. We all stepped off to school feeling brand new for the first time in our lives.

After the first day of school, I rushed home, changed my school clothes and hurried off to work. With my mind absent of any of the drama that jumped off the day before, I went on with doing my job until I saw Hughes standing behind the cashier's counter, his broken jaw wired shut. I couldn't even make out his mumbled words in the conversation he was having with a female customer, as he handed her a pack of cigarettes.

"Hey Sessie-Gal!" Mac called from the open doorway to the main back storeroom where he quietly stood watching over me. I hadn't noticed Mac until that moment he grinned at me and waved me over to him. I could feel Hughes eyeing me through the dark sunglasses that hid his black eye when I crossed the floor and went into the storeroom with Mac.

"Babygirl, you ain't gone be havin' no more issues with Hughes, ya hear?" Mac said. "He and I done reached an understanding the way men sometimes have to do. So you go on and get working on balancing them books for ya Uncle Mac Daddy." Mac said with a grin. Mac always had this way about him that made me light up when he grinned like that, and I'd give him what he called a big O' Colgate tooth-paste smile. That was all I could do as I strolled off to the manager's office.

At day's end, I had all the books in order for Mac and was ready to go home. Hughes never looked in my direction and that was fine by me.

When I got home that evening, Yorkie told me that she had gotten a call from the school. They said I had tested too high to continue at grammar school. So at the top of the following week, the school board had advanced me to Junior High school.

Monday morning, I headed off to the new school—Thomas Edison Junior High. That's where I met Debra Bovaise, who insisted I call her Deb. She just knew that she was the shit; thirteen years old going on thirty. She took me under her wing and laced me on fashion, how boys move and how I should move when it came to them. She taught me how to get them to do anything I wanted them to without giving them any more than a conversation for it. She called herself the Queen Mack in the game and charging and discarding chumps was her claim to fame. I once watched Deb stick her tongue in a boy's ear, while she rifled her hands through all his pockets and picked them for anything of value before he could catch his breath and realize that she was long gone with whatever chump change he owned.

Deb had an after-school job working at Cheap Charlie's; a nickel and dime store not far from Mac and Hughes, owned by an old Jewish man everyone called Charlie. Deb was always coming to school dressed in the latest fashions. Charlie kept her suited and booted; perks of the job that came out of sitting on Charlie's lap and listening to his problem. To be so young, Deb was very experienced in life; she was what adults called fast-assed; too fast for her own good.

After working several low paying temporary jobs, Yorkie landed a permanent job working for the County USC Medical Center also known as General Hospital. It's where I first learned about a job with benefits.

"They ain't got a dental plan, but I got us all full medical coverage and Mac done put me down on how we can keep our food stamps and still collect the welfare checks at the same time," Yorkie told me after dinner one night as I washed the dishes while she dried them.

"But Mama, won't they put us in jail for that?" Yorkie looked at me with that now I know that you know better than what you asking me expression she gives whenever she's about to put me up on game.

"Huh girl, the catchin' always got to come before the hangin', and chances of that are slim to none... child Mama got this, you just keep the game under yo' hat if them folks from downtown come snoopin' around with they sneaky asses tryin' to catch us slippin', you tell them little ones to look at em' like they crazy, while you hit em' with, our Mama's po' as Job's turkey from the Bible".

I laid in bed that night thinking about everything Yorkie had taught me about a job with benefits, and I knew as I one day would have me one.

Deb on the other hand was getting her benefits from a job any way she could. She and I were tight all through junior high and high school, and when we were not working, we were hanging out together. I never saw Deb broke; but she always played broke. The girl was a jack of all sorts of felonious street hustles; bitch had more slick moves for your ass than a box of Ex-lax. She was heavily into pick-pocketing people. She would clip broad's wallets out of their purses while it hung on their shoulder. I don't know who taught Deb this shit but she was at the top of the game for sure, even in shooting the pea game, shootin' craps and Three Card Molly.

She would say, "Sessie, peep game girl, I'm uh do the talking; while you collect the cabbage with a smile". I loved watching Deb work the Three Card Molly con at school, we always set up shop beneath a large tree that sat in one corner of the lunch patio; with branches that hung over one of the furthest tables out of view of any faculty member looking to peep game and snitch us off. She would take three brand new cards from a freshly opened deck in front of the victims, and fold them the long way down the center, so that they would stand up on the table like the roofs of houses. Two black queens and a red queen, all standing open ended beside one another. "The trap to this game is that people are always looking for some free shit Sessie; whatever it is government cheese, powdered milk so long as it's free, people want it Sessie, Somethin' fo' nothin' will trap you every time." Deb always set the game off letting the victims win every hand, until the crowd grew so large that the victims were all jockeying to place a bet.

"We ain't got much time; win your lunch money on me. It's your moment to shine on my dime have faith in what Ya' eyes say they see. Pick uh card it ain't hard, in the Gypsy twist where the red you win, and the black you miss." Deb would say in a poetic flow.

She never stopped talking in that flow, while her hands seemed to move in time with her words as she moved the cards with her finger-tips, over and under one another, from left to right and back again, repeating the motion again and again until all of the suckers were spellbound by her hocus-pocus bullshit and magician's sleight of a hand. When the cards dropped on the table, Deb would slap her hands and rub her palms together as if releasing them from her spell, the money would fall before each of the cards.

"Everybody is a winner!" Deb would shout. And everyone was a winner; but none a bigger winner than Deb and I, because we won one hand with every bet. The dealer always pockets the winnings from one of the three hands played, while paying the winner of the second hand from the money generated by the third hand… Deb and I never knew a broke day in school.

Shortly after high school graduation, I reluctantly told Mac that I was looking to interview for a new job over the summer, that I had heard about in school –the job was located in the deep end of my East-side Los Angeles ghetto neighborhood, called the Low-Bottoms, turned out that Mac knew the owner. Benzo Green, and with Mac's blessing he set up an interview for me.

"Now you know that if thang's don't work out for you over at Benzo's joint for any reason at all, you always got a job here," Mac said to me as he hung up the phone with Benzo Green.

Mac put on a straight face but I could tell that he wasn't feeling my leaving. I hugged Mac, and told him I'd drop in to help him out whenever he needed me and we both knew we'd see one another regularly.

Chapter 3

The following morning on the first day of summer, I rode the Compton Avenue city bus into the heart of my Low-Bottom neighborhood. From a bus window, I could see a crowd of people beginning to form near the corner of 55th Street and Compton Avenue. At first I thought that something bad had happened, as the bus came closer to my stop, I realized that all of the people where customers at Super Fry, the Burger Pushers burger stand, and it wasn't even 10 o' clock in the morning yet. I got off the bus at the corner of 55th street. The scent of hamburgers filled the air. The sound of DeBarge's hit song "I *Call Your Name"* was blowing out the little sidewalk front hamburger-stand. It was no larger than my Mama's small kitchen in her apartment.

The fancy cars parked along both sides of Compton Avenue stood out for the first time as I walked towards the hamburger-stand. They were mostly Cadillac's, each clean enough that you could eat off their hoods, with polished rims sparkling in the sunlight.

As I made my way through the crowd of the somebodies that were from all walks of life, who made up the energetic clientele, I was charged up by the time I made it to the side-door entrance. I could see through the open top half of the double door, that a large grill took up most of the room inside and was covered by sizzling hamburgers with grilled onions on one side of it, and toasting buns on the other side.

The three women who worked inside weren't much older than me, and I noted right off that each was a different shade of black, beautiful, sophistication, and well-dressed under their aprons in the spotless little place. They all worked non-stop; one on the cash register, another on the grill and the third dressing the buns, wrapping and bagging the finished burgers. I loved the rhythm the women moved in as they worked.

"Excuse me," I said. "My name is Sessie Jones and I'm supposed to meet Mr. Benzo Green for a --," was all I got out of my mouth before the woman on the cash register opened the doors bottom half, while one of the women on the grill beckoned for me to step inside. I shut the door behind me.

"Benzo told us you were coming. So, can you chew gum, work this grill, count money, take orders and kick game with the clientele all at the same time?" the woman flipping the burgers asked. I stood off to one side behind her, while she watched me through a small mirror that hung above the grill.

I took a moment to think about what she asked me. I cut my eyes over at all the people standing on the sidewalk front who were in ear shot, and I knew they were waiting to hear my answer. "Yeah, I can handle that."

"Then watcha holding up the wall for girl," said the woman who was dressing the buns, a chipper voice that immediately relaxed the tension and caused everyone within ear- shot to erupt in laughter.

I fell right into the program, and the women taught me everything. Before I realized it, I was moving around inside the small space in rhythm with the other three women, who had all totally embraced me. I was conversing with the customers outside and enjoying every minute of it.

By the time Benzo Green arrived that evening; I hadn't taken a lunch break. I wasn't even aware that eight whole hours had passed. Benzo Green parked his brand new Cadillac out in front of his place of business. He stepped out looking every bit of the player of the year heavy in the game, as he did the owner of a legitimate successful business. He was in his mid-thirties, and took obvious care of himself: permed hair, clean shaven except for his mustache. He wore gold rim sunglasses and I could tell he spent lots of time in the gym.

"Clean, ain't he?" AB, said to me. She was the women working the cash register. I had learned all of their names by this time; Lexie was working the grill, and Shae was the burger bagger.

"Clean as the board of health," Came my response. He wore five hundred dollar snake skin shoes, designer jeans with a matching snake skin belt. His silk shirt was unbuttoned at the collar halfway down his bird-chest; a gold lion head medallion on a gold rope chain draped from his neck with diamond stone eyes. A large diamond stud sparkled in one of his pierced ear along with his whole swagger walk and manners, said to all, that he was the shit, as he stepped into the small space.

"You got to be Mac's niece, Sessie-girl?" Benzo said as he stuck one of his hands out to shake mines. I immediately noticed how soft his hands felt, and the way he studied me.

"Nice to meet you Mr. Green," I responded.

"Me and Mac go back to when he first came out here from the big Apple. We both was out in the street back then," Benzo said in reflection. "Anyway, he told me you were family and on the strength of that, I got a full time spot here for you. That is if you want it?" Benzo said questioningly.

"Yes, I want it."

"Well here's what it is. I'm gone separate yours from mine every time it comes to bread breaking. All I ask for is eight hour work days a week. Starting salary is one hundred five dollars a week flat-rate. You work out your own schedule with your co-workers, meaning get in where you fit in."

He paused to be certain that I heard and understood everything that he had blown by me so far, and when I nodded that I understood him, he stepped right back into the suave matter of fact tone that he spoke in. "If ya in school; are have plans on attending school, that ain't a problem, like I say just manage your schedule so that it don't clash with my pursuit of cash, cause if you fall off you gone get laid off; nothing personal, just business. All the overtime you won't is yours for the taken."

Benzo Green went on to tell me how the customers are always right when it comes to the food, and how just smiling and being pleasant with the clientele will pass the day. Listening to Benzo's conversation left no illusion of the fact that Benzo Green was a mack: his nails were manicured, with three fingers on one hand sporting gold rings of clustered diamonds, and a gold pave bracelet. Two fingers on his opposite hand covered by a gold ring of clustered diamonds with a Lon gene wrist watch.

I enrolled full time at West LA College in the mornings, studying psychology, and working evenings and nights at the burger-stand. I couldn't believe the amounts of money that was being made every day, and I worked all the overtime I wanted. Between college and the new job, Deb and I sort of just fell off until we drifted further and further apart, and we lost contact all together. Benzo Green kept it real with all us girls who worked for him. He treated us like we were his little sisters; he loved talking to us, and we loved listening to him.

Benzo came up hustling hard in the streets; a jack of all trades who'd gone legit about ten years ago. Between the game Benzo laced us with and what I ear-hustled from regular customers who was all walks of life-- straight honest working stiffs, the pimps, hoes, gamblers, gangstas, dope dealers, dope fiends, players and hustlers of every kind, there wasn't too much about life that escaped me.

"The major drawback about moving illicit mind altering substances on the Black Market, is that the paper you stack, is money classified by the State Federal Government criminal codes, as ill-gotten gains; and the law is always laying low to break you for the paper you stack, and bounce that ass down to the bottom rack in a prison cell with no get back to where you're now standing in the real world." Benzo said to us one night about a dope dealer who was flashing his bankroll on us, in full high-sign mode to impress.

Benzo went on to tell us. "Young bloods, money stacks tall no doubt. I know cause them gators he kickin' on his feet, they fresh off of a reptile's ass killed and skinned down in the Florida Everglades in the not too distant past. His pants come from the same tailor as mines. The shirt on his back be spent from the finest silk-worms in China, and that coat came from the same gator's ass his kicks came from. Yeah, his jewels are real too. And that El Dorado he sliding about town in; it's the year. He can afford to pay the note on it every month, but the name on the registration be his Mama's, his sisters or some other relative, cause he ain't got neither job nor bank account with anything more than a few grand in it."

"Lace 'em then Benzo, lace 'em "said a jazzy elder sister, who was obviously coming from a Sunday night church service.

"So he hustling for the police is what you're saying," AB said from the cash register."

"Basically. Peep it, the D-game and most other get-rich-quick shit jumping outside the law, not getting a tax out of it, aint got a 401K retirement plan, and you can't draw pension or social security from it. Oh yeah, and should you get a home out of it; best believe it's in someone else's name, because there's no paper trail, and the tax code get you in the end, and there goes your home, gone!" Benzo said.

"Now, that's ugly," I found myself saying.

"Hustling in the game topsy-turvy, but if you do manage to play, it's imperative that you understand you have to pay the tax on every illegal dime obtained."

"Fo' sho' doe," came a familiar voice; I turned to find Mac standing at the window.

"Mac Daddy!" I squealed in delight..

The conversation turned into a lesson on ways to launder money between Mac, Benzo and the other elders. All of us girls could recognize that what we were getting for free, was what they paid to learn in some way or another.

Chapter 4

By that first year's end, Yorkie and I had stacked enough money between the two of us to make a down payment on a house. I introduced Yorkie to a realtor who was a regular at the hamburger stand. Wimpy Boston was a dapper old dude in his mid-forties, who was always kicking the business of commercial and residential real-estate with us. He had a small office on Crenshaw Boulevard and was more than happy to show Yorkie how to stay out of all the industry traps.

Yorkie found us a spot across town over on west 58th Place and Normandie Avenue, a three bedroom and one bathroom with a large backyard. We never lived in a house before; so I never knew what a backyard was, except for those we saw in houses on TV shows or in the movies. The backyard was the coolest; it had an old swing set in it. Mac made refurbishing the swing set his special project, along with putting a new roof on the house.

Everyone in the family worked on repairing the house-- By the time we were done the house was one of the nicest on the block, if not the nicest. Yorkie took special care with the front yard. She re-seeded the lawn, and laid the surrounding landscape with several kinds of flowers.

Between us, there was always money left over for the extra stuff in the house. Yorkie and I had no problem making the monthly house note.

Mac, with a couple of guys he hired, did most of the renovation. In the beginning Mac was spending a lot of family time with us, and nearly every holiday. But as time passed, keeping up with the day to day maintenance of our individual lives, began to pull us in different directions.

Mac bought Hughes out, so he was spending most of his time at the store, while Yorkie was working longer and longer hours until she began coming home well after me. I worked every day after school until mid-night. I was close to getting my degree in psychology and another in business management.

I felt uneasy about Yorkie riding the bus all the way from work by herself after working the graveyard shift up in East LA, so I took a Thursday off from work and went looking for a hoopty with the little money I had saved up. I found a cool little Subaru in mint-condition; but I was short a few hundred so I convinced the owner to hold it until Saturday morning, until I come back for it.

When I got home I called up the one person who I knew would show me some love if he had it to give.

"Hey Mac Daddy!" I shouted into the phone before he could say hello.

"Hey now is this my Sassafras?" Mac asked excitedly.

"Yes it is, and how are you doing?" I joyfully responded.

Mac went on to tell me about all the renovations he was making in the store now that Hughes was gone, and about a couple of young brothers he had working for him. He told me how good of a job they were doing; but how no one has ever done a better job than me.

"So, what's up? You need a job?" Mac asked me.

I told him that I didn't need a job, but that I was trying to bum a few hundred off of him to make up the difference I needed to buy the Subaru. Mac told me that he should have helped me get a car a lot sooner but it just got past him. He told me that the money was no problem He asked me for the car location, and then told me that he needed to go with me to make sure everything was on the up and up.

"I just need to check out all the paper work, and make sure you ain't getting mixed up with no shade-tree mechanic" Mac said.

I laughed at Mac's mechanic jokes as he went on to tell me that he'll picked me up on Saturday, and that he loved me.

That night I fell asleep thinking about the little Subaru. The following morning I awoke to the sound of Yorkie coming home and went into the kitchen where I found her putting some groceries away in the pantry that she bought the night before. As I helped her, we got to chopping it up about Mac until I just flat out asked her, "Mama why you and Mac never got together? He would have been a good man for you."

Yorkie told me that he probably would have been her man had it not been for them being such tight friends as kids. She told me how she used to play with Mac and his homeboys back in Brooklyn growing up; and they treated her just like one of the fellas. She told me how Mac and his crew, had never looked at her in any other way than as one of the homies.

"Back in high school, I actual hooked Mac up with my friend Delores, and he ended up marrying him." Yorkie thoughtfully said to me. "They didn't have any kids though, cause she couldn't. They stayed together inspite of that and had a lot of good, good years, until she passed away from breast cancer," Yorkie softly said.

"O wow! Mac's a good man. I hope I can find a man like him when I'm ready to settle down," I said out loud.

Yorkie looked at me and answered, "Yeah child, you have to really seek, cause the good ones are really hard to find."

It was a moment of silence as thoughts of quiet reflection on her past filled Yorkie's expression.

"But first you got to fit a social life between all that working and schooling you been doing," Yorkie said in a light hearted tone. "You ain't never once had a boy come calling on you. You ain't swinging in the other direction are you?" Yorkie asked her brow furrowing as she threw one of her hands on her hips and looked at me."

"Mama, I just know you don't mean that."

"I don't know. I ain't never seen you with nobody but Deb. Hell, no boys aint never even called here for you. For as far back as I can remember, it's just been Deb and you." Yorkie said jokingly.

"You crazy for that Mama. I had a couple of boyfriends just not good enough for me to bring home. And for what it's worth, your daughter is strictly-dickly."

Yorkie laughed so hard tears came from her eyes as I walked out the door headed for school.

That night after work as I got off the bus to walk home, I looked over at its tail lights, thought out loud, "now that's the last time I'll ride the bus."

I turned the corner and saw a little car parked out in front of my house that seemed out of place. It didn't belong to anyone on my block I thought. It must be someone visiting the neighbor across the street. But why did it look so familiar? And then I knew why, it was a Subaru exactly like the one I was getting tomorrow.

That morning I awoke to find my little brother Nookie standing at my night stand shaking a pair of keys in my face.

"Oh Sassafras, wake up. Wake up, wake up, my little Sassafras," Nookie said to me in that little sing-song voice that little kids do, while continuously shaking the keys in my face.

"Nookie it's Saturday. Let me get a little more sleep before I kill you," I said as I ducked under the pillow. "And whose keys you got anyway?"

"Yours" Nookie said.

"Mines?".

"Yeah, Mac told me to give them to you when you wake up they to your car parked outside."

I sprung from my bed so fast; that I never gave thought to putting some shoes on my feet, as I went out the door with Nookie right behind me. We woke up the whole house as we danced around the car. Yorkie watched us kids in the street from the porch.

I got dressed and called Mac while my little brothers and sisters cleaned out the car.

"Mac, thank you soooo much!" I screamed into the phone."

"You're more than welcome," Mac said.

I'll bring you the money I have down to the store," I told Mac.

"No you don't. The car is your school present. Now you take the money you got, get the car registered, buy some new tires for it, new brakes, an oil change and a tune-up. Cause the car's been sitting up now for a year," Mac said to me. Mac went on to speak with Yorkie while I headed on back outside to help with cleaning up the car.

Once my ride was sparkling like new money, I paused for a moment while sitting in the car, just tripping off the fact that I now had a car.

My brother Nookie was fifteen at the time, we were very tight in our relationship. He was closet to my age, and more responsible than the other kids, so I had him ride shot-gun with me.

Mac was a great influence in Nookie's life. He use to pick him up and take him to run errands with him, and all the while Mac would lace Nookie on the facts of life, mostly dealing with girls.

Nookie said to me "Come on Sassafras, I'm rolling with you. We gone roll till the wheels fall off." We laughed. I told Nookie, "Come on boy, let's do this."

I told the other kids they couldn't ride today with us. My reason for not letting them ride with me was, I really didn't know how to drive a stick-shift my damn self. But I knew I was ready to die trying.

As Nookie and I got into the car, I looked over at him and said, "You know I don't know how to drive a stick-shift Nookie!"

"What? Girl you gone kill us! Did you ever watch Mac when you were rolling with him?" Nookie said.

"I did but still I ain't drove one boy! I know what I need to do, but shit can I do it. And you bet not tell Mac or Mama."

"Man come on, only girls talk too much. Let's roll." Nookie said.

As I started up the car, I put it in first gear and tried to take off. For about six minutes, I couldn't get going because the car kept jerking and cutting off on us.

Nookie couldn't take it anymore, "Sessie, listen to me man, when you put it in first gear, don't take your foot off the clutch so fast. Mac use to ease his foot off and then he would ride that first shift for a few seconds before he switch gears. He told me you don't switch gears until you are ready to pick up speed. Now stop trying to take off so dang-gone fast."

"Okay Nookie, I got this." We finally got on the way jerking and cutting off on down the street while Nookie coached me through the gears and laughed like crazy; clowning me the whole way. Once we got to Arlington and Adams, the signal light caught me right on the hill and I was scared as hell trying to ease off the clutch to get up the hill without rolling back into the car behind me.

I turned and looked at Nookie, "You know we done fucked up now. I can't move Nookie."

"Sessie, just wait and let the other car go around you then just try it, we ain't got no choice but to climb this bitch, I'm gone flag the car to go around, then you better go for it before more cars come."

"Ok! Ok! I'm ready," I told Nookie as I revved up the gas while holding down the clutch.

The car rolled back a little as it was trying to cut off on me, but I held my ground, sweating like crazy, praying for God to step in right then because I got myself into some shit now.

Nookie, with his crazy ass, just started laughing harder and said, "You got faith, don't you?"

"Yeah boy," I answered him.

"Then stop panicking before you shit on yourself and get this car up the hill man 'cause I see some more cars coming."

"Ok. God step in right now and pull me up out of this. I need you Lord." As I spoke to the Lord it seemed as if he jumped in the driver's seat and shifted us on up the hill. Then I turned east on Adams, smooth sailing at this point. We rolled all over town and didn't get back home until 8 o'clock that evening. This ride was truly an experience for me and I have God and Nookie to thank. Anywhere that Nookie wanted to go on my days off, I didn't mind taking him because he not only put his life in jeopardy with me, but he taught me how to drive my car, reminded me how to have faith in God and most importantly, he never snitched on me to anyone about our face with death.

Chapter 5

Mac had got sick with a stomach virus, so I rushed over to take care of him, ran some errands, paid some bills, and made sure he got hot meals. While on one of the errands, I stopped at the old neighborhood Safeway Market and did Mac's grocery shopping where I bumped into my old high school girlfriend Deb, who was a cashier there.

As soon as Deb and I saw one another, she reached over and hugged me. "Sessie! How you been doing?"

"I'm good. I'm good." I said.

Deb stood back and looked at me, "Girl, you still look the same; cute as hell, with yo' wide behind." Deb said as I emptied my shopping cart onto the counter.

Deb's mouth started working like she had a motor in it, as she voiced her thoughts about how gorgeous the shape of my ass had gotten since she last saw me. It was like old times, and we were really glad to see one another.

"I'm telling you if I had yo' ass Sessie, I wouldn't be working at this damn grocery store. Shit, I put an ass like yours on the meat market if it was mine to sale. Advertise it for the prime porterhouse steak it is. You got the cash, I got the beefy ass," Deb said, and we both broke out into laughter.

"Girl, you are so crazy," I said.

Deb closed her register to the other customers and let her bagboy take an early break, as she rang up my groceries with us bagging them together. "Yeah, well I ain't so crazy that my shit don't be the truth. A bitch with a fat trunk like yourns needs to treat it like luggage and make it take her places. Make the thing pay like it weigh" Deb said.

Listening to Deb pop that shit, was like when we was kids on the school yard, and Deb was getting her clown on back when again.

"Girl do you know of any jobs hiring right now that are offering benefits because I'm about to graduate and receive my degree in Psychology and another in Business Management," I told Deb.

She told me how she had come up on an application to work for the CDC, and at first I thought she was talking about the Center for Disease Control down in Atlanta Georgia. Me with my slow ass. I told her that I wasn't interested in going all the way to Atlanta for a job.

"Sessie, you damn fool, I'm talking about the California Department of Corrections. They're hiring C.O.'s- Correctional Officers Prison guards."

Deb went on to say how the State of California was world renowned as the great industrial prison complex; how the CDC controls thirty-three prisons, and counting, how the prison guards union is the most powerful public union in the United States, and offers the finest benefits, all at the tax payers' expense. Full medical, dental, a pension plan, and all sorts of other perks and shit. She told me how she researched that the CO's union was responsible for all kinds of laws on the books that were written to lock that ass up, and keep it locked up forever, starting at age fourteen. She said that California's prisons held over two-hundred thousand people and the prison guards union played it that way in the name of long term job security guarantee.

"So come with me. We could ride the bus together down to their recruitment center," Deb said.

"Bus my ass! I got a car. Call me so I can come get the application. I'll fill it out, and we can roll together, girlfriend," I told Deb.

Later that night I laid awake in bed. I couldn't sleep for thinking, what if I could get this job, I would have some real benefits. I could really take care of Yorkie and my sisters and brothers. Then I started thinking about the down sides of working in the prison system; the crazy shit that goes on in there. I wonder what I would do if there was a riot and I be taken prisoner? Beaten down? Would I be gang raped, and then killed? What if I fell for one of the prisoners?"

"It could happen, I saw it on the news time after time," I thought out loud.

The last thought I had as I closed my eyes and drifted off to sleep was a quote I heard in school; life without risk is life not worth living. I couldn't recall who said it though. What the fuck. I gotta' do what I gotta' do to get paid.

Chapter 6

Driving out to the exam site, Deb and I tripped on if we both passed the test, and our request to work together in the same prison was possible. How cool would that be?

Deb turned to me with a blank look in her eyes that I never knew in all the years I'd known her, and she ask me "Do you think we're really cut out for this kind of work, Sessie?"

"Girl, look at our shapes, didn't you say with a fat trunk like mines it needs to be treated like luggage, make it take me places? Shit, we're definitely cut out to be around nothing but men," I jokingly told her. With that statement we both laughed and chopped it up on a more relaxed note to give one another confidence to go in and pass the Correctional Officers exam.

Before we knew it, we were at the exam site, and seated in a classroom with about forty other male and female applicants. This tall, dark hair, white chick gave us the scoop on being a CO. She broke down all the benefits we would be good for, and it all registered like the smell of gravy to me. Inspite of all that though, I still had this thought in the back of my mind; this fear that comes with drama of the unknown behind prison walls. Deb had it in the back of her mind as well.

On the ride back home we were silent for the longest part of the way, each of us locked in our own thoughts. For the most part, the test seemed easy. I mean the shit on it wasn't nowhere near rocket science, just basic common sense stuff that any average high school student would know their junior year.

Deb broke the silence between us, "Girl, how did you feel about the test we took?"

"Same as you, it was pretty easy."

"I hope we passed," Deb said.

Deb then turned to me with a questioning look in her eyes that I had never seen from her, and she asked me, "But what if we both didn't pass? I mean I know we both need this job bad, me more than you probably. But, I won't take it without you, Sessie. You're my homegirl and the only true friend that I ever had. Seeing you in the grocery store, and our driving up here to test for this job, just made me realize how much you really mean to me, Sessie."

As I listen to Deb, I could feel her emotions, and I knew that it wasn't what Deb was saying, but how she was saying it to me, that made me pull over to the shoulder, and stop in a rest area. I cut off the engine and I just listened to her ramble on. She told me how she wanted us to be best friends for life. She asked me if I thought we could be like that with one another; never allowing anyone or anything to divide us, never lie to one another, and never forsake one another no matter what. The truth of the matter was that Deb didn't really have anybody. Her mom had passed away, she never knew who her daddy was and she didn't have any sisters and brothers. Her Grannie was the only family she had, and she was a drunk for as long as I had known Deb. She didn't want Deb staying with her in her senior living home, because her Grannie was scared the folks downtown was going to find out that Deb was living there and bounce both their asses out on the curve.

It was then that we decided to make a blood pact.

"What is a blood pact?" Deb asked.

As I searched my purse for the switchblade that I kept for protection, I told her, "A blood pact means that each of us have to stick one of our fingertips, swear an oath to never forsake nor lie to one another no matter what, and then suck the blood from each other's finger."

In the instance I finished my explanation I found my knife, released its blade and Deb jumped at the sound and site of the blade popping out! Her eyes bucked at the sight of its catching the glitter of the sunlight's reflection, and I couldn't help but laugh.

"Ugh, you gone have to cut us both girl, cause I can't stand the sight of blood, especially mines," Deb said.

Deb reluctantly gave me her hand and looked away; her eyes closed and face twisted all up like she had to go pee real bad. I grabbed her hand, pricked her finger and then my own before she ever realized it was done.

"Take my hand, and look at me," I told Deb.

She took my hand, a spot of blood formed on my upward pointing fingertip, as she turned and looked into my eyes. With my other hand I held the hand of her bleeding fingertip in the same way.

"Repeat after me," I told Deb. "By the grace of God, I Sessie Jones, pledge to you in sisterhood."

"By the grace of God, I, Deb Bovaise, pledge to you in sisterhood," Deb repeated.

"Never to let anyone or anything come between us," I said to Deb.

"Never to let anyone or anything come between us," Deb repeated.

"I pledge I'll never lie to you and never to forsake this pledge of our sisterhood."

"I pledge I'll never lie to you and never to forsake our pledge of our sisterhood." Deb said.

"That's not exactly what I said; but it's close enough."

"Repeat it then? Cause I want to get it right," Deb requested.

"That's fine, just get this part right: as we go with God into hell on earth, against all odds," I said.

"As we go with God into hell on earth, against all odds" Deb repeated back to me.

I stuck Debs bloody fingertip into my mouth and sucked it.

"Ugh!" Deb said as she looked at me disgustedly, before taking my own bleeding finger into her mouth and sucking it.

I pulled Deb's finger from my mouth, and there was no blood on it. "Now, that ain't hurt at all. Did it bitch?" I asked her.

She pulled my finger from her mouth and responded, "Yeah it did."

"Well you better shake that shit off, stop whining and toughen up, 'cause pain is probably the norm where we heading," I told Deb. As I fired up the engine and eased back into freeway traffic, Ice Cube's "*Bonnie and Clyde thing*" came over the radio.

"Crank that shit up!" Deb said as she turned up the volume and started dancing in her seat.

"If one of the inmates get hold of your ass and starts running dick to the nuts, are you gone start whinny and crying like a chump? Or are you gone women up and take the dick like a champ, bitch?" I asked Deb as we laughed.

"Depends on how big the dick is," Deb shot back.

"You know some of them men up there ain't felt no real pussy since the one they fell out of at birth," I said. And we laughed so hard that we kept it going back and forth like that all the way home.

The days turned into weeks before we heard any word on how we had done on the exam. I told Benzo I had taken the CDC officers exam and was waiting on the results. He got a kick out of the whole me becoming a peace officer thing, and was always kidding me about it.

I focused on finals and school, and got my degree in psychology and business management. Yorkie framed them both and stuck them in her curial cabinet along with all the other family pictures.

Chapter 7

Two months passed, and then I got a letter from the State telling me I had passed the initial phase of the exam. I thought to myself, "Wow! I'm on my way to some benefits." I called Deb to see if she had gotten a letter. As I listened to the phone ringing, I hoped and prayed that she had because I needed the job, and I didn't know if I could stick to our blood pact, if I got the job and she didn't.

Deb answered the phone, "Deb, this Sessie, You get a letter?"

"Hell yeah I got one and I passed. How about you?" Deb asked.

"Girl, I passed too. We got to go out and celebrate, but first I think we need to write down everything to get prepared. Remember all the paperwork the lady said we have to fill out, and then talk to an investigator."

Deb got quiet after hearing that for a brief moment. Then she asked. "What's that all about Sessie?" I mean talking to an investigator, talk about what?"

"Deb, you mean to tell me that you didn't pay attention to what the lady was saying before she gave the test? She said that if we passed, we'd be given a date and time to report to the County Sheriff testing center, where we'd have to fill out a series of forms, and then we'd be assigned to an investigator who would do a background check on us. We'd also have to do more tests as to our drug use history and then a polygraph test you know, a lie detector test. And then a blood and hair follicle test for illegal drug use. And if we clear all of those, we will receive notification to report to formal training in northern California. You don't remember?" I asked.

"I must have been in la la land, 'cause I don't remember hearing a thing that bitch was saying," Deb said through her laughter.

"You gotta' stop cursing so much, Deb. We need to change our lingo if we're going to step up our game in this real work world. They already have us stereo-typed on some hood-rat sista' shit. Hear what I'm saying to you?" I asked.

Deb sarcastically replied, "Sessie don't yo' ass start getting all brand new on a bitch. As I remember back in school, it was you who had the foul mouth that wouldn't quit."

"There you go Deb, I'm just saying we need to step it up before we get there and be too comfortable saying shit that will get us into trouble, if not fired before we are ever hired. I think that we should even down-play knowing each other, to increase the chance of our getting placed in the same location. So use your head is all I'm trying to tell you."

"I'll use my head when I'm suckin' a dick," Deb said as she laughed."

"Funny bitch," I sarcastically told her.

"You need to practice what you preach," she hit me back with.

"Shut up Deb. Hey you wanna go out and have a drink?"

"Bet."

At the bar, three business suit dressed white men approached us. "What's up ladies," the lead man spoke. "I'm Michael," he introduced himself with that familiar hand shake that successful white men do, as he shook Deb's hand and then mines. Michael was tall and athletic build, in his late forties, had a perfect smile, intelligent blue eyes and a confidence that well-traveled educated white men possess. He introduced the other two as Jim and Seth. Both were in the same age group as Michael. Jim was wiry built, but equally handsome, with green eyes behind his Burberry spectacles, and sandy color hair that complimented his tan. Seth looked every bit the professional baseball player, except for the spots of gray in his jet black hair that complimented his gray eyes.

"And what are you ladies having to drink?" Jim asked.

"What y'all buying?" came Deb's response.

Michael beckoned to the bartender who quickly came over, "Long Island Ice Tea for the ladies and the three of us my good man," says Jim to the bartender.

Deb slid over and Michael sat at the bar between us, with Jim sitting on Deb's other side, and Seth on my other side. It was Michael who immediately took on the lead in command of the conversation. I could tell right off that he was the kind of man would saw what he wanted, and went for it.

"We're from out of town, San Diego to be specific, here for a business conference that was over at the Bonaventure Hotel." said Michael.

"And is yo' business one of buying or selling," Deb seductively shout back at Michael with a light brush of her hand across his hand.

Michael blushed, "Well I'm usually buying what's being sold," Michael said as he first slowly looked me up and down, before repeating the action on Deb. Just for an instance, it crossed my mind that Deb had better be careful. She was always so bold and so daring that I forgot how nervous she could make me feel and get excited at the same time by her audacity for taking risk. I wondered with my eyes as I had done so often when we were kids. She caught my look, but I knew she'd ignore it as she had always done.

"If your money is long enough, then we could start selling you some conversation," Deb said with a look at Michael and to Jim.

Michael grinned so wide that I thought his face would crack as he rested one of his hands on Deb's thigh, "Well little lady, in my world, conversation is an art in negotiation of a deal."

Deb glanced down at Michael's hand resting on her thigh and then rested her hand on top of his. "The deal is done if the price be right," Deb stated as she slip Michael's hand underneath her skirt and smiled broadly at him.

My mind began to race "I heard enough from the pimps and hoes all those nights working at Super Fry's hamburger stand, to know that Deb had just made a solicitation for prostitution, and if those guys were cops she was a done deal any minute.

"Would you gentlemen excuse us please? We need to run off to the ladies' room for a moment," I said to the men.

I slid from my seat and snatched Deb's ass from hers. We hurried off to the restroom, where once inside, I cracked the door open to see if we were being followed, before peeking over at the bar. The three men seem to just be innocently conversing with one another, but then if they were undercover cops, they would know how to make their shit look good for just this reason.

I closed the door, locked it, and turned to Deb who was standing at the sink looking in the mirror laughing. I checked under the stalls to make sure we were alone before I spoke.

"What the hell are you doing? I mean correct me if I'm wrong Deb, but it sounds like you're selling pussy, girl!"

Deb just looked at herself in the mirror, and began freshening up her makeup while answering me in that calm, cool and collected tone of hers, when she was in game mode. "Girl, calm the fuck down! I got this. Them tricks got pockets so fat, they calling me to trim some off. And yes, Sessie, I'm with it 'cause I need the money.

"I believe you been selling pussy for a while Deb."

"What female ain't? Hell wives sell it to their husbands on an installment plan. Every time he brings home his paycheck, he's buying the pussy. Dude takes female on a date; buys her dinner and a movie. He's buying the pussy. Dude pays a female's phone bill, utility bills and car note. Same thang, he's buying the pussy, period. Females been selling pussy since the pre-historic times Now, you got a problem with a female taking care of herself, Miss Sessie?" Deb asked.

"Come on Deb, kill the Miss Sessie shit, I don't knock anybody for taking care of themselves. It's just that you don't have to do this anymore. We have action at a good job, a real J.O.B., you feel me?"

Deb threw the lipstick back in her purse, and looked at me with that rubber-neck thing that only we sista's can do just before we're about to speak our minds. She folded her arms across her chest, "We ain't got shit yet, not until we are collecting paychecks. In the meantime I'm broke and need to eat, so are you down for getting this money or not?"

She waited for my response, but I didn't answer her, and it seemed as though the seconds were minutes, as we held one another's gaze. Then

Deb spoke again, "If not, then leave me the fuck alone, and I will catch up with you later."

Deb smiled, and started towards the restroom exit. When she reached the door, she unlocked it, and then turned to me as she opened it.

"Deb, I just want better for us. I just want you to move better than you are doing right now. If you get this wrong and these are undercover cops then there goes your CO career."

"Alright sis, go home and I'll hit you later to tell you all about it," Deb said with a wink at me, and walked out.

Chapter 8

I went straight home and dosed off to sleep. When I awoke that night it was 2a.m. and I never heard the phone ring if Deb had called, so I felt an immediate sense of worry, and called Deb. She answered after the second ring. "Hey Deb, I dosed off girl, are you alright?"

"Happy as a lark, girl. I'm sitting here well fed, well fucked and well paid," Deb said with satisfaction.

"So, how did it go down? What did you have to do?"
"Well girl, after I made up some sob story about why you shook me – I can't remember what I told them, Michael asked me if I'd like to join him in his hotel. I did, and when I got there he gave me five hundred for everything I was selling" Deb said,

and I found myself giggling and encouraging her to tell me more. "I turned on the hotel's room radio, and I did a little strip-tease for him. He poured himself a glass of Scotch and sipped as he watched. He tried to get me to drink with him but I didn't want to get so drunk that I wasn't all the way up on every move jumping off in the room, so I didn't drink anymore. By the time the record ended I was laid out on the bed, flat on my back, patting my pussy and thinking to myself; "Yeah I know I got it good." And girl let me tell you, that white man was as naked as a newborn fresh into the world in under a minute at the site of this hot fudge Sunday staring him in the face from in between these thighs of mine."

I found myself getting seriously aroused by what Deb was telling me. In my mind, I could see it all as clear as if I was standing in the room with them watching. "Go ahead hooker, tell the story!" I anxiously blurted out.

"Don't rush me, hell had yo' ass stayed, this would have been our story, and I wouldn't have to tell you at all," Deb said. "Any way, Michael slid into the bed beside me and ordered me to roll over onto my stomach. He was so into the way my ass looked and felt that he couldn't stop touching me. He was obsessed with it. He was lying on his side, his face eye level to my ass, his head propped up by one of his hands, bent at the elbow while he gently rubbed my lower back. At first I was watching his eyes trained on my ass as he licked his lips, and then I couldn't help but close my own eyes as his hand cupped one of my ass cheeks. The thumb of his hand slid between my butt crack. He kissed me on my opposite butt cheek and I felt my kitty-kat get instantly wet. I been around the world, but what he was doing to me, was brand new, and I found myself wanting him."

Listening to Deb, I hadn't even realized that I had kicked my bedspread off, I could hear my own heavy breathing, and my free hand was down inside of my panties touching myself. I was hot and wet, and I didn't want Deb to stop telling me what happened. "Why do you keep stopping?" I managed to get out to Deb, without letting on to what I was doing.

I could hear the radio playing softly over the phone in the background at Deb's who was listening to the same radio station playing slow jams, and in that moment T.L.C's *"I Ain't Afraid To Touch Myself,"* was the dedication of choice.

"Between Michael's kisses on my ass, he told me how he always watched the asses of Black women when they walk, and he knew that our pussy would be good, but he had no idea how good. Sessie, before I knew it, his finger was up in my pussy and he was touching something up in me that I never knew was there. He was gently putting his finger further and further up inside me with every stroke of his hand; his finger-tip touching that new spot up inside me. When all of a sudden girl, my pussy lips started jumping and tightening up on his finger, until all I saw was white light, and my pussy got wetter than ever. Girl, I heard myself scream."

The more Deb talked, I found myself really turned up, and I could feel my pussy getting fat. It started jumping and I didn't want Deb to stop talking. I got up out of the bed and locked my room door before I hurried back into the bed. "What else happened girl?" I asked.

"Sessie, I just know this ain't turning you on bitch,"

"Girl, hell naw."

Deb laugh, "alright you better not be on no freaky stuff while I'm talking to you."

"Just tell the damn story Deb, will you?"

"Ok, ok."

I slipped my panties off, and lay in bed naked as I listened to Deb. I had never done what I was doing, and I dare not tell Deb. She'd laugh at me and that would be totally embarrassing.

"Sessie, I'm telling you girl, the spot he touched up inside me was against the front inside of my stuff above my little thing-a-ma-gingy. Anyway, Michael climbed up on top of me, and he was kissing me on my shoulder and neck as he slipped his dick up in my kitty-kat from behind. I didn't even know it could be done like that Sessie. I'm telling you girl, he was all the way up inside of me. And then he stuck his tongue in my ear and I climaxed," Deb squealed. In that instances I found the spot Deb had just described. My finger-tip touched it and I threw my legs back to my shoulders as I felt my stuff tighten up on my finger. I pulled my finger out of me, because I knew if I didn't, I would scream, wake up the whole house, and be busted by Deb. "Then Sessie, he told me that if I let Jim and Seth come on up to the room, that they'd give me another five hundred each for a taste of this hot chocolate. I had to think quick girl, so I told him to let me check in with my boys who follow me everywhere I go; that they knew what room we were in already. He was impressed about how professional I was. He said he knew I was a business woman as soon as he saw me. I told him that I needed to let our boys know that it was all just business, so that they wouldn't think I was up in this piece getting raped, but that they are paying me, and that I would give them their cut when I come out. And then Michael called Jim and Seth on the phone."

Well, who was watching out for you Deb?" I asked.

"Did you not hear me Sessie? I said that I had to think fast girl. I made that up so that they wouldn't try anything crazy on me."

"That was dangerous Deb, dumb and dangerous," I snapped at her!

"I know, but at the same time, I thought it was smart. I mean I know how dumb it actually was. Once Jim and Seth showed up I got so nervous that I damn near ran out of there several times butt-ass naked. But then Jim and Seth gave me five-hundred a piece and before I knew it, everybody, was naked and I was in a get down straight out the devils play book of fun. Girl I'm telling you now, it ain't true what they say about white men, all three of these had nice size dicks."

As Deb kept talking, I was beginning to get hot all over again. My nipples were getting hard, and when I touched one, I could feel it down in between my thighs. And I found myself encouraging Deb to tell me more of the intimate details.

"Michael had slipped on a robe and sat in a chair watching as Jim and Seth had me in bed sandwiched between them. They were feeling, licking and kissing on me. I didn't know I could get so turned up. I forgot all about my nervousness, and before I knew it Jim was going up in me from behind while Seth was sucking one of my titties and rubbing the nipple of the other between the tips of his fingers. Michael told me to keep my eyes on him while Jim and Seth were having me. Michael's dick popped out of his robe, as he began to jack it off, and Sessie I got so turned on watching Michael. I felt like I was out of my body watching this whole get down with myself and them."

By now I could hardly hide the sound of my heavy breathing from Deb, so I gently laid the phone down between my breasts for a second and turned up the radio a bit. I never missed a stroke in the rhythm I was rubbing the tip of my pussy with my other hand. Deb never even knew that I had set the phone down in the time that it took me to turn up the radio.

"Sessie, I'm telling you, Michael's eyes had this glassy look in them that I've never seen in a man. He was moaning and stroking his dick, his head moving all over the place, but he never took his eyes off the action happening in the bed with Jim, Seth and I. Jim pulled back out of me, and lifted me onto my knees doggy style, and honey hush! It felt like he was hittin' the bottom of my stuff. I was trying to keep my eyes on Michael, but

Seth was up on his knees in front of me with his hand in my mouth pulling my jaw down, while he was pulling my head up by my hair in his other hand. He wasn't hurting me though. It was really kind of gentle the way he was doing it, while at the same time he was pumping his dick in and out of my mouth."

My finger slipped inside of me, and I touched that spot again that Deb had turned me on to. I thought I saw the flash of white lights she mention and I didn't want to touch it again too quickly so I just opened my legs really wide, and let my finger slide half way up inside of me with every slow stroke of my hand sure to rub along my brand new little friend. I closed my eyes and visualized Deb in the room with Michael, Jim and Seth as I listened to her voice.

"Jim tried to go up in my ass; but that was a no-go girl, and he respected my having none of that as soon as he asked me. With that, Seth turned me around and had me sit backwards on his dick while I sucked Jim off. I was holding Jims balls in one of my hands and rubbing his ass with my other, while I slow bounced up and down on Seth's thang girl. I could feel my climax coming on, and Seth must have felt my pussy tighten up, because he suddenly sat behind me. Jim came, I came and Seth bit me on my shoulder as he came, while Michael shot his off and in that moment girl I saw stars and damn near lost consciousness. Sessie, you still there? Sessie?"

The sound of Deb's calling my name seemed to come from some distant place, as I reached my finger deep up inside of me and hit that special spot. I heard myself scream, and then I saw the white light.

"Sessie! Sessie! Sessie what's wrong girl? Is somebody in your house? Sessie!"

I heard Deb screaming my name, and when I opened my eyes the phone was on the floor; and I heard Yorkie pounding on my bedroom door!

"Sessie, what's the matter? You ok?" Yorkie yelled from outside my room door.

Oh shit! What the hell? I thought. "Yeah Mama, I'm fine it was just a dream," go back to sleep Mama." I picked the phone up from the floor, "Deb you still there?"

"I'm here girl. What the hell you do?"

I caught my breath before I answered, "Nothing sis."

"Nothing sis my ass. You breathing like you been running or fuckin' ooo Sessie, I know what you did you nasty little bitch," Deb said as we both cracked up laughing.

"Girl, I don't believe I did that." And we laughed some more.

"Sessie I don't think I want another brother anymore, if he can't make me see the stars that white man turned me on to. From here out, I'm taken fools to school when they fuck me, and if they don't give it to me right, then they gets none of this for free; and I can't have it no other way."

"I think them white men turned both our asses out, and I wasn't even in the room."

"And to top it off Sessie, they were real gentlemen about it, and that they gave me their number and said for me to let them know if my sister changes her mind."

"Deb, don't get side tracked remember, we did pass the exam to work a legitimate job with full benefits. If you want to get paid by who you lay with on the side, then do yo thang. I mean that kind of money was a real cool payday, but never lose sight of the big picture, as my Mama always said."

Chapter 9

I thought that we would move into the CO jobs fast, but a month had passed since we heard any word. I kept slinging burgers, while Deb held onto her job at Safeway. And then we got our notifications in the mail telling us what day and time to report to the county testing center to begin or investigations.

On the morning of our investigations, I drove over to the senior living complex to pick up Deb, and when I got there I found her standing next to this bright red Camaro that she obviously wanted me to notice. She had this big smile on her face that would block out the sun if it was any brighter.

"What are you smiling about? And whose car is this?"

"Don't act like you don't know," Deb replied.

"Are you serious Deb? But how?"

"Gotta let-uh-ho' be -uh-ho', fo' the price Jim, Seth and Michael will pay on a regular fo' some black P' hole," Deb said. I looked over the Camaro, and it was damn-near brand new."I keep telling you Sessie, you gotta treat that ass like the trunk that it is, and let it take you where you want to go in this world girl. Ain't nothing wrong about peddling pussy when it's done right. And not a broad on this planet can market it better than me. Put me in a room full of men, and I'm gone sell 'em a scheme or a wet dream with this hot young sticky thing, know what I mean? We could make a real run out of slanging pussy. Set up a dating service, some call girls. Shit hell, sell it to the stars for top dollars. Be our own bosses, Sessie. I got an idea for pulling some other broads into the mix. We could be madams, you know, hire some protection, be rich in no time."

"We could or we could be really smart, and live a square, well paid life that has a pension plan at the end of our thirty years of punching a clock, the kind of life this CO job can give us. We can make a lifelong career out of guarding the people they throw away in this prison shit." I said to Deb.

"My dear prissy blood-sista wants to be legit I get it Sessie and I'm taking this job for these crumbs we gone get paid, only because there's nothing I wouldn't do for you. But I'm telling you now, if there's any low-risk, no taxable income to be generated up in this spot, I'm having it. And don't let that be selling pussy at my price to the police if that be the case, I'm serving 'em."

"Just be careful Deb. Just be safe."

"I always use protection; no glove no love, now take the wheel and get us where we got to go hoe." Deb said.

As I sat behind the wheel I told Deb, "That is not what I meant about being careful, and you know that."

As we arrived at the sheriff's county testing center, we saw a long line of people waiting to be interviewed. We parked and got in line with everyone else. I sort of just took in the site of all the people in the line who was there to be interview.

I had been having some mixed feelings about going to work in a prison and those mixed feelings had given me some real regular nightmares: about being gang raped, taken hostage and stabbed to death. I even had one nightmare where the prisoners cut my head off with a sword. I wondered if Deb was having reservations of her own, but when I really looked at her, I knew the answer to that because for the first time I could read it in the lines of her face.

"Deb, you know that if we get this job; we are going to see some really crazy shit that we can't even imagine yet."

"Oh, I don't know about that because I got a vivid imagination if I ain't got nothing else and I done had some real crazy dreams about some of what could happen in the pen," Deb answered.

"And here I thought it was just me."

"Shit naw," Deb nervously said. "I just been quiet about all the nightmares because I ain't want you to take me for a coward. We both know I can't stand the site of blood. Hell, I damn near peed in my panties the day we became blood-sisters."

I couldn't help but laugh at the memory of the way Deb the acted that day in the car at the site of my switch blade and our blood. Deb lightened up a bit, and laughed herself.

"Well, don't let 'em know how scared you are of blood. Don't tell 'em about your nightmares, and no cursing Deb. I need you to sound square, you know what I mean? You hear me Deb?"

She nodded that she did.

"I don't know how I'm going to pack my switch blade, but best believe me you, that I ain't leaving my heat behind when I step up in that bitch," I nervously said.

"No point worrying about it now. I mean this is what you want to do, so I'm down with it," remarked Deb.

Looking at Deb, I couldn't believe she had just said that. "What do you mean this is what I want to do? As if you have nothing to do with it at all. As I recall, it was you who gave me the application because you was looking for a job."

"I did and I was up until I got paid real swell for this pussy." Deb softly said with a pat on her pussy.

"Look, that's all fine and dandy Deb but flat-backing got occupational hazards that you really ain't ready for. I know 'cause as a kid I watched my Mama slang pussy out of both legs of her draws, and she could tell you that she ain't got shit to show for it but a deep throat, blowed out guts and scared knees, Now let's kill the negativity because we both need this job and that's that," I banged on Deb.

Deb stood in line quietly for a while, before she finally looked over at me and said "You're right

Sessie, I'm out of line, and I apologize for getting at you like that. I just didn't think I would get any further in life than working at that damn market and fucking fleas down on my knees for pennies. I just can't get over how much those white men paid me and how they turned me on to something new. They showed me what I was really worth, Sessie."

"If you want to put a fifteen hundred dollar price on your sex that's your right, but you as a person are worth more than all the money in the world, and I ain't gone ever let you forget that,- " I told Deb.

"True that But I do feel that I really don't need this prison job after what I've learned. I feel I'm going into the wrong business. I want the finer things in life and I want them fast, Sessie. I'm talking right now and my car is proof that I could have them right now."

I rested my hand on her shoulder and looked in her eyes. "I know you do and so do I, but let's give ourselves a chance to get it the legal way, is all I'm sayin'."

Deb rested one of her hands atop mines on her shoulder, "Ok Sessie, We gone see what this do."

"I'm not saying I'm totally dismissing your plan, oh no, you hold that hoe thought, if I can't cut this CO thang, I just may take you up on that You're just going to have to school me on how to fuck," I laughed.

"Girl, what do you mean by I'm going to have to show you how to fuck? You mean to tell me you don't know how to grab hold on the pole and put it up in your hole? And sucking a dick show ain't rocket-science. When we leave here we gone stop at the store and get us a couple of big stick ice creams and by the time you get down to the stick; you'll be a pro at sucking a dick."

Two white women standing directly in front of us, heard the last part of what Deb said they looked back at us, and they cracked up laughing. I thought to myself, what am I gone do with Deb's crazy ass."

"I know how to open my legs and lay there Deb; I've only been up in by one boy, more than once of course, and that was last year. And do you know, it didn't feel like much of nothing to me at all. I was waiting for some big explosion to come and I would suddenly be in love with the first boy I experienced, but nothing. No explosion, not even a poof!" Deb and the two white women laughed even harder. "That's why I got so turned on when you were telling me about Michael, Jim and Seth tossing you up; and this big stick you buying me is as close as I've ever been to even thinking about what it's like to suck a dick. I just thought that was nasty."

"Girl you got a lot to learn. A whole lot to learn Sessie," Deb said as she slowly shook her head with a smile.

"Ok Deb, don't act like you always been a pro at it. As I recall you saying you didn't really know what getting your fire lit was like either, until those white men introduced your ass to the joy of sex."

"True that! True that! But still don't take credit from yo' girl, I did have that go-gedda spirit in me to be adventurous enough to let them have their way with me. I allowed myself to relax and think as nasty as my mind could, and before I knew it I was the one tossing their asses up!"

We laughed so much that we both forgot all about the tension that was up in the air between us earlier. Deb always had a way with making me laugh, in some of the worst situations.

Before we knew it we were inside the building, and they were calling us in separate waiting rooms. "Remember, be on your best behavior," I told Deb as we split up.

I walked into the small interview room, and the investigator stood up from behind his desk, with his hand out-stretched to shake mines. "Hello, I'm Officer Dickerson and I'll be handling your investigation."

I shook his hand and found it to be so much larger than my own. He was a tall, athletic build Black man with a thick mustache, and short wavy black hair that shined by the over-head light. His teeth were perfect, and everything about him put me in the mind of the brutishly handsome brothers who always played the part of the no nonsense black drill sergeant in army movies. All I could think about during my interview was pulling off my panties, and sitting on his lap like Deb had said she did with Seth that night in the hotel. I kept starring at his crouch area trying to get a glimpse of what the imprint of his beef sack looked like in his pants. I wanted to flirt with him so bad but I dare not risk being over familiar just yet. So I found something else in the room to fix my eyes on, so that he wouldn't notice that I had the hots for him. I thought, "I could think of a million ways to play with this Dickerson."

Investigator Dickerson was all professional in the series of questions he asked me. Ten minutes into the interview I forgot all about sitting in his lap, and I found my focus on the questions; my every answer thought out before I responded. I was looking for traps and trick questions. He asked me why I had chosen to work in prison, as well as things into my past. Thank God I was able to answer all those questions in a steady relaxed manner. He wanted to know if I had ever committed any crimes as a kid; if I had ever been accused of a crime. He asked me if I had ever thrown a rock at someone or something, then hid my hands behind my back. Of course my answer was "no" to every question, but the last one about the rock had just seemed to lighten up the whole process.

He told me that I did well, and that he was scheduling my polygraph today. I was totally caught off guard, as he picked up the phone and made a call that sent me across the hall into another room. As I entered the room, my palms began to sweat and I felt my lips quiver.

The agent administering the exam was a short beetie-eyed man, with a half bald head, and gold rim spectacles whose alabaster skin and coffee stained teeth put me in the mind of a mortician. He was a methodical little bastard. His suit looked a size too small at the ankles and wrist, and his shoes squeaked when he walked, but he was surprisingly nice in a nerdy kind of way. He told me to relax as he hooked me up to the polygraph machine and after a while I managed to calm down. I told him I was ready and we began.

When the exam was over, the agent told me to go back across the hall to Investigator Dickerson's office. I did, and as I opened Dickerson's office door, I could smell cologne – that wasn't there before. "You smell really nice," I said to Dickerson in a voice that was so husky, I didn't recognize it as my own.

"Sit down," he ordered me.

Dickerson leaned over his desk really close to me and whispered, "You look nice."

Now I didn't know if Dickerson was testing me or really coming on to me, so I just down played the action he was giving me I thanked him, and then asked him what I needed to do at this point?

He slid a pen and clipboard of forms across the desktop to me, "I need you to fill out all of these forms and sign up to take a physical tomorrow." My nerves begin to unravel with the realization that this job was happening, and I lost my focus, I forgot everything that I had told Deb about checking herself on the cussing, and I began to talk to myself, repeatedly saying, "this shit is going too fast now. This shit is going to fast now. I'm getting scared."

"Hey, it's cool," Dickerson said. "I'm going to help you get through this." Dickerson then gave me his business card and told me, if I had any questions or if I just wanted to talk, that he would be available to me at any time. I couldn't read if he was flirting with me or just keeping to protocol until I walked out of his office and I thought I got a glimpse of him checking out my ass. But even then I couldn't be sure.

I walked out in the lobby and looked for Deb. When I didn't see her, I assumed that she was still caught up in the process, so I took a seat and waited for her. After thirty-five minutes, I decided I would go outside and wait by the car for Deb only to get there, and find her standing by the car talking to some guy.

"Deb!" I shouted.

She looked over and saw me as I walked over to her, and the guy walked off by the time I reached her. "Girl, how long have you been standing out here?"

"About an hour and a half. What took you so long?"

"They had me take a polygraph exam—you know a lie-detector test. And I had to calm down before I got started, because I wasn't expecting that. Then I had to go back to fill out some more forms, and schedule my physical exam for tomorrow. Didn't you do the same?"

"Naw, they just asked me a bunch of questions and then she told me that I would have to call this number on a card she gave me to set up a poly-lie-detector test."

"Are you serious?"

"Dead serious so, whose socks did you blow off to get preferential treatment?"

"Nobody's – not yet, but I did have one fine ass Investigator black guy, and I could swear he was flirting with me. He gave me his card and told me to call him anytime I wanted to talk."

Deb got in the car behind the wheel with me getting into the passenger side. I pulled the card out of my purse and showed it to Deb as she pulled off.

"Damn Sessie, you came up girl. You could work this dude – holla at him for me. I had some ugly foreign white bitch who acted like she was on her period, and look like she was raised on horse meat and beer, and pisses out vinegar."

I laughed so hard that I cried as Deb went on.

"I'm telling you this bitch had a mustache no titties, no ass with arms as big as my thighs, and her voice was deeper than Berry Whites. Hell, I probably could have gotten my lie-detector test done today also, had I reached under this broad's dress and stuffed a rag in her ass. Deb had to laugh at herself by then, right alone with me.

"You got to get at ole-boy."

"Okay Deb, I think I could ask him to do something for you. I did get the impression that he was flirting with me towards the end. I want to see what he's working with between his legs anyway."

"Then, let me hurry up and find a store so I could get you some condoms and that big stick ice cream again, and get you laced on suckin'-uh-dick," Deb said in her most seductive voice. "See girl, you're finally getting the hang of what that thang you totting around is worth," Deb shouted as she turned up the music and put the pedal to the metal.

Chapter 10

After I arrived home, I went straight to my room and called Investigator Dickerson, who answered on the third ring. "Officer Dickerson, Special Investigations Unit," He said in a most professional voice.

"Hello sir, this is Sessie Jones. I interviewed with you today," I mustered in my most sexy voice.

"Oh, say no more Miss Jones, I know exactly who you are. And how are you?"

"I'm good; I'm good, and yourself?"

"I'm fine. Listen, if I've offended you in any manner today, I apologize and it will not happen again."

"What do you mean you apologize for offending me?"

"Well I did put on some cologne and it seems as if you had a little adverse reaction to it."

"Yes, I did have a reaction, but it was just the opposite of adverse. And all truthfulness I found it seductive, but I didn't want a compliment to be misunderstood as my getting over-familiar with you while you were in the performance of your duty," I said.

"What do you mean seductive?"

I knew I had him then because out of all I said, the only thing that he latched on to was the word "seductive". "Oh I'm sorry, I didn't mean to say seductive. What I meant to say was, you just smelled so nice to me, that I momentarily lost my focus, and nothing like that has ever happen to me."

"Tell you what, we're both adults here so let's just be open in our conversation: mean what we say, and say what we mean Mrs. Jones, ok?

"Okay. And it's Miss Jones but I prefer you call me Sessie."

"Now that you told me you're not married."

"Did I do that?" I responded playfully.

"Yes you did and neither am I. – Married I mean. I'm on the clock right now but on my way out the office. And in case you didn't notice, I gave you my cell phone number on that card as well as this office number. Call me right back on it, I'd really like to continue along this line of conversation to see where it takes us."

"Okay," I said.

I called him right back on his cellular phone, and we continued the conversation right where we left off. My confidence wasn't in the least bit strained, in spite of the fact that he was at least fifteen years older than me, and the first fully grown man who I had ever stepped to. The advantage was all mines though, because Dickerson knew that I was young and he had mistakenly assumed that I was naive about life while I knew that sex was my only naivety, and then only in areas of the actual acts.

I played up my shyness and introduced a level of hesitation in my voice, as I told him that I worried about how my friend had done on her interview today, had given me a second excuse for calling him. "I was wondering if you could pull my friends information, Deb Bovaise. She and I did everything the same today up until the polygraph exam. Is it in your power to have her take her polygraph exam tomorrow, or as soon as possible? We really would like to go through the process together, to be there supporting and encouraging one another. I can't take this job without her sir."

"What do you mean you can't take this job without her? You would let this job go because your friend may not be able to start when you start? That's crazy young lady." Dickerson quickly stated, never giving me a chance to answer.

"I may have misstated what I'm trying to say, and that is, I've never been away on my own, and my friend Deb is the one who turned me on to the job. She's my best friend, I was just hoping that your offer to help me get through this in your office today could be counted on. Or did you not mean it?"

"No,No. I meant it; I just -."

I cut him off. I felt him slipping away, and this was it. Deb needed me, and I decided to go all out. "Maybe we could get together over dinner my treat of course --and you could offer me some insight into what options I could tell Deb about."

"I think I could offer you some advice on the matter. Tell you what, how 'bout I pick you up at eight tonight for dinner– my treat, and I could help you figure out a plan for your friend."

"That works for me. You have my address: I'll see you then. And again I really appreciate this Mr. Dickerson."

As soon as I hung up I called Deb and told her what had just gone down so that we could put our heads together on how to best play this. With Deb answering the phone we went back and forth on some slick shit of how I could make this happen for Deb, and get paid as well.

"You got to be crafty with your conversation Sessie, you don't know what his ass could be up to. I mean he could be a damn good trick or he could be on some investigative shit. Hell he could even bust you and haul your ass off to jail."

"Naw, I got a feeling that he's more on some slick stuff than me. I'm just playing him to the left at every move, and he's trying to counter me so that I don't try playing for a lawsuit or something, blindside him and blow his career with some sex charge stuff."

"He's the police. They're trained to trap that ass Sessie, don't get comfortable with this cop. Whatever you do, always remember this is the police you got by the nut sack."

"So, what should I do then Deb?"

"Go head and take the date. But don't crack at him for what you want until you get him butt ass naked and he's all hot and bothered. You see, if he's naked, he can't hide any wire. You know a listening device for other police to hear if he is on some "bust you" operation. You got it?"

"I got all of that. Now, tell me how do I turn this beast on to the point that he pushes your paperwork, pays me, and gets my rocks off?"

"Damn you greedy bitch. It's your first night out, and you want the whole get-down," Deb said and began to laugh.

"Uh! Yeah."

"Once his dick is standing at attention with him butt ass naked following behind it, trust me, grab it by the head in one of your hands, take him by the ear in your other hand, look him in his eyes and softly bite on his bottom lip. Trust me he'll slap his Mama if that's what you want from him."

All I could do was laugh, as Deb continued on. "Remember, what I told you. Just think real nasty as you can, and the rest will come naturally."

Chapter 11

From my living-room window I watched the gray color Mercedes Benz SE sedan pull up and park curve-side in front of my house. Before the car had even come to a full stop, I glanced at the clock and noticed that it was 8 o'clock on the dot, and I knew that it was Officer Dickerson before he revealed himself.

As soon as Dickerson stepped from his car, for the first time I was struck by the fact that Dickerson was a long way from the few boys that I had dated up to this point in my life. He moved with a sense of confidence and he was carrying flowers in one hand. None of the boys had ever been to my house to this date nor had I ever received flowers from any of them. Dickerson wore an immaculate double-breasted, dark blue color suit with a burgundy color tie and black leather loafers. He looked nothing like the officer of the law that he was, but that of the consummate professional city official. Everything about him so far said, responsible grown man.

He couldn't see me as I watched him from one side of the living room window drawn drapes. Dickerson rang the doorbell as I looked into a mirror of a curio cabinet for a final check on my come-up. I was pleasantly stunned at a never before now seen mature me smiling back from the mirror. I knew that my powder blue mini-skirt and snakeskin stiletto pumps would complement his suit. I knew that the people we would come in contact with that night would see us as some high profile couple.

Dickerson rang the doorbell a second time as I stepped out to the porch lightly shutting the door behind me. He took a step back from me, and seemed to slowly take the full sight of me in from head to toe and back again.

He couldn't help himself and whistled in appreciation, at what he saw before he caught himself. "You're beautiful Miss Jones."

"And you look very handsome Dickerson and you smell as good as you did when I caught your drift at the testing center."

"Thank you," Dickerson said, and extended his arm out to me in that way I had only saw in the movies. I inner-locked my arm in his as he escorted me to the passenger side of his car he opened the car door; I got inside with him closing it behind me as he hurried in behind the wheel to drive off. The stereo system in the Mercedes was the clearest sound I ever heard. It was jazz, that had no singing, it was one of the most beautiful pieces of music I had ever heard.

"This is beautiful who is he?" I asked.

"Joe Samples 'Ashes to Ashes', he answered. I could tell that he was thoroughly impressed by my taste for his choice in music. But then I was impressed by all of him so far but mostly by the car. It moved like it was floating and turned

corners like it was on rails. The leather seat was like nothing I had ever sat on, and I thought one day, I will have me one of these.

Dickerson and I continued to make small talk as we drove to our destination. We arrived at Crustacean's restaurant in Beverly Hills. As the maître-d' escorted us through the restaurant, I could see fish swimming in the floor. It was a trip to see something so way out. I knew that this was what being a grown up and dating a man with some money was about. This is what Deb was talking about. She was always saying what we as women are worth how we need to use what we been physically blessed with to pay some of our way if not all of our way through life. And now for the first time I agree and it's this moment that has made a believer out of me.

With our being seated, Dickerson pulled back my chair, as I sat down he pushed my chair up to the table and kissed my forehead. "Wow, I'm being treated like a lady for the first time in my life," I thought.

I held my composure because I didn't want him to know that I had never been treated like this before. We were served champagne with lobster in a creamy sauce that was simply out of this world. Officer Dickerson slid his chair close enough to me so that he could whisper in my ear. He said, "May I taste you?"

"Yes you may," I answered and puckered up my lips to kiss him. Dickerson eased his hand up my skirt and I was startled. But I didn't move as he slipped his finger past the crotch of my panties, up inside of my vagina. He withdrew his hand from beneath my skirt, and I was somewhat startled by what he next did. He put his finger in his mouth, and tasted my feminine juice. A look of pure pleasure came over his face as if he had just tasted the best thing life had to offer.

"Ugh!" I thought, and damn near said as much. But I knew that this was one of the big girl moments that came with the night that I was going to let this man make me a woman. And as the night went on, my legs began to move nervously, to the point that Dickerson asked me if I was nervous or if he had offended me at some point. I told him that I was fine and he hadn't offended me. I told him that I was just ready to have some private time with him.

"Wow, thank you. Thank you I can't wait to be alone with you," Dickerson said to me upon hearing that.

His response and the way he looked at me, really made me nervous until my thoughts shifted to I just may have overstepped my boundaries with this man sexually, because I just didn't have any experience in none of this grown up shit – this big girl get down that's about to go down. Thankfully for me, he just took my whole nervousness as my anticipation of wanting to be alone with him.

When dinner was over, we drove to the Nikko, a big fancy hotel that I never knew about until that night. I had never been in a hotel before and looking at the Nikko, I had made it to the big time. Dickerson paid for our suite with his credit card. For the night he was charged two-hundred fifty dollars. "Damn!" I thought as the price of the room registered to me that was, this is a lot of money for one night; but worth every penny based on what I have seen of the place so far.

As we stepped onto an empty elevator --as soon as the doors closed --Dickerson immediately made a move on me, pressing himself up against me, with his arms around my waist, I could feel his stiffness against my behind. I was trying to gage its size: but I was still kinda' nervous, but he really couldn't tell. I had to get a sense of what was in store for me, so I just reached around behind me and began massaging and measuring it through his pants. I was glad that he made a move on the elevator before we got to the room. This gave me the chance I needed to satisfy the curiosity that had begun from the moment I met him, and couldn't take my eyes off of his crouch, back in his office.

It wasn't what I expected from a grown man. He was shorter than many of the boys that I had let grind on me, and nowhere near the size of the one boy whom I had given myself to on the few occasions where I was sexually active. And I was really disappointed at Dickerson's size. From the point I touched him, it became all about the money I could earn first, and getting Deb's paperwork pushed along. And to think I was really getting into him I felt he could really be the kind of guy I would have liked as the man in my life, based on his looks and his gentleman's standing, but now my fantasy was ruined.

As soon as the room door closed behind us, Dickerson was ushering me towards the bed, his hands pulling up my skirt.

"Hold on, why are you rushing sweetie?" I said as I took hold of his hand, and stopped him.

"I thought you wanted it right away. Didn't you say you were anxious to leave the restaurant," he panted.

"That I did, and I'm anxious to give myself to you so get naked and show me whatcha working with."

Before I could get my second shoe off, Dickerson was standing in front of me just as naked as he was on the day he was born. His erection stood on end, pointed straight at me. He drew both hands behind the back of his head in a body-builders pose and said in his best Al Pacino as Scarface impersonation, "Say hello to my not so little friend Mommy," and grinned. It took every bit of control that I had in me, not to break out laughing at his muscle bound, little dick ass standing there like the pride of the party. His was not the dick of a grown man but one of a middle school boy.

"You have to slow your roll, and talk dollars to me before I grant you the privilege of full access to this young tight pussy I'm packing in these panties of mine," I told him.

Dickerson's grin abruptly turned to an expression of bewilderment and he brought to mind a young kid to go along with his little dick. "I'm certain it's a privilege but you didn't tell me that you're a whore," Dickerson said in astonishment.

"I'm not a Hoe. I never sold myself to any man. I've only been sexually active with one boy in my life --a schoolmate in high school. And it's because of that fact that you have to pay. See, it's a blessing for you – a grown ass man --to get my youth. Hell, I'm brand new to what you been getting up in for a long time now, am I right?"

"Okay whatever. I still don't get it, I mean it's not like you're a virgin. You said it yourself you been fucked by one boy already." He scoffed!

I walked over to him really slow took his dick in my hand, and looked in his eyes. His eyes seemed to gloss over at the touch of my hand and the feel of my hot breath against his chest. I didn't feel that I had reduced him to the trick that Deb had laced me on yet, but I was damn close.

"I like you Dickerson, and I think you're very attractive. But if you want to be the man who makes me a woman tonight, then start talking dollars to me that makes sense. You get what I'm saying? Because if you don't then I think we should leave."

I reached up and rubbed his earlobe in the fingers of my other hand, then I gently bit his bottom lip while I cupped his balls in the hand I held his dick with. For a second, I thought he might faint.

"One hundred, "Dickerson groaned.

"Two hundred and you look out for my girl Deb."

"D – D – Deal" Dickerson stammered.

"Give me a minute," I told Dickerson as I let go of him. "I have to call home and let my family know that I'm okay, where I am." And I walked off into the living room to use the phone.

"Hold on now, I don't need someone coming in here on some bullshit."

"Not to worry honey, this is just for my safety," I shouted back over my shoulder to him from the living room.

"Shit I'm the law sugar; you never been safer than you are now." Dickerson said.

Deb picked up her phone on the second ring, "Hello."

"Hey Deb!"

"Hey my ass you fuck 'em yet?"

"No, but it's about to happen. I'm at the Hotel Nikko."

"Get the fuck out of here. For real girl?"

"Yeah but Deb listen I got a problem – rather he got one. His dick is so small it's no wonder he could find it when he goes to pee – real doe. So how in the hell am I supposed to think nasty if I ain't turned on by him?" I whispered into the phone.

"Girl, listen to me just because he's short don't mean he can't pleasure you. He's fine as hell and he smells good. Keep that in mind and stay focused on your getting paid, not to mention you're getting my paperwork pushed. He just might surprise you, and turn your ass out. Now, just concentrate on the mission girl, and if the Negro ain't pleasing you then tell him as much and once you let him know that he ain't handling his business, he gone damn near kill himself trying to. And you need to get really sexual with him, act like the harder he pounds up in you, the more turned on you become. Talk dirty to him. Get aggressive, spank his ass a bit. You got it?" Deb asked.

"Yeah, I got it."

"And Sessie?"

"What?"

"No glove no love girl. You make sure that you slip the condom on his dick."

"Okay Deb, I'll do what you say, I gotta' go now and I'll hit you later when I get home," I said and hung up the phone.

Chapter 12

Walking back into the bedroom, I took my time, each step made in the most seductive sway of my hips that I could without being obvious, and Dickerson couldn't take his eyes off of me. He was lying in the bed atop the covers like he was King-Ding-Dong with his little dick in his hand. I kept my eyes on his face and chest, so that I could maintain my focus on his good looks, and not his shortcomings.

I turned the radio on the slow jam station like Deb had earlier told me to careful to give Dickerson a full view of my ass as I searched out the correct station. Glancing at the dresser top mirror, I could see Dickerson was completely focused on me and he took on a new appeal to me in the dim light as I let my mind slip further and further into the nasty place that Deb told me to go to. I slowly crawled onto the bed and stood over him. He began kissing my legs, while I took off my bra with him looking at me and I tossed it onto the floor. Dickerson leaned up into a seated position, slowly pulled down my panties and pressed his face close to my crouch, as he slowly inhaled with closed eyes, liken to that of a chef taking in the aroma of a gourmet dish, then stuck his middle finger up inside my pussy, and moved it around in a way that caused a warm sensation to creep through my whole body. That was brand new to me. I stepped out of my panties and I felt his lips tugging at and kissing the fat part of the sides of my vagina, and I grabbed hold on to the headboard to keep from losing my balance. "Oh my goodness," I found myself saying.

His tongue began to probe my opening between the tugs and kisses along the sides of my vagina, when all at once I felt his tongue going up inside me along my clitoris and I felt my knees slightly buckle. I wasn't even aware that I had closed my eyes, and the sounds of my own moans were momentarily unrecognizable to me.

Dickerson was giving me a whole new meaning to that old Black folk saying about talking in tongue, as I tried to distinguish what he was mumbling to my pussy. I grabbed hold onto the headboard with one hand to sturdy myself, while I rested my other hand on one of my hips and threw my head back to stare at the ceiling while I slow grind in time with the soft sounds of that song called 'Whip Appeal' playing over the radio station. My mind was gone; my sense of reality blown, I knew that this was what Deb had called the erotic zone. Where Dickerson was short on dick, he was making up for with this gift. My moaning and groaning was out of control now, and Dickerson knew that he had taken charge. I could feel it in the way that he held my ass cheeks in each of his hands, he was dominating the moment, and I needed to regain control.

"Come down from there sexy," said Dickerson.

I stepped down off from the bed, and he bent me positioned over the bed on my stomach. I instantly thought that he was readying to enter me from behind and I was about to stop him so that I could put the condom on that Deb had bought, but I held back for a moment, and it was a good thing that I did because he hit me with the totally unexpected. I felt his tongue lick and kiss the top of my right butt cheek and then my left cheek, which made me think back to the experience Deb had with Michael, Jim and Seth her first night with them. But what Dickerson did next was so far from the story Deb told me, that I was taken by total surprise! I wasn't really sure if what I knew was happening to me, in fact what was really happening at all. But then I felt the tip of his tongue probe between my butt cheeks, and I tried to let my mind lose itself in that nasty place that Deb had taught me about. I couldn't do it. Suddenly, I lurched forward across the bed, like a bullet fired from a pistol to the sound of my inner voice saying, "Ugh! this nasty mother fucker!"

I landed on the floor along the beds opposite side, where I heard Dickerson ask, "What's with this?"

I got up from the floor, and turned to find Dickerson standing there with a dumfounded look on his face, where he was standing across the bed.

"I'm sorry Dickerson, but I just ain't feeling the booty-hole thang."

"But I paid to have it my way," Dickerson pitifully said.

It wasn't what he said, but the way that he said it that made me feel a sudden sense of sorrow for him.

He dropped his head as I walked around the bed towards him. I knew this was a chance for me to retake control of the situation, "I know you paid baby, but I'm just not down with this."

I took his hand and gently nudged him towards the bed. My psychology degree just seemed to come into play from out of nowhere, as he sat on the edge of the bed, his whole posture mindful of a sullen tempered child. Arms folded tightly across his chest, penned down, his bottom lip poked out, his whole authority persona was gone.

"I got this," I heard myself saying. I was turning up my game on instinct, and I knew it. The cop that he was is now missed on me as I kneeled down between his legs and rolled the condom onto his semi-erect little dick. "Let Mama look out for you big daddy, show you what I can do with this big dick you got," I said as I slipped it into my mouth, and followed Deb's big stick ice cream teaching instructions down to every memorized detail.

Dickerson began to moan and grind in my face, as he grabbed me by the hair with both his hands, and the thrust of his hips becoming more forceful. If he would have had any size about him, I knew that he would have been choking me now as he began to mumble that same unintelligible shit as before. The more I moaned and pretended he had it going on, the rougher he got. I began to think I might lose control of the situation, when all of a sudden he got up on his knees and turned his behind to my face. "What is it with this man and ass?" I thought. That's when I saw the butterfly wings tattooed on each butt cheek opposite of his hole.

"I've been a bad boy Miss. Jones, and I should be spanked," he whimpered.

I damn near busted out laughing, but I didn't want to offend him because I needed him—I needed him to do what he could for Deb, and I had a feeling he might come in handy for something unknown in the future. So I began to spank him and the harder I spanked him on his ass, the more this freaky-meeky son-of-a-bitch became turned on. He started wiggling his ass at me, "Harder Miss. Jones, please baby, baby, baby harder please," he growled.

I began to enjoy the whipping that I was giving him. I found myself slapping his ass so hard that my hands begin to hurt while thinking, "He's the police and twisted beyond belief. You just never know about people, or what they got going on behind bedroom doors."

"Kiss it! Oh great googily-woogily kiss it will you please!" He quivered.

I stopped and took a step back, "That ain't happening man."

"Please, I'll pay you more money," he panted.

"It's not about the money I'm not putting my face, let alone my tongue, up in your bootyhole.

"But I did you!"

"Oh no you didn't and you ain't going to either. Now if you want some pussy I'm game, but the booty-hole thang —uh-uh."

Dickerson abruptly turned angry. His face twisted up in a frown, and before I knew it he was in my face. I thought about my switchblade down in my purse, and I knew that with one kick to his tiny balls I could get to it before he could hurt me. That's when I saw it in his eyes. I saw that he wasn't going to attack me; I just sensed that it wasn't in him to harm me in that way.

"Ok chicken shit ass bitch! The pussy will do," He yelled as he grabbed me by my arms and slammed me back onto the bed. Even though he was acting out of anger, I felt more in control now than I had been at any point in the evening, and to cap it off I liked his new roughness. I was actually turned on as he climbed on top of me, grabbed me by my throat applying enough pressure that I at first became a bit worried, and in that instant I again thought about my purse —my survival instincts were in full swing.

He took his little dick in hand and he forced it inside of me. "I need you Dickerson. Fuck me daddy, oooh yes, yes big dick Dickerson daddy, give it to me baby."

He released his hold from around my throat as he began to pound between my thighs. Though I couldn't feel him up inside of me, I couldn't help but moan in agony at the pressure of his weight banging against my pelvis, causing my breast to bounce so hard that they hurt as well. I turned my head to stay away from his mouth, because I was not going to put his ass kissing mouth on my face, let alone his tongue in my mouth. He began growling like an animal as he pounded into me with all his might, while he called me his little whore, his bitch asking me who was my daddy."

"You're my daddy! I'm your bitch, I'm your whore. Ooh yes, yes, yes." I screamed, and the louder I became the more pain he tried to inflict on me, the more turned on he became. I wrapped my legs around his waist to absorb some of the pounding while acting as if he was really satisfying me until I faked him into climaxing. He rolled off of me as if he had truly sexually satisfied me. "You really surprised me Dickerson. You good dick daddy. Maybe we can do this again real soon," I said to the back of his head, stroking his ego, and setting the stage to escape this crazy, kinky son-of-a-bitch.

"You'll never get this dick again, you fucking tramp."

Normally, I would have responded to this with the sassy mouth that I'm known for, but instead I checked my tongue, slipped out of bed, grabbed up my clothes and went into the bathroom where I got dressed.

On my return to the room, Dickerson was sound asleep. I saw his pants on the floor, his wallet hanging out, so, I thought to myself "well the bastard under paid me, disrespected me, and scared the hell out of me. Ole short dick undercover punk. So why not exit this stage of the game on his page." I opened up his wallet and emptied it for all its cash money, and his investigator's identification. I crept back into the bathroom, and wrote on the mirror in lipstick, "NEXT TIME YOU WANT TO FUCK SOMETHING; GO WITH SOMETHING THAT FITS YOUR DICK SIZE, TRY FUCKING A NAT, THEY LIKE FRUIT YOU FREAK!"

I took his clothes and dropped them in the trash on my way to the elevator. Deb answered her phone after several rings, and I told her some of what had happened to me and where I was waiting for her to pick me up at.

Deb pulled up in less than twenty minutes, and we were in the car laughing about Dickerson's fruit-cake ass. I told her everything that took place the entire evening, between Dickerson and I. Deb told me how proud of me she was for how I had managed the situation with what she had taught me. I told her how I had a plan for making Dickerson push her paperwork through the process; for her to be ready to roll, and to leave shit to me.

As soon as I stepped through my front door, I heard the faint sound of my bedroom phone ringing. I knew that it was Dickerson before I answered it. My first thought was to let the bastard sweat; but I went with my second mind, and answered his call. Because I needed to know where he was coming from, I needed to know if he was a threat to my chances at getting the new job.

"Hello," I answered.

Dickerson's tone was sad, "Why did you take my clothes, my money and my identification?"

"Because you treated me like trash, and I felt you owed me more for what you took me through."

"What do you mean, what I took you through? I treated you to an expensive dinner, took you to a fancy hotel, and paid you for a sexual escaped that you thoroughly enjoyed."

"Enjoyed? Enjoyed my ass man, you scared me shitless. You were the one enjoying it."

"You know you enjoyed it, because you were moaning and begging for more. You're my daddy, I'm your bitch, I'm your whore. Fuck me big dick daddy, is what you said to me. Did you not?"

"I was faking –like in the porn flicks. I just wanted you to cum so that I could be done with your little dick ass."

"Why you fucking little bitch, you tramp you whore! You just tell me what you did with my identification, so that I could forget that I ever met you," Dickerson yelled.

"You wish. I got your I.D. and you can get it back after you take care of my girl's paperwork and we're on the job. The faster you make it happen, the faster you get your shit back. And if you try anything, I'll tell about this night, and for proof I'll tell about that butterfly tattooed on your ass. Bye, bye!"

I sat there watching the phone for a moment, and when he didn't call back I laughed till tears streamed down my cheeks.

Chapter 13

Deb and I finally finished the whole employment process. After eight weeks of training up north at the California Training Facility in Soledad Prison, we were issued our gold star California Correctional Officers badges, and notified of our posting at C.I.M: the California Institution for Men, at Chino prison just outside of Pomona, California.

My first order of business was to square things with Dickerson, so I dressed in blue jeans that really accentuated the shape of my ass and the contour of my pussy a pair of black leather stiletto heel boots, with a matching quarter length black leather coat, and a tight V-neck silk white t-shirt with no bra so that my nipples could be seen through it. I clipped my badge to my belt in a way that when I move my coat, my badge would be visible. I drove out to the Sheriffs Testing Center and surprised Dickerson. I walked into his office, to find him seated at his desk, so immersed in paperwork that he hadn't noticed me until I slid the brand new alligator wallet I brought him with his credentials inside, across the table.

He looked up at me and I opened my coat to reveal the badge clip to my belt, and my hard nipples beneath my t-shirt. He looked from my fat pussy past my badge up to my titties and back to my face with his tongue hanging out the side of his mouth.

"I brought you back your i.d."

"Damn you woman; if I wasn't so crazy about you, I could kill your black ass."

We both laughed. He was genuinely glad to see me; he loved the new wallet I bought him, and we ate lunch in his office together while I told him all about the academy, and where I was assigned. I dick teased him, and we talked shit. He told me if ever I needed him for anything, that I knew where to find him. We parted on good terms, and I felt really good about it.

···

I awoke before the crack of dawn on my first day. The instant my feet hit the floor, my mind shifted from peaceful dreams the night before, to thoughts of what in the hell have I gotten myself into? I went through my toiletries dressed in my new uniform with a black ball cap, baring the Correctional Officers insignia patch on its face. Looking in the mirror, my image staring back at me sparked thoughts of me being a commando, then a Correctional Officer in my dark green jumpsuit, with black leather gloves and jump boots. The gold Correctional Officer's badge worn on my utility belt stood out the most. I didn't have much of an appetite so I packed a light lunch in the igloo I had bought for this job. Then I was out the door.

Deb and I had decided that we would drive our own cars, and pretend that we didn't know each other until after we got our bearings. We were in low profile mode. We had to be because this was only our ninety day observation point's probationary period. We had to get past this before we could move any further to full Peace Officer's status. Driving along the highway leading into the prison, my first thoughts were of how wide spread it was. Its razor wire top fencings went on for several miles and then there were the watch towers spread along the fence line. But the towers were more than just an observation post. They were the high ground points for guards armed with semiautomatics, high-powered mini – 14 riffles, and they were charged with maiming or killing any man who dare attempt an escape. The tower guard was also armed with a thirty-eight special pistol. Tinted glass obstructed the view of any person looking from the ground, while the tower had a Birdseye view of anything on the ground. To protect the public from the imprisoned at all cost, was the tower shooter's sole objective. It's what our instructors at the academy repeatedly drilled in us.

When I turned onto the prison grounds, of all the signs that I noticed, it was the one that read enter at your own risk, hostages will not be recognized for bargaining purposes pursuant to C.C.R. 3304. Suddenly I felt a new fear at the thought of being taken hostage. I'd be on my own because the official position is not to trade a prisoner's freedom for the life of any hostage taken on prison grounds. I parked near the employee's entrance and I sat quietly in my car looking out the front windshield up into the dark gray overcast of the sky where I thought of God. "God now you know I ain't big on bothering you with begging but please if you're listening, your girl is begging you right now for a sign that you got me covered up in here today." I grabbed my igloo container, stepped from the car and walked towards the staff entrance. Off to my right side just for a moment, the clouds parted and the sun broke through and shined a rainbow above the cold, colorless prison below.

Once inside the prison I was directed by a black male Sergeant, who looked and moved about a day away from retirement on a full pension. He directed me to tag along with security and escort, Officer Sheldon who stored my lunch container and lead me off to a secured room where I was issued a P4 baton and handcuffs. Then S & E 1 Officer Sheldon lead me out into the central corridor where we walked down its center with inmates to the right wall of us moving in one direction, and inmates to the left wall of us moving in the opposite direction. Officer Sheldon was a stern, stone-face Caucasian of thirty years old. He stood over 6 feet on his well-built frame. He wore his full head of blonde hair close cropped under his uniform cap, and his steel blue color eyes where hidden behind dark shades. Everything about the man conveyed the essence of a pure hard ass cop on first impression, except for the periodic glances that he stole at my ass.

"All of the bullshit you learned during the academy, forget it, except for two things: the first is, never ever bail out on your partner because your partner is your only true friend in this bitch; two, never rat out your fellow officers no matter what when it comes to the animals, understood?"

"Yes sir."

"Be certain about it because you forget either and you're dead, understood?" Sheldon said without as much as a glance at me. His attention completely changed, trained on the inmates walking along the wall in traffic that moved towards us.

"Yes sir," I answered.

I took in the corridor as we walked for a while in silence. All officers and other personnel moved down the center of the corridor. It was the personal space of staff. Large iron doors stood along the sides of the corridor sign above them stating where they led to.

For the most part, the inmates seemed to look me over from head to toe with little to no interest in Officer Sheldon. But at times there were certain inmates who stood out to me; the ones who passed me without seeming to notice us, yet I knew they had. Those inmates all conveyed a fearlessness about them that wasn't missed on me.

A corridor PA system, which randomly broke the soft tone of chatter that filled the air with the directives from a unseen female, paged various inmates by last name, last two prison numbers and housing. We came to one of the steel doors and paused. Its overhead sign read Palm Hall.

Sheldon turned to me and sternly said, "Stay off the cell bars, keep your back to the walls where possible. Watch your back and make a mental inventory of every one of these guy's hands and feet at all times. If anyone in here asks you a question, pretend you don't hear them at first and if they persist, respectfully tell them to get at their floor officer, and show no fear. Be courteous, lose the smile and look everyone in the eye that makes eye contact with you."

Sheldon's key open the large iron door and we proceeded to the officer's station of the hole. A sign above the desk read "Ad/Seg." There were several desks with officers seated at them. All five of the officers were me: four whites and one black. A large caged area contained riot helmets, protective shields and other gear behind lock and key. The sound of hundreds of men in unison followed the calls of a single man in a military cadence, "How do you feel?" Shouted the lead man! "fine sir!" came the chorus of the men.

"What do you want?" shouted the lead man! "Freedom sir!" Came the chorus of the men.

I had never heard such fearlessness in men; they sounded like soldiers in a standing army ready for war.

"Oh most of them will kill you if given the chance –so don't give them the chance," Sheldon said. "This is where we keep the worst of the worst: Black Guerilla Family, Mexican Mafia, La Emmy, Crips, Bloods, Fruit of Islam, Notorious None Affiliates, Arian Brotherhood, and few Northern Familia, but there's not a lot of them down on this end of the state to make the kind of noise your listening to now: Those are the monkeys you're hearing now, Sheldon said in a tone of respectful distain.

"Mutiyari," said the single voice.

"Mutiyari," came the chorus.

"Undelaya," said the single voice.

"Undelaya," came the chorus.

"Anza," Said the single voice.

"Anza," came the chorus.

"What are they saying?" I asked.

"Ready, set, go. They're just saying it in the African language of Swahili," Came the response of a heavy, yet feminine voice from behind me.

I turned to see an open door to a small dark office, where robust built black woman of forty years old walked out onto the light, carrying a clipboard in hand. Her collar held the double gold bars on each that identified her rank as Captain. I knew immediately that she was a lesbian. She was Captain Gains, a nonsense butch of a bitch, with a pretty face and moves about her that would likely give an average man a good squabble on her worst day. Her hands looked like mitts and her feet were way too large for any woman, while her gold teeth told everyone that she was from the Dirty South.

"You're a long way from flipping burgers and working department store registers little girl," she said to me with an up and down stare.

"Beg your pardon?" I stated.

"You got heart. Good, cause you gone need all of that. Hell, you gone need a gun-slinger's heart up in here," she smiled. "Show her the menagerie animals Sheldon," she said.

"Yes, Captain."

The other officers all chuckled as Sheldon unlocked a second iron bar door that let us into a three tiered cell block, each with some fifty cells on each tier. We walked up three flights of stairs to the third tier were Sheldon paused, and we looked down on a prison exercise yard where at least forty black inmates exercised with military precision to the cadence call of a lone man standing faced-off to them. Most were wearing cheap tennis-shoes, their boxer underwear, and maybe a t-shirt.

"In excellent shape, aren't they?" Sheldon asked.

"Yes."

"They function like a military unit, in theory at least. When they are released, most go back to the world we know and fall right back into an undisciplined life style of sex, drugs, drinking and fast cash … all this shit ain't even a memory, until they're return to custody on a parole violation or a new beef. Then it all begins all over again. If it wasn't for overwhelming fire power…" Sheldon points at the Gunner's post, protruding from an adjacent building. Halfway up it, the guard watched them from behind dark shades, a mini-14 assault rifle in hand. "they'd over run us in less than the time it takes you to piss," Sheldon finishes.

We continued on down the third tier past the filled single cells of Mexican inmates, all dressed as the men out on the exercise yard. Each seemed silently disciplined, their faces buried in books. All of them were covered in elaborate tattoos that reflected prison life, pretty girls and low-rider cars. They played it off like they weren't interested in me but I knew different, simply because you can't bullshit a bullshitter.

As soon as we were off of the tier, Sheldon said to me "those guys there are the Mexican Mafia; very cordial, extremely disciplined as they are lethal. They will lie in wait with the patience of a crocodile to make the kill.

"So how long will they stay locked up like this? "I asked.

"Til hell freezes over if they don't die, go home or some fucking liberal court doesn't order their release back into the general population," Sheldon said as he spat on the ground. "Crips coming up. Not as organized from what you've seen so far. Administratively them and the bloods are classified as disruptive groups, but I got 'em noted as disorganized noise: but dangerous none the less, and they will tear up shit when they go off.

As soon as we walked on the tier someone yelled, "Back door coming at you!" The taps of a manual typewriter sounded from somewhere along the tier. I knew it was a look out that we were on the tier.

"Yo,yo, yo hey shorty, put some breaks on that thang!" said a Black inmate to me as he looked up from a magazine he was reading from while seated on the toilet taking a shit.

"Cuz check the pooper on this trooper marching from the rear. Damn dog, oooH weee!" another Black inmate said, as we passed him casing in his cell.

"Pardon me officer" one of the inmates said. Sheldon stopped in front of his cell. He was the most muscle bound man I had ever seen in my life. From his head to his toes he left nothing to the imagination as he stood there in nothing but his boxer underwear and tennis shoes. His chest muscles jumped up and down as he put his hands on his hips, and looked me straight in my eyes with a smile.

"I need a couple of 602 forms," he said to me. Sheldon looked to me.

"I'm talking to you lady," he said.

I turned to him, "Officer Jones," I pointed to my name tag. "And you have to see your Floor Officer about that request sir."

"Very good Jones," Sheldon said to me over his shoulder as we continued on.

"Me and Mrs. Jones, we 'bout to have a thang going on, going on, going on" The inmate suddenly belted out in song. The other inmates all joined in to the song, and I had to crack a smile that I was thankful Sheldon didn't see.

"This next tier is where the Bloods are housed. They're not much different than, Sheldon falls abruptly silent at the sound of an alarm.

The PA system blares "Code one, Sycamore! Code one, Sycamore!" the announcer's sense of urgency rings out.

"Follow me!" Sheldon shouts to me, and starts out running. By the time we clear the stairs to the ground floor, the Ad/Seg Officers have the bar door open and we're running down the corridor center with our batons drawn, as the inmates are all seated on the floor along the walls.

I had no idea what I was running into as I followed officers filing through the open iron door with the sign above it that read "Sycamore." We ran through a second bar gate, where we found a number of officers at the rear of the cell block gathered around a White inmate lying on the floor. A number of inmates were seated on the floor along the walls and the cell doors; but none were near the White inmate, and then I saw why. He was obviously dead, lying in his own blood pool that was so red it looked purple. His throat was open ear to ear, his head nearly severed off, with eyes wide open in death's gaze of nothingness. It was as if his eyes had turned gray. At that moment I thought of something I had read in school about the eyes being the windows to the soul, and that the grayness of his eyes signified his soul was long gone.

Medical staff rushed in and began trying to revive the dead guy, but everyone on the tier knew that only God could revive this guy and that was most unlikely. I backed away from the scene of death towards a wall with all of the officers seemingly looking at me, but I heard someone behind me coughing. I turned to find it wasn't me who they were looking at but Deb, standing behind me with her back to everyone, and the palms of her hands resting against the wall as she was throwing up.

"I got you. Come on," I said to Deb who looked up and realized it was I who was talking to her. I took her around the waist and lead her down the tier towards the exit.

"Soft ass bitch shouldn't be here in the first place," one of the Black inmates said from where he sat against the wall, as Deb and I approached him.

With my arm around Deb as she leaned on my shoulder, I paused next to the Black inmate, "Shut your mouth smart ass, before you find yourself in Ad/Seg," I stated to the inmate, the smug look on his face suddenly lost.

I looked over my shoulder and Sheldon smiled at me with a slight nod of his head. I continued with Deb out into the central corridor to a staff restroom, where she ran into the toilet and threw up again. I stood before a mirror staring back at my out stretched hand trembling before me. I turned on the sink tap.

"Deb, shake that shit off and get your ass over here. Now Deb, it's just blood girl, you see it from out your ass once a month, and it don't make you sick then, now getcha' your ass over here."

Deb staggered over to the sink and cupped hands full of water that she repeatedly splashed in her face. "I saw it happen, Sessie. Two of them grabbed his arms and the other one came from behind him and cut his throat. I thought they were playing. I was touring the third tier, oh shit I can't. I can't even remember what they look like," Deb stammered out between splashes of water to her face.

The door opens and into the restroom walks two more officers. The first is a White Sergeant with an obvious implant boob job, platinum blonde hair worn in a Cleopatra cut, heavy eye mascara, with wine-red lipstick and cheap perfume. At thirty-two years old, Sergeant Donna Deloach. In spite of her functioning alcoholism, Sergeant Deloach was still somewhat attractive and physically in shape. A fifteen year veteran she had been married and divorced five times in the last fifteen years, all to other officers in the three prisons she had worked in --I would later learn. She had a tough manner, spoke her mind, and was reputable as a team player by her colleagues.

The second woman was Officer Rhonda Tubbs a twenty-eight year old four year veteran from Compton, California. Tubbs was six feet tall, and very attractive with unblemished extremely dark skin, clear brown eyes, and pearl white teeth. She wore her nails short and well-kept; with hair so short she was near balled. She had played for the WNBA out of college on one of the eastern teams; before a knee injury took her out of the game. She returned to the C.P.T where she became a Correctional Officer, Deb would later tell me.

"Which one of these would be your tag alone?" Deloach asked.

"She would be Bovaise," Tubbs answered.

Deb wiped her face with paper towels as her composure slowing returned to calm.

"What did you see?" Deloach asked Deb.

Standing behind Deloach, Tubbs shook her head no to Deb, and then dropped her head rubbing the back of her neck as if fatigue, as Deloach glanced back over her shoulder at Tubbs and then returned her attention to Deb.

"Nothing Ma'am, Sergeant. Nothing at all. When I looked down from the third tier, the inmate was just lying there," Deb nervously answered.

"I see. You can't stand the sight of blood uh Bovaise?" Deloach asked Deb.

"No, no I can't."

"Well, you better get used to it real fast, because you're going to see a whole lot of it on a regular in here. Same thang leaks out of your tail is all it is. Think about it like that, and before long you won't even notice it," Deloach stated to Deb, and then turned to Tubbs. "See to it that she writes it up on the report the same as you, understand it?"

Tubbs nods her head in the affirmative.

"And who are you?" Deloach asked me.

"Jones."

"I saw how you came to her aid, good job. Sheldon is out in the corridor waiting on you," Deloach said as she shook my hand. "And this is Tubbs. I schooled her myself", Deloach said with a pat to Tubbs back, as she too, shook my hand.

Chapter 14

At shift's end, I walked to my car. I ran into Tubbs, Deloach and Deb all standing in the parking lot.

"Hey Jones, some of us girls are about to hook up at the hangout for drinks. Are you game?" Deloach asked me.

"Yeah, yeah. I'm game lead the way."

I followed the caravan to a Pomona bar full of off duty CO's, where we shot pool and drank over conversation. Deb and I played it low key social, like we were brand new. Tubbs introduced Deb and I to Lucy Velasco and Glenda Joy.

Lucy Velasco was barley five feet tall; a Filipino and Black woman with a petite stature, beautiful shiny black hair and bronze completion, with an outgoing manner.

Officer Glenda Joy was twenty-nine years old five feet ten inches, light completion Black woman with green eyes. Glenda had a very bubbly personality with a sassy mouth when she spoke.

Latanya Yizar walked into the bar with Sally Ramirez and Lenard McCoy, none of them were officers; but they joined our party. Latanya Yizar, a Caucasian woman who was the Chief Dietician for the prison, stood five feet- six and a half inches, medium athletic built with a very soft spoken manner. Sally Ramirez wore her M.T.A (medical training assistant) credentials pinned to her scrubs, above her breast and I read on it that she was twenty five years old. She was born in Puerto Rico, Boriken a province of the United States, as she was so quickly to point out, in her second language of English. Sally was five feet-eight with smooth tan-tone skin. She had a personality of a bull: very stubborn but very smart and thorough.

Lenard McCoy was thirty years old and from Utah, the Mormon State, he told us. He was tall and handsome with alabaster skin, sandy brown curly hair. His face cleanly shaven his eyes green from behind his designer spectacles. He was a Registered Nurse at the prison, and a student attending UCLA's Medical School where he was studying to be a doctor.

Yizar, Ramirez, and McCoy were regulars at the bar in the company of Deloach, Tubbs, Velasco and Joy. They welcomed Deb and me into their clique.

"Everyone is cliqued up at the prison even the prisoners," Sergeant Deloach said to Deb and I.

Deloach pointed out "Captain Gains, with her boys from Ad/Seg". She called Deb's and my attention to a corner table in the shadows where three large body builder type men and a lone woman sat taking in the movements of all. All four were wearing civilian clothes.

"The big red son-of-a-gun is Lieutenant Mark Zimmerman, the Black guy across from him is Buddy Cox, the Mexican is Antony Solece and the broad; that's Suti Ali, they are the black patches –

I.S.U. Institutional Security Unit, the Warden's crew and they answer to no one except him. Don't you girls get your boots in their shit, because if you do, there ain't no getting it off," Deloach said.

Mark Zimmerman, I guessed to be about forty-five years old, an ex-Marine type who still wore his hair in a buzz cut. He stood at six feet-seven inches tall, and weighted at least two-hundred, forty-seven pounds, legs like tree-trunks, with arms larger then my thighs with a neck the size of my waist. His expression was intense and he was extremely intimidating to look at.

Buddy Cox looked to be about forty years old and he too stood as tall as Zimmerman, but he seemed much wider at two-hundred, sixty-five pounds of all muscle. He wore a handle-bar mustache like that of a cartoon character, with bulging eyes and a clean shaved head. He drank in silence, all the while his big eyes shifting about.

Antony Solece was equal in size to his crew, poster child for a muscle magazine. His arms were so large that I wondered how he was able to wipe his ass when he shit. He seems so much younger than the other two. I thought I saw him smile-a time or two ever so slightly.

Deloach told me that Sergeant Suti Ali was thirty years old and that she had defected from Libya where she was one of Moammar Gadahafi's private bodyguards. She told me that the broad was a black belt, and once fought with three inmates in the hole on the second tier at San

Quentin where she started eight years ago. Deloach said that Sergeant Ali got the best of the inmates until they tossed her over the tier where she broke her collar bone. She told me that it was said the bitch never cried. I got the feeling that Deloach admired Sergeant Suti Ali.

"Coming through the door, that be Officer Sheldon who you already know. The piece of chorizo beef behind him is Officer Hymie Mendez. Now that gorgeous Black stud he's with is Officer Norman Lane. They say he got a dick like a mule, and if you let him fuck you, you're ruined for life, so if you ever plan on having kids stay clear of him." Deloach said, and we all cracked up laughing. "That last thing in their clique, he be Officer Hite. I can't be certain but he just may be -," Deloach holds one of her hands out and rocks it with a whistle. And we laughed so hard that I think Hite sensed that Deloach was talking about him. Sheldon, Mendez, Lane and Hite headed over to a pool table.

As soon as he saw me, Officer Sheldon acknowledged me with a slight nod of his head for which I, in turn, did the same. The evening went on with Officer Tubbs, Sergeant Deloach, Officer Velasco, Officer Joy, M.T.A Ramirez, Dietician Yizar and the only guy in our clique, R.N. McCoy filling Deb and I in on who was who until we parted ways for home.

Deb and I took different freeways home that night. Once I was home she called me. "I'll admit I'm scared of the place. I mean, it looks so cold colorless and creepy. It's as if no human should be living in there," I told Deb.

"That's because that ain't living. Hell, they just existing on hope that they will come out and live again. But then it's prison Sessie. Get over it. It's not supposed to be colorful and soft looking. Most all society has deemed them animals less than human. That's why they're in cages, Hello! Wake up and smell the coffee."

"All of that from a bitch who threw up at the sight of a little blood, and probably peed in her panties," I told Deb, and we laughed. Coming up together, Deb and I always had to be tough girls. We had to be supportive of one another; our characters complimenting each other in a shared sisterhood. Deb is street savvy and strong willed, but at times her street savvy needs to be checked, and her roll slowed a bit. She knows how to get her money for the sake of survival. While I balance her street savvy with critical thinking, and slow strategic planning. Where Deb first jumps in and thinks later; I think it out first, and then jump in. We each acknowledge that I'm the decision maker in our relationship, without ever saying as much. If we stay on track with her game and my leadership skills, we can truly be successful in whatever endeavor we embark upon.

Chapter 15

The ninety day probation period passed, and we were granted our peace officers status, licensed to carry firearms, and assigned to our wings. I was assigned to Sycamore Hall while Deb was assigned down the corridor from me to Cypress Hall. We waited until we were able to get from behind the desk at the front of the cell block, and assigned onto the cell block floor, before we begin setting in motion our plan to come together.

I wanted to be on the same wing as Deb. She said not to worry, she can make it happen. And before I knew it, I was transferred down to Cypress Hall with Deb, Velasco, Joy, and Deloach as our wing Sergeant. We had the only all-female wing in the entire prison. Sergeant Deloach was at the top of her game. We worked well together, and just as it was back in high school, people gravitated to Deb, and the staff here was no different. I on the other hand, was very observant of my surroundings and I never attempted to make friends as Deb did.

The guys wanted to get with Deb and I because of our shapes. It just so happened, we both have really unusually large butts with very small waist and nice proportional boobs; not to mention our attractive faces.

Deb's motto in life is using what you got to get what you want, so having the figure that she has, is why she feels that she can get it. Judging from her encounter with Michael, Jim and Seth before we landed this job, just goes to show she's right to think just that.

Truly, I don't knock anyone who has to do what they need to do to survive. My mother did what she needed to do to make sure she kept us going. Sometimes you have to look past the surface of your life, as opposed to those who possess the finer things but could be the most unhappy, stressed out and at times the most maniacal in life. When you have to struggle as a family, you learn to appreciate life and each other. You learn to make it happen for yourself by any means necessary, even though some things you do can cost you, you still can't help but think it was worth it, especially when you can see how it may benefit those you love.

Deb and Lucy worked side-by-side, and they hit it off really well together. Deb told me that Lucy had shared some of her personal life. She told Deb about a sexual relationship that she was having with a Lieutenant, and how they would sneak off together to get down in a secret spot where they meet whenever the urge struck them. It sounded risky to me, yet tempting to be under fire like that. And I wondered what being spontaneous felt like, and knew that I would have to try it someday.

Chapter 16

Three months into the job and I was feeling the paychecks. The money was good, so good that I was beginning to be somewhat numb to the ever presence of tension and possible drama. But still the money wasn't enough and I found that the more money I made, the more I felt I needed to make. We were making the transition from young inner-city girls of the hood, to responsible women.

The one thing that I was unable to get a handle on was some transportation for Yorkie. Our schedules were to the point that we hardly saw each other. Our schedules were set to where I'd come in from work and she would be gone, or when I'm leaving for work she would be coming in. I mean we were doing what we had to do in order to pay our bills and keep a roof over our heads; but we were missing family time together. I just wasn't feeling her hours. She needed a car to get around and that was that. It was too dangerous for her to be catching the bus out of East LA in the wee-hours of the morning.

But with each week of time's passage, I became more frustrated at not being able to help Yorkie with some wheels. My siblings were straight though; enjoying their new clothes and toys that I was showering them with at each paycheck. My little sister's grades improved and she was placed on the honor roll. She told me that she felt her good grades were due to the new clothes and shoes that she was now wearing to school, no longer sharing with her sisters.

She told me that nobody looks at her like she was poor and raggedy anymore, and that the kids had stopped teasing her. She told me that she had friends and how looking good, made her feel good. When she told me that, my heart was so filled with joy. I really felt the difference that I was now making in their lives, and I could see it in them as well. I was paying for braces and other stuff, and the bills were mounting.

There was no way that I could ever stop providing for them now but I knew that I couldn't take care of us on my salary alone. I made up my mind that it was time to holla' at Deb about a little talk she and I had about checking some more money on a Hoe tip. But I had to put a plan together or Deb would just go willy-nilly and put us at risk of being crashed.

...

On the job I thought about how and when I would cut into Deb about pulling some paper out the pussy. I held off until things kind of lightened up. Joy took a break in Deloach's office, so I slid over to Deb and Velasco's side of the wing were the inmates were having dayroom leisure time.

"Hey Deb, I'm about to start looking for a second job. Well, a hustle on the weekends for the most part. I need another car, like yesterday," I told her.

"What's up, you finally tired of pushing that bucket of yours?"

"Naw, my baby runs like a race horse. I'm tired of my Mama catching the bus late nights from work. She needs a car."

"So, what's the problem with you letting her use yours, and you riding to work with me."

"Nothing at all, but it's more than that. I'm paying for the kids braces and the whole nine right now, so I need to check some more paper, and I need it like yesterday," I said and I knew where her mind was going to go before Deb opened her mouth.

"You know you sitting on a gold mine already. You can mine what you need out of it and sit back down on it til you need it again. Look at what I did in two days of lying on my back busting nuts; cumin' all the way to the bank," Deb said softly laughing. I just smiled and shook my head at her.

After hearing Deb out, I told her I was down but that I would decide when and where we would do it, because the stakes were just too high. We could protect ourselves now, we were licensed to carry firearms, but if we got busted it would mean the end of our careers and we'd probably spend some time in jail for Hoeing while armed with pistols.

Chapter 17

After work that evening, Deb and I got dressed up in our stilettos and mini-dresses. We went out to the bar that we celebrated in when we first passed our test… the same bar where we met Michael, Jim and Seth at. But it was a different place now and I felt uncomfortable with propositioning any of the guys we saw in there. Most didn't look like they had much money, and the few that did, had a police look about them.

"Let's go home Deb. This doesn't feel right. I need to rethink some shit. I may just have a better hunting ground in mind. Just let me think on it."

Back in the car, I began to tell Deb how it was just too risky to be out in the open like that pushing up on men.

"We could hit up prisoners," I told Deb.

"Bitch are you crazy? You lost your rabbit ass mind!"

"No listen just hear me out Deb, the street shit is just too risky."

"Oh and you think fucking prisoners in prison is less jeopardizing than that bar? What the hell are you thinking? They're most likely to snitch us off or worst, cut our fucking throats, than one of those guys in the bar," Deb ranted.

"Tone it down and just hear me out. We know they got cash in there. Hell the Gooners just ran in on that big crazy White boy they call Pin Cushion; shook his cage down, ripped his mattress open and found what seven, no eight grand. Uh?"

I could see Deb's mind was racing. She was too quiet, and when she finally did speak she said, "Yeah, true-dat, but I wouldn't be caught dead in a room by myself with that beast. He ain't been fucking nothin' but butt-boys his whole life. He don't even like girls," Deb shivered. "Son of a bitch gives me the willies just thinkin' bout his ass," Deb went on to say.

"I know, I know but hear me out. I'm not talkin' about him perse. I'm just using the money that they found in his cell as an example of what kind of money that is in here. They ain't all monsters. Most of them are just crooks out for their paper. The one thing for damn sure ain't none of them cops. Some of them is snitches for sure, but them that are not, ain't trying to get no rat-jacket put on them. Secondly, they want some pussy too bad to be giving up a good thang."

"Well how are you going to know who we can and can't trust Sessie? How are you going to know which one of them won't try to kill us or just fuck us, and tell us we paid? Basically, rape us."

I let the question linger for a while as we rode along. And then it came to me. I snapped my finger at the realization, "I got it! Lucy has already shown us that she's cool. We get at her about a good spot to take an inmate and toss him up? You did tell me she knows where all the locations are for getting-down didn't you? "

"Yeah, I did,"

"Okay then, I'm going to line up the clientele, and I know just the inmate to holla' at. I stumbled on him selling weed a week ago. Instead of busting his ass and rolling him up, I just told him that I knew my mind was playing tricks on me, and I didn't see what I thought I did. But if I saw it again, then I will put the Gooner squad in his mix. He thanked me for warning him and then smiled at me. And now I got a friend for life."

"Well Sessie I ain't convinced yet, but I'm going to trust that you got this and I'm game as usual."

"Do you have Lucy's number? I don't want to discuss this with her at work until I fill her out."

"I got her number right here." Deb pulled out her phone, dialed up Lucy and handed me the phone.

"Hey Lucy, this is Sessie Jones from the job girl."

"Hey girl what's up?" Lucy's voice came back over the phone.

"I had Deb call you up for me."

"Make sure you get my number so you can get at me direct next time okay?"

"I got it! Check this, there's an inmate I need to get in an isolated spot where I can get at him. Do you think you could help me out with that?"

"Sure, but if it's something that can get you caught up, then you need to go over to records and check out his C-File, it will give you some insight into him. The crime shit could say anything; don't concern yourself with that, what you want to look at is the C-File's confidential section. It will have a big red stamp across it that reads CONFIDENTIAL; if he's an informant or if he's ever told on anyone, you'll find it there. And girl once a rat always a rat."

"Records won't raise any red flags on me or the inmate whose file I'm requesting, will they?"

"Not at all, you can request and review as many C-Files as you want but only on your off hours. The department encourages it in the interest of inmate identification," Lucy said.

"Good looking out girl. We gone talk some more tomorrow."

We said our goodbyes, and Deb started talking to me to see where I was headed with this. I could hear her talking to me but I wasn't paying attention, and she knew me well enough to know it. I was formulating the plan. It was game time money to be made, but it had to be played right. I knew going into this, that once it got rolling, it would take on a life of its own and I had to control it. I knew that Deb would want to push it to the limit and I was going to have to balance her get-down.

"Sessie Jones?"

"Yeah Deb."

"You ain't heard shit I said."

"My bad. I'm puttin' this shit together in my head and when I get it right it's on."

Chapter 18

I arrived at work with a feeling that my life was again about to take on a dramatic change. I had the plan now it was all about who the players would be in the game... my game, and what shape it would take. During that mornings work release of the prisoners, the first thing that I noticed was that our; Joy's and my, wing side cage gunner was new. The old, by-the-book white man was gone. Joy told me that she thought Deloach had him booted for rating her out.

"Deloach is not a person to get into a pissing contest with in here, because the girl's got juice that flows all the way down from the Warden's office. You rat her out and she will know about it. Once she knows you crossed her, you assed out!" Joy said as we walked the third tier together un-keying the cell doors for the inmates to get out for work.

The new gunner was a young Asian guy. Maybe twenty-five years old, he was Officer Winn Tag, an all American Vietnamese who miss nothing from behind his dark tint Ray ban sunglasses. The mini 14-assault rifle always draped from the shoulder strap as he cradled it in his arms. There was something about the way Officer Tag handled the rifle, that told anyone who half-ass paid attention to him, that he would put a spark to you and make shit dark to you real fast.

After the work release unlock was completed, Joy and I headed up to the Wing front where Velasco and Deb where seated at their desk on a short break before yard release. As Joy and I sat at our desk, Deloach came out of her office with a box of pastries.

"The wing staff assignments are now complete. I gather all of you have met the new gunners. If not make it so and I'll tell you now, they are us and we are them. It took me a minute to work Officer Tag up on the A-Wing gun, and Officer Mendez up on the B-Wing gun. And now that I have, if we run into any situation on my wing, we work them out through me. We don't take our dirty laundry past my office, am I understood?"

A chorus of understanding rang out. Deloach went on to say, "Cause if whatever happens on this wing is aired outside my office, your ass will be booted off to gun tower seventy-three, out by the sewage plant where you can guard shit floating around in a cesspool. Now, eat my pastries and make sure both gunners get their issues." With that Deloach walked back into her office, kicked her heels atop her desk and got on her institutional office phone.

"Okay, Your-Highness," Deb said in a low voice.

"I heard that Bovaise," Deloach gave Deb the finger from behind the pictured window to her office, and we all laughed.

"The woman's ears can hear a mouse pissing on cotton," Joy said.

"So what you got for me Velasco?" I asked.

"During first yard release, go over to records. I already had the inmate's file pulled, and if it's good when you get back, we'll go from there," Velasco answered.

The PA system announced yard release. Sergeant Deloach called out from her office for us to pull the bars and let them out. She closed her office door and turned off the light. We climbed the stairs up to the third tier and began our release of the cell block from the third tier down.

I was in records thirty minutes later reading inmate Don Ford's C-File. I went straight to his confidential file and I read that he was a non-affiliated gang member, who had been in multiple incidents over his ten years of imprisonment. It also included an over seven years to life sentence for a credit union robbery. The file read that he had been stabbed on two occasions and was suspected of having stabbed three inmates himself, as a result of his suspected involvement in the prison drug trade.

The file read that he offered no information in each of the incidents where he was stabbed and in three incidents where he was the suspect in the stabbings, all three victims failed to identify him.

The subject's informant potential; is unlikely. For confidential enemy listing see continuous pages.

It was nearly voluntary inline from the yard, so I returned the file and headed back to my post, just in time for lock-ups.

"So what did you learn girl?" Velasco ask me.

"Informant potential unlikely," I said with a smile.

Velasco gave me a handwritten pass, "On your next security check give this to the inmate. It's to the diet kitchen."

On my security check; when I arrived at inmate Ford's cell up on the third tier, Tupac's 'Me Against The World' softly sounded from a CD player on his shelf as he did push-ups down on the floor. He was in excellent shape. He was sweaty, and bare chested, wearing sweatpants. His body was decorated with several beautiful tattoos. Then there was a scar to one side of his lower back that I knew was from one of the stabbings I'd read about in the confidential section of his C-File.

He looked up at me as he was doing his pushups.

"Give me your last two Ford?"

"Twenty-two Denver twenty-two Why what's up?" he asked as he rose from the floor to stand at the cell door.

I gave him the pass that Velasco had written out. He took it and looked at it.

"The cost of living is what's up and it's time for you to pay for it."

"Pay for it. Pay for what?" he ask puzzled.

"Bring a hundred dollars cash with you, and find out but if you're broke, well you need not even come out the cell," I said and walked off leaving him standing there.

Velasco had prearranged Ford's pass to the diet kitchen to coincide with my break. I got there before him. Officer Tubbs was waiting for me seated at the desk of her post.

"Hey Jones, stand on deck. When your boy comes through the grill gate pat him down, cuff him from behind and have him step to the door over there to the right." Tubbs said and pointed to a door. "I'm going to lock you in there with him, you got twenty minutes to holla' at him. Don't knock when you want to get out, I'll come get you ok?"

"Yeah girl."

Ford walked through the grill gate a moment later with the pass in his hand. He looked at me then he looked cautiously about the room, and approached Officers Tubbs' desk where she was writing notations in her log book.

"Ford, Denver twenty-two. I don't know what this is about," Ford said to Tubbs.

I approached Ford. "Inmate Ford, I need to pat you down. Please step over to the wall, and put your hands on it for me." Ford complied and I pat-searched him, as Tubbs came from behind her desk. Her hand gingerly poised on her P-4 baton.

"What's this all about? What I do Officer Jones?"

"Did you bring what I told you to? " He glanced over his shoulder at me.

"Trust me. I'm the police," I told him.

He pulled the hundred dollars from the coin pocket of his Levi jeans. It was rolled up so small in saran-wrap, that it was no larger than the tip of my pinky finger. I gave it to Tubbs, and then handcuffed him behind his back.

"All man, this is a setup," he said.

"Be quiet," I said. And I walked him into the room with Tubbs locking the door behind us.

"Face me Ford. What it is? is that you ain't had no pussy since pussy had you and that hundred dollars just bought you fifteen minutes of fame," I told him.

He brought his cuffed hands under his feet before him some shit I would never have thought of, and then undid his pants before I could get the condom out its package. He was standing there grinning with his pants and boxers down around his ankles with his dick standing straight up pointing at me.

I let my jumpsuit fall down around my knees as I walked up to him. He put the condom on before I could get turned around and backed into him. He rested his cuffed hand on my lower back

and guided his hard dick up inside me. "Oh my goodness," he mumbled as he went
up inside me.

•••

    After work that day, our clique met up at the Pomona Bar & Grill where we got to meet our latest two members. Officer Winn Tag turned out to be the coolest. He was born in California. His parents had been evacuated from Vietnam during the 1975 fall of South Vietnam, where they were granted political asylum for their work in the American Embassy at Saigon.

    Officer Tag grew up in Long Beach in the same neighborhood as Snoop Dogg, the rapper. That day after work in the Pomona Bar & Grill, I learned that Officer Tag was a fan of the hip-hop culture and he had more swagger about him than most Black men in the hood. He was a pool shark who had hustled his way through high school behind a Que ball. By the time he made it to college he was supplementing his pool hall hustling with Mc'ing and d.j.'ing at clubs and parties.

    Seated at our table having drinks, were Officer Tubbs, Joy Velasco, Deb, myself along with Dietician Yizar, M.T.A Ramirez, R.N. McCoy and the new B-side wing Gunner Officer Sonia Mendez, a thirty year old Chicana woman out of South Central Los Angeles. Deb and I knew right off by the way officer Sonia Mendez spoke, what kind of chick she was. The way she spoke told us, she was a chola like the broads who ran with S.Aes who attended the same inner city schools as we attended. I got a glimpse of a tattoo under one of her sleeves as she drank her beer straight from the bottle. It was in the gang style writing that covered so many walls in the neighborhood. "Well, I was born in the barrio of Florencia Thirteen, I graduated from Gage Junior High and Huntington Park High. You know where that is? Mendez asked.

"Yeah, that ain't too far from where my girl Sessie and I grew up at," Deb answered.

"So, were you ever a gang-banger?" Officer Joy asked.

"Chaley, but I come from a family of eight; four boys and four girls. Two of my brothers and one of my sisters banged at one time and they still, to this day, represent the barrio, but they all settled down, hard working with families of their own." Officer Mendez answered.

I liked Mendez and so did Deb. We all did. Officer Tag and Sergeant Deloach went off to play a game of pool. Deb, Velasco and I decided to head on home, excusing ourselves for the evening. Once out in the parking lot, the three of us talked for a bit more.

"So, how was your meeting with Inmate Ford, Jones?" Velasco asked.

In that moment Officer Tubbs hurried out to the parking lot and handed me a folded hundred dollar bill. "Your money," Tubbs said to me.

"Money for what?"

"Today. This morning."

"I'm lost girl?"

"Ford. Hello."

"You made him pay you? A hundred dollars? Damn, you got screwed and he paid you," Velasco stated with an expression of disbelief."

"That's my girl," Deb said. "Don't nothing pay like good, hot pussy on a platter," Deb went on to say.

"Shit, you got a hundred dollars. Sold yourself short and undervalued the market," Tubbs said.

"Huh?" said Velasco.

Tubbs looked at her watch. "Oh shit, I have to get to my kids play. Talk to you tomorrow," Tubbs shouted over her shoulder as she hurried through the parking lot into her car, and drove away.

"Hey, I wanna try one of those Manaja twa parties you been going on all day about," Deb said to Officer Velasco.

"ManaHo' what parties?" I asked and Velasco laughed.

"Ménage' –trois," Velasco corrected us.

"Yeah that," Deb said.

"Are you for real?" Velasco asked.

"Hell yeah I'm for real. You made that shit sound cool. I had one with these White guys before, and I got paid some damn good money girl," Deb said.

"You got paid for that too," asked Velasco in disbelief.

"You mean to tell me you don't, especially given' the fact that you fucking more than one person all at the same time?" Deb asked.

"No, I don't get paid because it's all done for the fun of satisfying my freaky desires."

"For fun my ass, girl you trippin'." Don't you know what your pussy is worth? You are supposed to get paid anytime you get laid. Even if it's just a gift they give you; a dinner and a movie they pay for it. a bill they pay. Men expect to pay to fuck, so don't give your ass away for free girl and if it's about love, well that cost money too," Deb said to Velasco.

"Wow, you are something else Miss Bovaise. So, you know it's a swinger's party? And I've been invited to one tomorrow night, Frank and I."

"We're game. Right, Sess?" Deb asks me.

"Uh, okay," I answered.

"I'll call you tomorrow and give you the directions."

That night, Deb called me and we talked about my get down with inmate Ford. I told her that since it was the first time, I was too nervous to let him do anything other than hit it from behind. I couldn't stop looking at my watch and the door.

"Fuck all that, was the dick big?"

"Biggest one yet. He had to hold me by my hips to keep me on it, with the damn cuffs scratching my back. Next time it will be better."

"Next, time?"

"Yeah. I saw a brand new bed in one of the rooms over there. I'm going to get at Tubbs about moving it in the room she let us get busy in."

"Okay."

"Let me think it all the way out before we go full throttle Deb."

Chapter 19

On the following day I had inmate Ford to hang back in his cell on the morning yard release, so I could get at him. I told Officer Tag that I was cool on the gun coverage, and for him to cover Joy down on the second tier while she was doing a routine pruno search. I went up to the third tier to inmate Ford's cell.

When I got up there he was alone in the cell, his cellie was out on his job assignment. He was seated on his bed listening to the new Notorious B.I.G track *'The World is Filled with Pimps and Hoes.*

"Hey Ford, turn that shit up!" Officer Tag yelled from the gunner's cage.

"You don't know nothin' about that Tag!" Inmate Ford called back.

I got the feeling that Officer Tag was up on who's who and he knew inmate, Ford a lot better than anyone suspected. I keyed open Fords cell door, and I then looked to Officer Tag who gave me a thumbs up, that I returned as I stepped into the cell.

"So what blessing am I to be afforded this morning Miss. Jones?"

"The blessing is my gracing you with my mere presence." I said as I fingered the zipper-pull along the crouch of my jumpsuit.

Ford's eyes locked on my hand. Once I knew that I had his complete attention I cocked one of my black boots up and rested it along the corner foot of his bunk which positioned the contour of my fat pussy in plain view just an arm's length from his face.

"I want you to put it out that I got hot pussy on the line for a hundred dollars a pop. I want you to handle clientele. No sick puppies, 'cause all money ain't good money. You secure the paper, pass it to me with the buyers name and CDC number, and I'll give you the date and the time within seventy-two hours and you already know the place."

"What's in it for me?"

"You get to fuck me for free."

"Okay, that's doable, But first thing's first shorty. You dropping your panties below wholesale market value. See now, a ten minute ride on some pussy one-fourth as good as yours, bottom prices at two hundred bucks for a ten minute ride. And some hot brains on a fellas thang should hit 'em for no less than one hundred and fifty bucks for ten minutes. Now for a thirty minute ride cost four hundred dollars all day long. And them chittlins you packin' in that trunk, shit that deal be whatever you can feel with regards to a price. Now you got them figures locked on your brain?"

"I'm trying to understand something?"

"I'm good with handling your line. No sick puppies, but now I got to get mines."

"I told you. You get to fuck me for free."

"That's all good, believe me you Miss. Jones. And if I would just be inclined to trick my dick off, then you would be the shorty. But I'm tryin' to eat. So I'll tell you what. For my part you see me with half a pound of pot every two weeks. I'll drop you fifteen hundred every time, plus pay you for your pussy like every other stiff dick blowing off stress," He said with a grin.

The P.A system erupts "Code one Burch Hall! Code one Burch Hall!"

Ford grabbed me and stuck his tongue in my mouth. He told me to be safe, as I stepped out his cell. I watched him as I hurriedly keyed his cell door locked. He never broke eye contact with me before I took off running in response to the alarm.

Deb and I were the second floor officers in our post. All code one alarm were ours to respond to as part of our duties. When we got to Burch Hall, we were directed onto the second tier. When we got down its A-side wing, we found officers gathered around an open cell door midway down the tier. A sergeant was waving our run off and we slowed down to a brisk walk just to looky-look. There inside the open cell, sat a handsome Black man in his early forties on the toilet. A cigarette had burned out in the corner of his mouth, his head was slumped to his chest, and I could smell the burnt flesh of his lips from the cigarette. His feet were crossed at the ankle and my first thought was how nice the soft gray leather shoes looked on his feet. His gray silk socks, designer blue jeans and gray silk V-neck t-shirt made him a better dressrd guy than most men on the street. He was wearing a Gucci watch. There was a syringe still planted in the crook of his arm below a Gucci belt used to tie his arm with. He had overdosed on heroin. There was a gold rope chain around his neck with a small medallion in the likeness of Jesus' face.

"There was a curtain up since before yard release, and I just assumed that the guy was taken a dump. Making a pruno run. I saw the curtain still up, so I tell him to show me some movement. He doesn't. I un-keyed his door and tell him I'm coming in. I snatched the sheet down and walla!" said a White male officer of about thirty-five years of age that I had seen in the Pomona Bar & Grill with another clique of officers who were all unknown to me by name.

The officer was speaking to Lieutenant Frank. I knew immediately that he was Velasco's dude by the piercing blue eyes of his that she had described to me. He was in his early forties and stood over six feet tall with good looks and a mannerism that projected the all American Cop. He was in excellent physical shape. Lieutenant Frank cancelled the code one alarm and placed the prison under lockdown status. As he called off command into his radio, I watched him stealing glances at our Deb's and my asses as he took in the scene of death by overdose. Lieutenant Frank orders everyone back to their assigned wing as the I.S.U squad officers arrived on scene and took control.

Lieutenant Zimmerman, Officers Cox, Solece and Sergeant Ali were all business. Their uniforms bore correctional insignia that was absent of the bright colors that was standardized to everyone else. Their insignia patches were all black stitched in color, even the small American flag sewn above their name tags and sleeve patches. Even the crime scene tackle boxes they carried were black in color. "All non-essential personnel; clear the tier," Sergeant Ali commanded.

As I passed her I looked at her; studied her face. She had the darkest eyes that I had ever seen in another person. Her teeth were perfect and pearly white with unblemished skin the complexion of café-au-lait. But the cold black gaze of the bitch's eyes would not allow me to look her in the eyes. She was lethal and I knew it. She made me think of death, and I shuttered at the cold black lifelessness I had seen in her.

"Sessie did you see that Hoe's eyes; cold black like a fuckin cobra's. We need to miss that bitch at all cost".

"You damn sho' got that right".

Chapter 20

The prison stayed locked down for the remainder of that week. Deloach told us that she didn't think the Warden would order a major search, but that he was just operating under a standard procedure for drug overdoses. She told us that the Gooners –black patches were waiting for lab reports to come back on the heroin that they had found in the dead guy's cell. They were just crossing their T's and dotting their I's on the report to make it all look good on paper for Sacramento.

Friday came, and by our shift's end, Deloach told us that she had heard over the prison grapevine that the yard would be up and running Monday morning. As Deb and I made our way through the employee parking lot, I told her that Lieutenant Frank had offered to pick us up for the party tonight. Joy went off to the bathroom while I was in the supply room putting together a fish kit for an inmate who got cut loose from Ad/Seg, when I looked up and saw Lieutenant Frank standing in the room with me."

"What?"

"Yeah girl, he spooked me so bad I damn near fired on him. That's when he asked for our addresses to pick us up, but I told him that's okay, we'd drive ourselves if he just gave us the place and time."

"And?"

"Oh, he gave me the address, and then he tried to slip in a quick feel on the under."

"You bullshittin',Sessie."

"Naw I ain't. I'm telling you girl, the man's eyes never left my breast the whole time we were talking. I don't even think he would know what my face look like if he saw me again." We both laughed at that.

"Velasco really likes this horny fuck. I wonder if she knows he's that flirtatious."

"Come on now Deb, they are swingers."

Chapter 21

Deb and I arrived sometime after nine. The address turned out to be a large Mediterranean style place in the Mount Olympus area of Hollywood. Deb parked along the road leading up to the home, and as we walked towards it we can see that all of the cars were very expensive automobiles.

The closer we came to the front door, the clearer the music sounded. The song playing was the classic Rolling Stone's *"I Miss You"*. Deb rang the doorbell. The door which was opened by a white man in his mid-twenties, immediately brought to mind the model Fabio Lanzoni. He wore only a powder blue colored silk Roman toga, piped in gold with a gold rope tied about his waist that matched his sandals. The lights from the room behind him shined through his outfit, and revealed that he was naked beneath it. He smiled at us, with perfect teeth. "Ladies," he said with a gesture of his hand for us to come on in.

"Why, ain't you all that and then some Honey," Deb told him as we walked into the house.

I watched Deb as she reached beneath his little outfit, and caressed his genitals as we passed him. The man kissed her on the cheek and rubbed my ass as we continued on through the living room, taking in the sights as we walked. It was as if we had gone back in history to the reign of the

Roman Empire. That was the parties theme in the beautiful home of its obviously rich owner. We were the only Black people in the room of some thirty-five White people with a Filipino here and there. Everyone except Deb and I were dressed in the little silk togas and other silk gowns from the period. No one wore any underwear, self-apparent by the soft light that offered us peaks into what they were working with. There were lavish trays of meat and fruit, with plenty of wine.

      The pleasant smiles and the approving nods that Deb and I generated on sight, told us both that our fine Black asses were novelties up in the spot as we slowly made our way through the crowd in search of Velasco and Frank.

      A White woman of thirty years old approached us. She was carrying a platter of wine filled chalices. She offered us a drink and asked us if we'd like to change into what the other guest were wearing. We each took wine but declined to change; telling her that we would change later.

      "I certainly hope you shall," she said with a wink and a smile as she looked at us both; licking her lips at us like we were a sweet treat to eat, before walking off.

      "Ooo," Deb said as we walked on giggling.

      We continued into the den and were bathed in the glow of soft light from the flickering flame of a fire place, and a candelabrum. The entire floor was covered by large beautiful pillows, except for a path that cut through the room's center into a hallway. There were no less than thirty people spread about the pillows, in an orgiastic entanglement of passionate sex. The sight and sounds combined with the smell of their sweaty sex, perfume and chronic smoke was an intoxicating turn on for Deb and me.

Deb walked just behind me; one of her hands resting on one of my shoulders, as we slowly moved along the path between the pillows. I could feel my pussy getting wet as I took in the sights of asses, titties, pussies and dicks of people in every sexual position that I had never knew before then, let alone seen. The freaks were reaching out to us from both sides; asking for us to join in, as they touched us. I felt the warmest sensation at the touch of so many hands caressing my ankles up my legs, and beneath my skirt to fondle my ass and pussy. Before I realized it my panties had been pulled down and I simply walked out of them leaving them behind as we entered into the hallway.

"Deb I lost my panties back there," I panted and Deb cracked up laughing.

"You ain't by yourself. Shit I think I came, and I know that one of them stuck their finger in my butthole," Deb said.

"Oh Deb, that's just nasty." I laughed.

Walking through the hallway we began to pass the doors to open bedrooms, where one freak session after another was going down. Two women on one man in one of the rooms, several men on one another, in another room several women on one another, and several men on one woman. There were sex toys being played with. I even thought I saw Little Dick Dickerson being spanked by two women, but I was mistaken, the guy wasn't even Black he just had a dark suntan. No one minded that we stood in the open doorways watching them, and everyone seemed to want us to join in. We walked out into the backyard, where we found ourselves in the most beautiful tropical garden. There were flowers of every kind amidst the naked statues of people likened to ancient Roman deities.

We came upon a pool and Jacuzzi where we found Velasco and Frank standing along the deck with several other groups of men and women. An attractive redhead woman of about thirty years old was hanging on Franks arm. A dozen or so naked men and women were frolicking in the pool and Jacuzzi. Velasco saw us as we walked out of the garden onto the pool deck. We knew that she had a hot shape beneath her baggy uniform, but looking at her in the slinky, silk Roman costume left no mystery as to how good she really looked. Her pussy hairs were trimmed and the nipples of her small breast pointed straight ahead.

"You guys made it," Velasco happily said as she first embraced Deb and then me.

"Told you we were coming," Deb said.

"That you did. And where's my hug," said Frank, as he embraced me.

I could feel his dick pressed up against me through the little toga he was wearing. He slipped his hand down inside the open, low cut back of my dress, so deep that his finger slipped passt my butthole into my pussy before I had time to react, withdrawing his hand again and tasting his finger tip. I was both stung and at once turned on in a way that I could not believe.

"Very good," he said to me about his finger with a smile.

Deb never had time to react either, as Frank embraced her and kissed her on the cheek. He cupped her ass in one of his hands, and slipped his other up the front of Deb's dress. She lurched up on her tiptoes, and it was over in an instance.

Frank knew that neither of us was wearing panties; he was crafty. Neither I nor Deb said anything but as Frank tasted the fingertip of the other hand, each of us knew that he had tasted our pussies, and I suspected Velasco knew as well.

"Why don't you ladies get comfortable, our host has gowns for you both. Come on, I'll show you where they are," Frank volunteered.

"No thanks. We've already told the lady up front that we were fine with what we're wearing," I told Frank.

"Or not wearing," Frank said with a chuckle.

At that moment the redhead first looked Deb slowly up and down and then me. Deb and I looked to one another in disbelief and Velasco just laughed at what our expressions conveyed.

"Frank, why don't you take a walk with me, and bring the chocolate swirl to go with this strawberry," the redhead woman said with lust in her green eyes.

"Oh no baby, maybe later," I said.

"I'm going to hold you to that gorgeous," the woman smiled at us. "Coming Lucy?" she asked.

"No, you take Frank and treat him. I'm going to show my girls the garden," Velasco answered. The woman took Frank's hand and led him off to the garden towards the house. Once they were out of sight, Deb turned to Velasco.

"How are you ok with your man kissing somebody right in front of you like that?" Deb asked.

"Frank is not my man like that. He and I just have a fuck relationship."

Deb folded her arms across her chest and looked to Velasco with an expression that only a Black woman can muster. "Well, excuse me Miss Thang, I guess you got it going on better than I gave you credit for. Shit, you got just as much game as I got girlfriend," Deb said.

Velasco laughed. "Come on, let me show you guys this dude's place. You have to see it." Velasco said. She led us off into the garden, "The dude is some kind of big shot record executive. My girl fucked him off, and then she turned me on to these parties. I wasn't with it at first, but then I told

Frank about them and we've been coming to them ever since."

While Deb and Velasco chopping it up about some of the high rollers who were here on the under, my thoughts drifted off on how we could capitalize on this free fucking. As I listened to Velasco, I could tell she had been around the block a few times. She probably got paid and just didn't know how to tell us, because of how we might think about her. But she had seen me get paid already.

"Have you ever sold any pussy?" I asked Velasco.

She looked at me, then at Deb. She told us that she had only sold herself to one man way back when she first came to America. She told us that her father had been an enlisted U.S. service man stationed at Subic Bay's Naval Base, and after the base closed down her father returned to America. Her family had been out-casted because her Black father never married her mother.

Lucy Velasco told us that she was named after her mother. She told us that she had illegally entered the United States and settled in California where she searched for her father. She found herself working in McDonalds for minimum wage, but her money was running out faster than she could make it. The thirty dollar a night Motel she was living in eventually broke her and so she had sold herself to the motel manager in a tradeoff of rent for sex.

She told us how afraid she was the first few times she did it but it got easier as she went, because he wanted it from her more and more. Lucy said that she eventually started charging him money on top of the rent and he had paid with no problem. But then he found out that she was in the country illegally, the bastard stole all of the money she had, and threatened to turn her in to immigration if she didn't marry him. She said that she knew that once she married him, she was guaranteed a green card, so she married him for that reason. The abuse began before the ink dried on the certificate of marriage. She told us how he sexually devoured her in ways that made sex disgusting to her for a long time after him, until Frank came into her life. But it was his physical abuse that was the worst. She was his cook, his maid, his slave and he had called her a filthy whore bitch so many times, that she thought those three words where her first, middle and last name after a while.

It all had come to an end one day when he came home drunk and raped her, then beat her because she wouldn't let his German Sheppard lick her pussy. He had taken a bath and fallen asleep in the tub where his radio accidently fell in and fried his ass. She didn't have to tell us that it was no accident, because we all knew without saying what had really happened.

"And that's how I prostituted myself," Velasco said as we sat on a bench inside a gazebo in the garden.

"You had to do what you had to do to survive girl," Deb said to Velasco as she hugged her.

Deb shared her own story of a time when she had to sell herself back when we were in our first year of high school, to her boss Cheap Charlie to pay her grandmother's rent and utilities after her grandmother lost the money on horse racing.

"I never knew about that," I told Deb.

"No you didn't. It was the first time, but not the last. I kept you out of that end of the game," Deb answered.

"I guess you never had to sale yourself, uh Jones?" Velasco ask.

"Yeah, I did it so Deb could go through her training process with me at the same time and be placed at the same prison.

"Knock it off. You was gone fuck Little Dick Dickerson anyway, you just used me as an excuse," Deb playfully snapped off, inciting a moments lighthearted laughter from us all.

"She's right. But on the serious, while it's been a choice for me, it wasn't my choice as a child to watch my Mama back in Brooklyn, Hoe hustling in the dead of New York's winter to feed, clothe and keep a roof over her kid's head. I had to watch my Mama do what she had to for our survival; dragging herself in from the snow night after night just before the crack of dawn. She got robbed every so often, fucked over and beat down instead of being paid for her services. And I would often hear the neighbors talking about her, calling her hoes and tramps. My Mama was a damn good hoe, but she was never a tramp for doing what she had to out of the necessity to survive. She was stigmatized for it. Her only flaw was that she had bad choices in men. She got with all the wrong men for all the right reasons. She just wanted someone to love her and her children and for that someone to give us a better life. A better life is why we came to California."

Tears had welled up in Deb's eyes as she listened to how hard life was for my family back in Brooklyn. "I remember you talking about some of that when we were kids, and it made what I had to do a lot easier for me," Deb said.

"Okay girls, let's get off the sad wagon, and climb aboard the money train," I told them.

Velasco looked to me with a puzzled expression. "Look Velasco, we here on a paper chase. I mean we game for all the suckin' and fuckin', but we got to be paid for the chocolate sprinkles we droppin' on all this vanilla spread up in here. Translation we need money and most definitely don't believe in all this free fuckin', you feel me?" Deb said.

"Gosh I love the way you put your words Bovaise," said Velasco.

"That's because the bitch is a mack," I chimed in.

"Okay girlfriend, I'm with you just tell me how you're going to get some money for what their giving away for free here, when there are so many more women than men?" Velasco asks.

"Deb and I have an advantage. We are young, gifted and black, and ain't no other pussy up in the place better than ours. We pretty by the face, and packin' below the waist."

Velasco laughed and asked, "How do I fit in?"

"Lucy Velasco, you're absolutely gorgeous girl; you gotta' shake all that plain-Jane shit, put some swagger in your game. You'll kill 'em dead. Just do what I do," Deb said.

"And do as I say," I chimed in once more.

"But what about Frank? If he knows that I'm trying to charge people here, he'll be upset with me," Velasco stated.

"He'll get over it," I told her.

"Yeah girl, fuck Frank and feed him catfish, let him pay like any other. You ain't his broad. The free ride is over, and it's time to be about your money honey. Now are you ready to be paid for getting' laid?" Deb ran by her.

Velasco smiled and nodded her head yes. "Okay ladies, whatever the plan is to make the money, count me in."

We came together in a group hug when Velasco suddenly pointed out an elder White gentleman, wearing a gold crown with his toga and holding a golden wand in hand as he stood in a cluster of the most beautiful White women.

"He's the host of the party, and this is his home. He's worth millions," Velasco says to us.

"Then he ain't gone miss what he's about to pay us for the time of his life," Deb said and walked over to him.

She had his attention as soon as he caught sight of the sway in her hips as she approached him. It only took two minutes before he smiled and waved off all of the white women with Deb took hold of his arm, and interlocked hers in his as they waved us over to them.

Chapter 22

The following day everyone under Sergeant Deloach's supervision as well as Dietician Yizar, M.T.A Ramirez and R.N. McCoy were invited to Deloach's home for a barbecue. She had told us to bring our children and make it a family thing, to bring their bathing suits, and any food item that we wanted to add but she had assured us that she had it all covered, so we really didn't have to bring anything but ourselves.

I packed up my brothers and sisters, made a stop at a bakery, picked up several pies and other sweet treats, and followed the directions Deloach had given me. As we drove through the hills of Corona California where Deloach lived; my brothers and sisters were admiring all the new homes, and so was I. They marveled at the various boats, jet skis, snow mobiles, and other off road toys that were on trailers in the driveways in front of opened garages of most of the homes.

We came to Deloach's street. She lived at the end of a cul-de-sac in a contemporary two-story home; none of the homes in the new community were older than five years. Even the street had that freshly paved black top look. The track homes were all identical for the most part, and the suburban working middle class neighborhood of predominately White people, was a different world than where we came from.

I saw the cars of mostly everyone in our clique parked along the street, and as I squeezed in between Deb's and Velasco's cars, I gave instructions to my brothers and sisters. "I'm not going to say this shit but one time and one time only. Be on your best behaviors and mind your manners today, am I clear?" The chorus of yes sounded from everyone as Deloach emerged from out her front door to meet us.

"You didn't have any trouble finding the house?" Deloach asked as I popped the trunk open and my siblings carried the bags of food items I purchased into the house.

"I told you I had everything," Deloach said.

"Girl, these brothers and sisters of mine eat like machines," I said as Deloach laughed.

Everyone was in the backyard except for R.N. McCoy who was in the kitchen, watching football on a small T.V. as he was preparing various items for the barbecue. "Hey slow poke," McCoy said to me.

"Hey yourself. You need some help."

"I been done; I'm just trying to keep up with the money I bet on these games."

I sort of just took in the house and Deloach just let me for a while. "Go ahead I especially wanted you to see my home. Give yourself a tour, and feel free to explore every room. I'm going out in the backyard and let everyone know you're here," Deloach said before walking off.

McCoy had returned his attention back to the game and I was left standing there. Deloach had taste. Her living-room décor was beautiful. It sat sunk three feet beneath some stairs with plush shag carpeting and a gorgeous chandelier centered in its ceiling. The kitchen looked like it was one of the fancy displays at a Lowe's department store; all of its appliances were top of the line stainless steel. But it was the center island that stood out most to me. I looked over the dining room and made my way through the family room, where there was shag carpeting, a pool table, ping pong table, large screen T.V and a leather sofa set complete with two lazy boy chairs. There was even a movie theater style popcorn maker and two old fashion arcade pen-ball machines. Deloach was living. Passed the down stairs bathroom on my way to the second floor, where I found four bedrooms, but only three were occupied. The first two were obviously the rooms of teenage kids; a girl's room and a boy's room, both were really nice. There was another bathroom and a third room had been converted in two an office complete with a library, while the final room was obviously Deloach's and the bitch had her shit laid out. Canopy style bed, with a mahogany wood dresser set. The walk in closet had another bathroom connected to her bedroom. The largest of the three with its large oval shape tub and adjacent shower. There was no sign of Deloach's sharing her personal space with a significant other -she was doing her thing solo.

Back downstairs I stepped through the sliding patio door into her backyard where the kids were having a ball in the pool. Officer Tag was dressed like Chief Boyar-Dee or some damn body; as he barbequed on a grill that was made in a part of the backyard wall off to one side of the pool. Deloach had Mary J. Blige bumping out the stereo system and in that instance I recognized that she was on a whole different elevated level of the game. A long ways from what she had shown me before now.

Everyone from our clique was there all seated about the patio area. Joy pointed her kids out to me. They were a little boy of eight, and his six year old sister. Tubbs two, twin girls of ten years old were also there. Yizar's son was twelve, and Mendez's fourteen year old daughter was in a conversation with Deloach's fourteen year old son and fifteen year old daughter. While R.N. McCoy's six year old daughter was playing with Deloach's dog, a little Jack Russell, off to the opposite side of the yard with one of my little brothers.

"Man, your house is bomb Deloach," I told her.

"It ain't mine yet, but in the next fifteen years it will be, unless I come up with a way to close out the mortgage on it before then."

"I would love to have a house like this one day," I told her.

The girls all laughed.

"What? What's so funny?" I asked Deb.

"Your ass. I told them you would say that," Deb answered.

"And I was hoping she was right about you, that I was right about you," said Deloach.

I already knew Velasco's story and she knew Deb's and mine, but we told them again. Rhonda Tubbs told us how she had the twins before she went off to college. She told us that their father was a bum down on Skid Row and how his addiction to crack had took him out of their lives so long ago, that they didn't remember him. She told us that while the pay was good if she could find a second source of income, she could really take care of her kids. We listened to Sonia Mendez tell us how the medication that she was paying for every month, to treat a rare genetic condition that her only child had, was costing half of her pay. She told us that she knew that if her daughter didn't get the medication every day she would die a horrible death within a week. She told us how she was selling Mary Kay cosmetics door to door every day to make ends meet, but some weeks she sold nothing.

Glenda Joy told us that both her kids was by a guy who was married when she started an affair with him. She told us how she believed that the guy would leave his wife, and marry her after the first kid was born. But by the time her second kid was born, she accepted the fact that she had wishful thinking, so she cut off the sexual get down' with him. She told us how if she wanted him to do for her kids, she had to put up with his being in her face, and if he couldn't get face-time with her to talk about himself, the negro would act funny with his money, and she was tired of his shit. By the conversations end I knew everyone's struggle.

"Everybody here had short money and there ain't a damn thang funny about that," Deloach said.

Everyone agreed.

"You sold yourself short on that hundred dollars you made off inmate Ford," Deloach said.

I looked at her in disbelief.

"Pick your bottom lip up girlfriend. I told you, you're in my house, don't nothing move in it that I'm not privileged to outright or have an inkling into. So where's my twenty-five percent of that?" Deloach said with an outstretched open palm of her hand to me. Everyone laughed. I went into my bra and pulled my money out.

"Go on and put that back in your bra. The first one is all profit and on me. Well not all profit considering the little Black so and so short changed you," Deloach continued. The laughter became harder with Tubbs beginning to cry from it.

"And this one," Deloach pointed at Velasco. "She played both you and Bovaise with her simple-minded ass, up in them freakfest just giving her snatch and grab away for free to old blue-eye Frank, the stank chaser," Deloach said, inciting our laughter.

Velasco pulled a check out her purse and laid it on the table. It was made out for two-thousand dollars.

"I got paid," Velasco said.

Deloach picked up the check. "Two-thousand dollars! Girl you shittin' me. Two-thousand a piece?" asked Deloach.

All the laughter suddenly stopped.

"Damn, when is the next freaky thing?" Yizar asked.

"Bovaise got us an audience with the big man himself, and Jones closed the deal. All the guy wanted to do, was watch us dance naked while he jerked himself off." Velasco said.

"He paid you for your discretion. All Hollywood types and public officials are like that," Deloach said.

Chapter 23

After all the kids had been fed and left to the entertaining distraction of Deloach's family room, the adults sat around in the living room listening to Deloach lace us on the differences between a convict and an inmate. "A convict mentality held a respect for officers but that they demanded the same in return, and that a convict would bleed a slow and painful death in a puddle of their own blood, before they dishonor the convict code about ratting. "A rat to them is hand-and-hand with the convicted child molester, where the inmate's mentality was one of everything goes. Ratting, turning out other men, embracing rapist and child molesters all beneath the convict. You see, an inmate is loud and obnoxious; all bark and no bite. Where a convict is silent and deadly; no bark and all bite. Cross him and he'll play the coward; smile in your face, swear its cool then take pleasure in killing you. I've watched two convicts go in a cell; each carrying a knife, where they fought like dogs to the death, winner takes all. Don't get the differences between them twisted, because if you make that mistake, shit goes all wrong real fast."

Deloach went on to say. "Now you got some insight into the players, let me tell you about the game being played and the money being made. Tens of thousands of dollars a month are divvied out between the cons, cops and us; keepers on organized gambling, drug smuggling, prostitution, liquor sales of the real stuff and that two hundred proof shit they moonshine from the pruno they brew, and all sorts of black marketed items like you wouldn't believe that we take for granted everyday out here. Hell they even have a system for turning books of postage stamps into thousands of dollars."

Then Deloach turned to me and said, "So, you want to sale them some kitty-cat; and how do you propose to do that?"

I broke down how I would select referrals from inmate Don Ford, who would also collect their money for me. I would check their C-File confidential section for informant factors, and review their crimes to weave out the rats and the whack-o's, before setting up the date by a ducat (pass) issued through the diet kitchen.

"I like it," Deloach said. "And what about the officers?" she asked.

"We run the same getdown' just X-out the ducat part of it," I answered.

"It works for me, but if we're going to do this, then we may as well go for the whole enchilada, que no' chica?" Deloach bumped Ramirez.

"Si," Ramirez answered.

"I want to corner it all; the meat market, the gambling, the liquor, the dope and everything else that's Black-market related," Deloach said.

I told the group how the record executive had given me his private number for a special clientele of people, who would pay top dollar for their secrecy in parties with the whole clique.

Deloach told me to make it happen and then she told me about some very special friends she had at the top of the prison machine, who would be very much interested in those same kind of services. And what went from selling a little pussy to a few prisoners and a few officers had evolved into a full blown criminal operation complete with drug trafficking, illegal gambling and no telling what else. Deloach wanted to sew up the whole damn prison. Deloach was no dummy by a long shot, she knew that with success the money would pose certain problems. The more you made, the greater the problem of holding on to it.

I explained to everyone how I could launder their money through dividend reinvestment programs with major corporations that sounded no state or federal alarm. I could do this in their names, their children's names and any other person they so desired. The only catch was if the money was withdrawn prematurely there would be a heavy broker's fee, and the holder would lose on the dollar. I broke down how mutual funds worked, I.R.A's and certificates of deposits. I told them how they could bank their checks with credit unions instead of banks and in return the credit union would give them lines of credit, while they could stash their cash in safety deposit boxes, and use it for paying the everyday household items. I told them that I could flip our paper a hundred ways and our jobs made it all possible.

"Where did you learn all this? And what the fuck is you doing working as a CO?" Deloach astonishingly asked.

"I got a simple degree in business management, and I'm working in a prison for the benefits."

"And you've done some of the slick money shit you just kicked before?" Tubbs asks.

"Hell naw. But only because I ain't never had money enough to do it with."

Deloach looked at each and every one of us.

"I'm in," Tag announced with a raised hand.

"Me too," McCoy said.

"Then here's the game plan; we do this my way, and anybody got a problem with that can get off my wing. Speak up now and I'll have you transferred in a week to a new post. But know this, if you bounce, don't make the mistake of opening your mouth, because if you rat on anybody in this clique –my clique- I will bring more than hurt down on your ass. Now who's in?" Deloach ask.

Everyone acknowledged that they were in, and Deloach looked to Tag. "Do yo' thang," Deloach told Tag.

"Miss Jones, the half-pound that you've been trying to figure out how to get to inmate Ford…" Tag said to me. I looked at him unbelieving of what he had just said to me.

"Ford and I are out the same hood? Hell I could have been him, had it not been for my pool hustling and my spinning. I told him to hit you up to see if you were down for more than just slanging pussy. He knows that it's now a pound of chronic every other week, and the payment is four grand. You drop the package in his foot locker same place where you'll find the cash in an envelope, work it like a routine cell search while he's on the yard." Tag explained.

Deloach took over. I've got a girl over in assignments who's hooking our boy Ford up with an a.m. Wing Porter assignment now. He'll get his ducat tonight."

"Don Ford, don't run his mouth about his business. The homie straight up, and he wouldn't rat anyone out under any circumstances, not even under torture. Hell he's in there for not snitching on some shit another homie did," Tag said.

"Okay, I'm hearing and loving everything so far, except for how the fuck I am supposed to get a pound pass Central Control," came my response.

"I'm your boy now and I got you," McCoy said.

"You sure you ain't got no swirl in you like my girl Lucy here," Deb said to McCoy.

Everyone laughed as McCoy walked off into the kitchen returning with an igloo lunch container in which he had a custom false bottom made that was impossible to detect, unless it was known to be there.

"Sweet," Deb said.

"I want one," Tag said.

"We had them made for everybody," McCoy responded.

"Mendez," Deloach said.

"Yes."

"The South Sider who's been dropping lugs at you about being down?" Deloach asked Mendez.

"Angel Guzman," Mendez answered.

"Ain't he the one they call Bugsy?" Deb asks.

"Yeah. He got the line for the Soreno's. He's always getting at me in riddles about La Raza being down for one another, and crackin' at me on the under about the endless possibilities with Chiva up in here," Mendez said.

"What's Chiva?" Deb asked.

"Heroin," Joy answered.

Everyone looked to her in disbelief at her having known what was what.

"Hey, ain't nothing wrong with my ear hustling tier talk. I mean I don't know Spanish, but talk enough of it and I'll catch words enough to half-ass know what's being said," Joy continued.

"You go girl," Yizar said to the laughter of everyone.

"Mendez, here's what you tell him. It's going to cost him ten-grand a zone every other week," Deloach told her.

"If he's game, you give him this," McCoy said and tossed her a cellophane wrapped ounce of tar heroin that landed atop the table before Mendez. Tubbs picked it up; smelled it, then frowned with a cough and a scowl as she quickly passed it over to Mendez.

"Smells like vinegar," Tubbs hoarsely said.

"If Bugsy tries to hit you up for China White, that's not happenin', because they'll just kill themselves outright with that. That's what old man Bruce White just killed himself with over in Birch Hall last week," Deloach said.

I thought about the man who I saw in the cell sitting on the toilet, but this time as I reflected back on that day, it wasn't his nice shoes that stood out to me, nor the smell of his seared lips from the cigarette that burnt out in his mouth, but the gold medallion in the resemblance of Jesus Christ's face that he wore, and unlike before, the diamonds that where the medallions eyes, sparkled like a flash of white fire. The thought startled me and I snapped out of it to Deb's looking at me, absent of any spoken words, her expression asked me what was wrong? And I just dismissed her unspoken question with a slow shake of my head that answered nothing.

"Yizar, I got a boy over in Birch Hall that I need you to pass a sack to for me. Its crank. I'll bring it in, but it's not good for him to cross wings to pick it up, he'll get busted like that. He's housed in B 233, and his name is Gregory White," said Deloach

"You talking about that big muscle bound son of a bitch they call The Buffalo," Yizar asked.

" Yep! That's him," Deloach answered.

"Just make sure you don't forget the thirty-five hundred he has for us first, and then get the money to our girl Jones," Deloach states.

Deloach went on to tell us that we would rotate our movements and keep our public interactions on the low; never discuss the business with none but our own clique, and once the money starts rolling absolutely no one is to go over the top. Deloach told us that a low profile was everything, because the haters will take us down if they could find something to get jealous behind.

We worked out codes that sounded like work related shit to anyone listening and we made it a point to get together every forth Sunday, at Deloach's where I was to go over their finances and we would discuss whatever business we needed to.

Chapter 24

In the first month of operation the clique made just over a hundred grand, with each one of us pocketed ten grand a piece after the overhead. I began our individual portfolios by buying into various dividends reinvestment programs in some of the most profitable American corporations. By the second month into our operation, the Record Executives who Deb, Lucy and I turned out in the Mount Olympus home introduced our clique to an exclusive clientele of his rich and famous, freaky friends who were from all facets of the entertainment industry, which in turn led to our meeting political figures, international magnets and moguls of world industry, who all paid top dollar for our discretion.

The first quarter's earnings saw every member in our clique with a portfolio worth sixty grand; the largest percentage of our state pay checks were stacked away in our credit union savings accounts. But it was the venture capitalist investment group that we were dialed into that we generated our largest legitimate profits through anonymous investments in various small business startups, and independent film productions. And we each had a stash of petty cash that we spent on small everyday things.

Ninety days from the day we were hired, we were off probation and making full Peace Officer pay with union benefits. Deb had shook her G-mom's spot, and moved into her own Culver City apartment. I helped her decorate, and Deb insisted that I have a door key. The complex where she moved had a pool, fitness room and laundry. I used my new credit to put Yorkie in her own set of wheels. It wasn't new, but the payments on the Honda were low enough that she would have no problem making them.

I taught Yorkie how to drive in Inglewood, at The Great Western Forum parking lot on a weekend when it was empty Yorkie mastered the wheel in a day, and we had more fun than ever before in our lives. The cops came to investigate our little driving lesson as a suspicious activity call. I explained to them that I had bought my Mom's her first car and was teaching her how to drive. The cops were on some bullshit and they were interested in nothing except seeing our identification. Yorkie showed them hers and as soon as they discovered that I was a fellow Peace Officer, their whole attitudes changed. Yorkie took it all in with a sense of pride that everyone felt it.

•••

Inmate Don Ford and I had become so intimate with one another that, we were long past casual sex for pay. Hell, there wasn't being any money exchange between us anymore because we were now coming together in long love-making sessions. I learned everything about him, from him verses what the C-File said. And mostly what the State knew about him was based on official speculation with the twinge of facts. He had gotten arrested when he was seventeen years old. The State had charged him as an adult for an attempted murder charge in a drug deal gone badly. He was sentenced eight years to life and sent straight to state prison. He was all street in his swagger, but his conversation was that of an intelligent hoodlum. He was self-taught a well-read man, who had been laced by older convicts as a youngster. I was all he had and though the words had not yet been spoken, I was his woman and he was my man on the low.

Deloach had gotten Don the a.m. Porter's job assignment just as she said she would, and he moved around me like there was absolutely nothing going on between us. It bothered me at first that he could be so distant in public with me. He was sharp, in total control, always at the top of his game, watchful for rats who might be watching us. I took my break early I was waiting for him in another small room that Tubbs had set up off to one side of Yizar's office. It was more secure. The bed inside was concealed behind archive file boxes in a way that anyone looking in would have to know that the bed was there in order to see it. There was a barred up window that had been painted white so that anyone who looked in couldn't see anything, but it allowed the natural light of day to shine in. There was a prayer rug on the floor beside the bed. I sat on the bed wearing nothing but my pink lace Fredrick's of Hollywood panties and bra, with an open condom in hand when I heard the door open, and Tubbs let me know that it was she and Don.

"Sessie, its eleven-thirty right now. I'll come back in thirty minutes to get you," I heard her say on the way out.

"Okay," I told her.

Don made his way through the narrow maze of boxes back to where I was waiting. He stopped as soon as he saw me. It was the way he looked at me, that told me everything he was thinking, but had not yet put into words.

"You like what you see?" I asked.

He slowly nodded his head yes.

"Well you can have some if you pay me," I giggled.

As he slowly walked over to me I knew that he wasn't paying attention to nothing I was saying. I stood up as he reached me, taking me in his arms, rubbing my lower back as he was kissing me. He sucked my tongue as he held each one of my ass-cheeks in his hand. I could see him getting hard, as I unbuckled his belt and he undid his button fly 501 Blue Jeans, letting them fall down around his ankles.

I knew that Don wasn't intimate with any of the other woman in our clique, and there hadn't been a women tearing down the visitors door to visit him for the past seven of the ten years he'd had so far served in prison. I had been through all of Don's medical records, so I knew he was healthy in every way. And I had never allowed anyone to sex me unless they wore a condom, so I was cleaner then the Board of Health. With Don, the condom was all about my not getting pregnant, because no matter how much I was beginning to fall in love with him, I was not about to risk getting pregnant, unmarried at my age.

I sat on the bed's edge taking him in my hand. He stiffened his back and exhaled at my touch, as I rolled the condom onto his hard-on. I cupped his balls in the palm of one hand, and guided him into my mouth with my other. He dropped his hands at his sides, and clinched his fist as I glanced up into his face, to see his pleased expression.

"Oh God," he softly said as he closed his eyes.

The rays of the sun shined through the window down on us, and I could feel its warmth as I heard the faint sound of his heavy breathing and the birds outside nearby in song. He rested one of his hands on my shoulder, while he stroked the side of my face with his other hand as he listen to my mumbled endearment with him in my mouth.

"Sessie, oh baby you feel so good to me. Oh yes, oh yes, I love you, I love you." At first I could not believe my ears, but he had said it, not once but twice. In that instant, I glanced up at Don's face to see his eyes gloss over and his expression twist in an orgasm. I squeezed each of his butt cheeks in both my hands, and he moaned my name as he tensed up and exploded into the condom. His knee's buckled as he rested each of his hands atop my shoulders to sturdy himself, but the sensation of his orgasm was so intense that he suddenly withdrew from my mouth. I watched him for several moments as he gasped for breath, while the glossy look in his eyes slowly subsided in a slow calm return to him. Standing there before me with his pants down around his ankles and his hands still resting on my shoulders, I slipped the cum filled condom off of his Semi-hard dick, and let it fall to the floor. I pulled a fresh condom pack from my bra; ripped the package open with my teeth, and discarded the package. As I rolled the condom onto his dick, I could feel it begin to throb under the slow return of his erection. I loved holding him in my hand; feeling his warmth, and the blood coursing through it at every beat of his heart.

He slipped out of his shoes, stepped out of his pants and gently pushed me back onto the bed.

"Stop, Stop!" I ordered, and he froze in his tracks.

"What's wrong?" he whispered.

"Don't move until I tell you to," I told him.

Don stood there with a confused look on his face; dick pointing straight ahead on end of his throbbing erection. He watched me as I slid back onto the bed and removed my bra, the sight of my titties feeling him with obvious anticipation. He hurriedly took off his shirt and T-shirt, as he stood there before me completely naked.

I lay back on the bed and rubbed my pussy through my panties, and the sensation of the silk made me all wet and hot. I could see the anticipation building in Don. He wanted me, he took a step towards the bed.

"Stop I told you, don't move!" I ordered again.

He stood there watching me as I pulled my panties to one side of my hot, fat pussy and let him see its lips. It was bald except for the finger thin, short cut strip of hair that began at the top of my pussy lips, and ran up for a couple of inches towards my bikini line. I watched him as I took my hand, and placed it atop my pussy and spread its lips apart to reveal my clitoris to him.

"Help me out of my panties."

He had my panties off in a blink of an eye.

"Not yet," I told him.

Reluctantly he sat back on his knees atop the bed, and slowly raised my panties to his nose with a deep breath. The sight of this made me want him more than ever before. I raised my knees back to my chest, and slowly spread my legs open like a butterfly does his wings when it's at rest on a flower. The sight of this made his eyes gloss over in that lust filled gaze again.

"Ooo baby; your butterfly is so beautiful, and so wet. Please, can I touch it?" he asked.

I glanced down between my legs, and I saw what he saw, My pussy was so wet that its pink part glistened by the light of day shining through the window above us.

"Taste me and tell me what I taste like and if your table manners are up to part, I'll let you do with it whatever you want. It's ok. Go ahead. I'm safe." I said with a smile.

"Yes Ma'am," he answered.

His lips first kissed the right and than the left side of my pussy, he moved the tip of his tongue slowly up and down the slit, than I felt him softly blow on my clitoris. I heard the sound of my own moan, and I could not believe it was me. I wanted more I needed more, and I knew that control was no longer mines, but his.

"You can touch me. You can touch me baby. Touch me, touch me please," I found myself repeating through my own disbelief.

He took the lips of my vagina in each of his hands, gently massaging them between the thumb and index finger of each hand, as he used the tip of his tongue to toy with my clitoris. I could hear the sound of my moaning and my own voice sounded alien to me, animal like, as I felt the vibration of his moans coursing through my clitoris all through my body. I felt his tongue darting up inside of me, and it took every bit of self-control that I could find in me to keep from screaming.

Don was talking to me, but my mind couldn't distinguish exactly what he was saying. I felt one of his fingers slip up inside me and tickle that special place, while he simultaneously toyed with my clitoris with the tip of his tongue. All of a sudden his other hand was massaging one of my nipples between his thumb and index finger. I couldn't take it. I bit down on one of my hands to keep from screaming, and closed my eyes. I could hear my voice pleading for him to stop it but my mind didn't really mean it. I could feel my hips begin to move in slow circular motions by a will of their own. I heard my heart beating, my own hurried breathing and then there was the blinding white light with a relief like I had never known.

When I regained my senses, I opened my eyes to the realization that I had momentarily blacked out. From out of the darkness Don's face came into view he was in between my thighs, slowly riding me while he kissed my face over and over again. This was different for me. He was in no hurry and he looked me in my eyes as he spoke to me. This wasn't sex; this was love-making.

I threw my arms spread straight out at my sides to their full span, and wrapped my legs around his waist to rest my ankles crossed behind his back. He slowly stroked me deeper than any man had ever gone inside of me before; his every stroke rubbed along my clitoris and touched my G-spot with his every up and down. I had never felt what he was giving me at that moment in my life before, and I knew that everything from this moment on between us would be different, as I felt the muscles deep inside my vagina repeatedly constricting around his dick.

We both gave off a sound that I was sure someone must have heard, but neither of us in that moment cared. When I awoke, he was collapsed on top of me, and Tubbs was standing over us, her expression saying it all.

"Sessie, get your ass up girl! They're paging you to your post," Tubbs said.

"Oh shit!" I flipped Don's ass over and off of me.

"Damn I must have blanked out," Don said.

We both scrambled to get dress with Rhonda Tubbs looking on in laughter.

Chapter 25

Back at my post Deb, Velasco, Joy and Deloach continued to clown me. It was Deloach who made the call for Central Control to put me on blast over the PA system. She did it as a joke, but I was in real trouble for abandoning my post. But Deloach knew her shit though, and cleaned up my mess with a simple call to the watch commander about my having female problems and the drama disappeared as fast as it had begun with the joke being none stop on me all that day.

"Inmate Ford ain't spent money with nobody but you. What's up with that? And how's the dick anyway, I'm curious. Is it big or what?" Deb asked with Joy and Velasco laughing.

"To answer your first question, my product speaks for itself. Once you hit this, nothing but it will do." I answered, inciting more laughter from everyone. "And as for your second question, it's an average size." And even more laughter flowed from them. I managed my best effort at a fake laugh that was convincing to everyone except Deb, because Deb knew me all too well.

Later when no one else was around, Deb pulled me into a supply room and shut the door for privacy. "Sessie, I know that you're not getting sprung on this inmate Ford nigga. Tell me that ain't what I see coming?" Deb asked. She was waiting for any answer and she was pissed at me, her every

BRENDA FRANCES —HEARTS OF STEEL

mannerism said as much. She wasn't even trying to hide it. "So, he's got a big head dick. Fuck him when you want for free, and enjoy it. But don't get caught up on him. He's just a trick. Ain't no future with him. He got nothing to offer you. He ain't apart of the big picture right?" Deb asked.

"I'm not getting sprung and no he's not a part of the big picture. It's all about the benjamin's with me when it comes to him, and any other inmate in here," I told Deb.

"I got your word that you ain't about to lose sight of our priority?"

"You got my word Deb. I would never forsake the business for him."

Deb gave me a look that made me feel as though she was looking straight through me. It so disturbed me because I knew that she had me figured for having feelings for Don and I would have to be more careful in how I moved in the future, because the others in the clique wouldn't take too kind to me mixing business with pleasure.

"Do you remember, the White boy who got his throat cut that first day we did our tag along?" Deb asked.

"Of course I remember."

"Well, he got in the way of Deloach's business, and that's why he died. He wasn't a child molester as we were told. Lucy told me that was a jacket Deloach put on the guy, to get him up out of her mix because he put her money at risk," Deb said.

IN-HOUSE PRODUCTION   Page 179

"And you're telling me this now why?"

"Because, you're the brains of this whole damn thing and if Deloach feels that inmate Ford -- Don is a risk to her money, shit could go bad for him accidently. So you might want to think about that before you go getting sprung on this nigga, you feel me?"

I didn't answer. I didn't have to. Deb and I knew each other so well that we could damn near feel each other's feelings. I opened the door and stepped out to find Deloach standing in the doorway of her office looking at me.

"There's a really special party tonight with some very important people that I know, and we're all invited. It's along the lines of our Mount Olympus affairs, so dress to impress. I mean if you don't have something else planned!" Deloach asked.

"I'm there," I told Deloach.

"Good, shit just wouldn't be the same without you. Hey, there's an inmate Willis on your tier. Cell 127. He needs an escort to the kitchen. Officer Hite keeps calling over here for him and I told him I'd take care of it, at shift's end. So, I'd appreciate it if you would see him over there for me."

Deloach walked back inside of her office and closed the door. Deb walked out of the supply room and paused momentarily at my side.

"I think this party is at the Warden's mansion", Deb said.

"That's just crazy," I stated in disbelief.

"May be. But I wouldn't give a damn about all that, so long as they pay to play," Deb said with a laugh as she petted me on my behind and walked off.

I went to inmate Willis cell where to my surprise, I found myself looking at the he/she that I had seen moving through the central corridor on a number of occasions. He was from one of the other wings and every time I had seen him, there had been no cause for me to say anything to him that would allow me to strike up a conversation long enough with him to satisfy the curiosity he/she created in me. Kennard Willis and his cellmate had been housed in my wing sometime during the night before, on a simple cell move that I somehow had missed them on when I did my bed check that morning before I ducked off with Don. The inmates were always busting moves that custody was last to know about. Hell inmates lived here twenty four- seven. This is their world, while custody for the most put their eight and hit the gate for the real world beyond prison walls, unless overtime allowed them to bill the state for more than that extra eight hours.

Every once in a while an officer would forget his or her place and think they were running something more than their own mouths in prison, until something jumped off and brought them back to reality. Every time that would happen for me, I would come back to what Officer Sheldon told me on my tag along that day, "They'd over run us in less time than it takes you to piss if it wasn't for the Gunners.

•••

      Standing at inmate Willis cell, the sound of Michael Jackson's *"Dangerous"* poured from the cell's ghetto blaster radio as I looked in and took a mental inventory of what he/she and his cellie had done with so little space. There was a large mirror that had obviously been made in one of the prison's hobby craft shop, that hung on the wall above the cell desk where a fish tank that had also been made in one of the prison's hobby craft shops, that contained a pair of garden lizards. There was a beautiful prayer rug on the floor, with hand-crafted frames of magazine pictures of Pac, Biggy, Michael Jackson, Toni Braxton and Janet Jackson, star athletes, other celebrities and lots of fancy cars. Two thirteen inch color televisions several pairs of the latest basketball shoes were under the bed, and the wall lockers were stocked with food.

      Kenard Willis had his back to me, unaware that I was standing there watching he-she dancing to the music. He-she stood five-foot-eleven and had the build of a runway model fresh off of a Paris fashion show catwalk. He-she was the epitome of what my instructors back in the academy had lectured about on how some of the transvestites, homosexuals in the men's prisons looked. But nothing could have prepared me for inmate Kennard Willis. He-she's cold, black permed hair cascaded halfway down his back in a way that would put any beauty parlor hairdo to shame. As he danced, he moved to the rhythm of *'Dangerous'* like poetry in motion; hips gyrating, fingers snapping all in time with his bare toenail polished feet. He-she wore red leggings with a very short jean-shirt, that had to have been altered from a pair of stonewashed blue jeans, but one couldn't tell from simply looking at them. He-she wore a red colored silk T-shirt that was twisted and tied at his chest.

He-she suddenly turned and froze at the sight of me standing there. We just watched each other. I was studying him, and he-she was studying me. Inmate Willis slowly looked me up and down, then back again and I looked at him. Our eyes locked. There were no words spoken between us, only the words of Michael Jackson's. *"The Girl is so dangerous... you can have my money, but you're no damn lover friend of mine'*, oooh," is all I heard.

He-she's light completive skin was unblemished; his makeup impeccable. His eyebrow's had been arched to perfection, and the application of his eyeliner would put any woman's to shame. He-she was wearing red lipstick that was a perfect complement to his complexion. There was a light mole above his top lip at the far right corner. His high cheek bones reminded me of those I had seen on ancient marble statues in the textbooks from my Greek Mythology classes back in college and his clear brown eyes said to me that he/she was healthy and not into dope, as we were taught to look for in the academy.

Obvious years of hormone therapy had, in every way, softened inmate Willis facial features. There was no trace of any masculinity to be seen in him. His breast stood up with more vigor than my own God given breast; the nipples clearly visible through the sheerness of his silk t-shirt, and they were perfect. The polish on his fingernails matched that on his toes. I found myself looking directly at his crotch by no intention, for some sign of his manhood, only to find none.

"Is there something in particular that you are looking for, Officer?" Willis asked in a voice that was more feminine than my own.

"No, –uh, what's your name?" I asked.

"Katie," he answered. I didn't want to be hard on him for giving me a fake name. I wanted to really get to know him for some strange reason, on top of just being plain nosey. There was something about him that I couldn't put my finger on. He was unique, and just out of place in this environment.

"Okay then, give me your prison name and full CDC number please?" I commanded.

He-she crossed his arms and said, "Kennard Willis CDC number H52459, Officer Jones," He smiled and revealed perfect white teeth.

"We don't want to get off on the wrong foot here inmate Willis, so I've got no issue with your name Katie outside of ear-shot of anyone else, so long as you give me the same respect. Do we understand one another?"

"Yes, Officer Jones, I know exactly whatcha' mean girl," He answered in a way that was filled with an ultimate respect.

I couldn't do anything to him for taking such a personal tone with me. He seemed cool, and I couldn't help but laugh at his mannerism because they were more feminine than any bitch I knew.

"Officer Hite is asking that you be escorted to the kitchen."

"I'm not being bothered with him today. It's my off day, and Title 15 say I ain't got to go in on my ODR unless the joint is under lockdown and we ain't on lockdown," He/she said.

"Okay then," I said.

I turned to walk away when I heard a strong masculine voice say, "You could have missed us with all that bullshit."

I turned back to the cell, took a step back, as I looked past Katie to see his cellmate down on the bottom bunk for the first time. He had been hidden from view for the most part by a privacy curtain that was strung from the upper bunk.

"Beg your pardon?" I said.

"She wants to be addressed by Katie, so that's what you address her by at all times," the cellmate said in a sarcastic voice.

"Come from under that rack so I can see who I'm talking to," I responded.

He parted the privacy curtain and stepped from the bed to stand behind Katie. He was Stanley Clark, a giant of a man over Katie. He stood six-five of toned muscle, and beautiful blue-black African buck skin, clear eyes and a missing front tooth. The man's hands look like baseball gloves. I had seen him many of mornings out on the yard beating on the heavy bags with his bare fist. He reminded me of big, black Jack Johnson the heavyweight boxing champ who put Blacks in the history books for all the White men he whipped on, and all the White women he screwed back when they hung Black folks for that shit. I had read about him in my African- American studies class. This guy was scary; but I dare not show him any fear, because if I did then his sarcastic tone would be just the beginning of his bullshit.

"What's your name?" I asked him.

He just stood there. Katie glanced back over her shoulder at him, "You heard the lady, give her your name and number Stan," Katie commanded, as if she was a wife in her home, at her husband.

"Stanley Clark CDC number Charlie37443," He said in that baritone voice of his.

"Okay Clark, next time you speak to me in that tone of voice just because you think you can,

I'ma cut a one fourteen D' on your behind stating that I feel threatened, and they gone escort you over Ad/Seg. And while your over there for your ninety day investigation, Katie gone be out here on the line free as a bird, a loose-goose kinda' bird. You understand what I'm saying?"

Katie cracked up laughing.

"We good?" I asked Clark.

"Tell her you-all good, and sit yo' Black ass down with that tough shit, because you know you don't want that," Katie told him.

"We good. We good," Clark said as he rapidly nodded his head in approval and sat back down on the bed.

I walked off using every bit of self-constraint that I had to keep from bursting out laughing at how in checked he-she had that big Black negro in. Katie ran shit up in cell 127 and there was no doubt about it.

When I got to the front of the wing, I repeated to Deloach what Katie had said about not having to work on her ODR's, and Deloach laughed. "That bitch knows her Title 15. She's right. She ain't trying to be bothered with Hite and his freaky shit. He's probably trying to go up in that boy's butt," Deloach said through her laughter.

I was shocked. I couldn't believe what Deloach had said. Could it be true? Naw, an officer fucking-- naw. Damn I heard it all. Deloach just stood there in the doorway of her office just laughing at what must have been a puzzled expression I had on my face.

"It's shift change and it's Friday. Hell we got a party to go to, we're out of here." Deloach said, her laughter none stop as she gathered up her things.

Chapter 26

That evening after a nice hot bath, I sat laughing at my imaged visions of Katie butt-fucking Officer Hite. I dressed in a new slinky, silk, red-colored dress, with matching stilettos that I had been just waiting for an opportunity to get my hot ass in. I put on gold earrings, a gold chain with matching tennis bracelet I found on sale.

The Gucci clutch purse was a gift from Deb, probably boosted. I hadn't yet convinced her totally to stop stealing. But the purse did just kick my whole little get-down off.

I looked in the mirror, and I knew that I was about to be the belle of this ball. I looked at how the dress highlighted the shape of my ass, and I was glad that I thought to leave my panties off and just wear the pantyhose and garter belt underneath because I knew that when the light caught my dress just right, anyone looking would get an eye full of what I was working with. "Make it take me places," I thought with one last look over in the dressing mirror. And then my thoughts drifted to Don. I wondered what he was doing, and I wished he could see how I looked tonight.

It was just after nine when I pulled up to the Altadena address that Deloach gave me. The Warden's mansion turned out to be a completely restored, large Victorian that looks like it was straight out of a movie. It was absolutely beautiful.

A valet took possession of my car, and I hadn't received that kind of treatment from the Mount Olympus clientele. This was different and as soon as I stepped through the mansion's front door, I knew that Warden Russell Brennen's money was a lot longer than any simple civil servant who had worked his way to the position of Warden.

Deloach found me standing in the foyer before the grand staircase, my thoughts lost in wonder to the history told by the massive wall painting to the Brennen's family tree. Deloach was gorgeous in her egg-white chiffon dress that no expense was spared on, with its matching quarter length gloves, and soft butter leather stilettos that no woman dare not take notice of.

She was in full hoe splendor tonight, and it always amazed me how beautiful this bitch cleaned up out of our tired ass unattractive jumpsuit uniforms, and them damn unfeminine combat boots we had to wear. They fucked up my feet, made them sweat, hurt my arch and made me loose the sway in my hips when I walked.

Deloach knew Warden Brennen's family history in great detail and she used the paintings to break it down to me. She told me that Warden Russell Brennen had come from old money inherited from his father, who inherited from his own father. She told me that Grandfather Brennen was a major player in the textile industry beginning in the eighteen hundreds, and he had established the family fortune when he supplied uniforms to both the Union and Confederate armies, uniforms that were made by slave labor in his Lafayette Louisiana textile company. The company had never known a lost in profits, because it had supplied military uniforms to armies all over the world, until Warden Brennen, the last heir apparent to the family company and fortune, liquidated the entire company and all the family assets when his father died, and came west with his wife from an arranged marriage, who was part of his inheritance.

Deloach told me that the only thing Russell Brennen kept from his inheritance was the mansion we were standing in family historical paintings, and other heirlooms that he had come out west with when he was still a young man, where he attended the University of Southern California and mastered business law. He was a successful corporate lawyer in some really shady deals Deloach said, before being tapped by his friend, the state's Republican Governor, for the warden's post. Before his conformation last year he had been acting Warden for three years. Russell Brennen was definitely politically connected, and a man of privilege and taste who always got what he wanted. Deloach ended.

I knew that in-spite of my job at the prison, regular Officers rarely ever saw Warden Brennen let alone, mingled in his circle of friends. But Deloach knew him well I could tell by the way she spoke of him. He was in a league or class where commoners were only the hired help, and I had only seen him from a distance in passing. Looking at his larger-than life sized portrait, Russell Brennen was Napoleonic in stature, but at fifty years old he was strikingly handsome, and I could see the Creole in his family line. His short, shinny, wavy, black hair and piercing gray eyes, together with his sharply chiseled features, and regal nose all made him appear ten years younger than his age.

Deloach interlocked her arm in mine, and we walked further inside the mansion. "I want to tell you that you look the bomb Miss Jones," Deloach said with a smile.

"Why thank you and so do you."

"And trust me when I tell you that we're not the only broads here tonight who left their bras and draws at home," Deloach giggled.

I giggled along with her, because one quick look around the room confirmed what she said. Every woman there was dressed in her best and no bras and panties was their commitment to getting laid tonight. While getting paid was left to the pros, and every one of my clique was a pro.

Deloach lead me over to our entire clique where they were all together at one of the tables in a large ballroom that had a live bandstand, where R&B sensations Mint Condition performed one of their ballets for the couples out on the dance floor. Butlers and maids were moving about tending to the needs of all. All of the women in our clique were beautifully dressed; McCoy and Tag were black tie in their tuxedoes, and Deb was hoochied out the game in the flyest gear in the joint. My girl knew her Rodeo Drive shit and simply put, there's not a bitch on the planet who could out dress her.

"Everything has been prearranged," Deloach said.

She grabbed her clutch purse, opened it, and gave me a check for seventy thousand dollars made out to the LLC that we banked at the credit union under in our venture capitalist play. I had to hand it to Deloach; she was a money getting hoe, as self-sufficient and independent as a bitch could get. But she still wasn't on my level.

"Tag, McCoy, some paying woman is hoping that you beat her pussy to a point that she cums out it so much, that she can't sit on it for a week after tonight," Deloach said. Everyone at the table erupted in laughter. "Same thing ladies. Whoever the man is that comes to get you; you're his for the night. Enjoy him. He'll respect you, and he'll expect your confidentiality in return," Deloach went on to say.

In that moment an eloquent White woman of seventy years old with enough ice on to sink a cruise ship, walked over to Deloach and patted her on the shoulder.

"Professor, it's so nice to see you again," Deloach said.

The professor had aged gracefully; she looked damn good, and her body looked as if she worked out daily. Her jewelry was worth more than our combined annual salaries; she was loaded, and there was no doubt about it.

"Donna Dear, pleasure is all mines," the Professor said as Deloach stood and they embraced with a kiss flush on the mouth.

I caught Deb's glance at me through the corner of my eye. We each knew that Deloach and this old woman had shared something more than friendship. The Professor looked at each of us long and admirably. She looked at me for a really long time, and in spite of my un-comfortableness, I smiled at her.

"I think I would like something a little warmer and not as stiff this evening," the Professor said to me. She then took Tag by the hand and led him out onto the dance floor.

"What was that?" I ask Deloach. "I don't think I'm up for kissing coochie," I told Deloach.

Everyone at the table laughed. Deloach told us that the old broad was a Professor of law from the Stanford University, and her money was so long that she didn't know where it ended. Deloach told us that the Professor wasn't into women in the sense of lesbian sex, but that she loved for women to strap on the rubber dickey, and do her doggie-style and then massage her feet.

"Oh my goodness Donna! What have you gotten us into?" Yizar asked in her best impression of the Professor and still more laughter poured out from everyone.

"Listen guys, everything has been paid for by Warden Brennen but who we do or don't do is our choice. So, if someone approaches you that you are uncomfortable with, then just respectfully decline their offer," Deloach stated. She went on to tell us that some of the women were officers from anyone of the state's other thirty-two prisons and a lot of the men as well. She told us that everyone here tonight was either buying or selling some sexual or political favor.

"A favor implies a kind or obliging act – a small gift or token something for free," I said to Deloach.

"Well, that fat as check you got in your purse, we know ain't nothing here at this table for free, "Tubbs said, invoking more laughter from everyone.

In that moment an attractive Asian couple approached our table; he in his early fifties, and she in her late thirties. She was dressed in a Versace gown, and he in a Giorgio Armani suit. They introduced themselves as husband and wife, and thought that McCoy and Deb were a couple. They were swingers down from Sacramento who both worked in Politics. They pulled Deb and McCoy away from us just as soon as introductions and small talk was over.

One after another the members of our clique were pulled into the mix, each by someone of prominence and financial means. Until I was left alone at the table and no one else approached.

Then I saw him, Warden Brennen walked into the room and on cue the band fell silent. He walked onto the bandstand, and someone handed him a glass of Champagne.

"Thank you everyone. I'm delighted for the privilege of your company this evening. Here's a toast to a wonderful night and the joy of living." Warden Brennen said and raised his Champagne glass.

Everyone applauded and the band resumed their play. Warden Brennen, greeted people in a slow advance of hugs, laughter, pats on the back and handshakes that brought him ever closer to my position. I watched him. He was a supreme bullshitter; his laughter louder than everyone else, his smiles the broadest. He moved with all of the grace of a seasoned politician on the campaign trail for public office, and his confidence made him appear so much taller than his five-feet five inch height. And then it hit me, he reminded me of Prince. But for Brennen's steel gray eyes, he was dead on his purple majesty, except I knew that there was just no substitution for the Prince of passion, I thought with a smile as Warden Brennen came to stand before me.

"Miss Jones," he said.

I rose from my seat, "Yes." I answered.

"I apologize for having kept you waiting, but I had a bit of business to attend to first," he stated.

"Kept me waiting?" came my puzzled replied.

"Why yes, I saved the best for myself, "he answered with a smile as he took my hand in his and kissed the back of it.

Brennen was speaking to me while his eyes never left my breast. I was taller than him without heels, so the stilettos I was wearing placed his face squarely at my breast. He was so close to them that I thought I felt his breath through the sheerness of my dress, and my nipples got hard right before his eyes. "Your home is beautiful Warden Brennen sir," I told him.

"I'm only the Warden while on the grounds of the prison, in my home and off of prison grounds, why I'm simply Russell. Come; let me give you a tour."

Russell's tour lead through a series of doors and hallways that ended on the second floor in a bedroom, that I had no sense of the direction that I had taken to get to. The bedroom was larger than my mother's living room, and its furnishings were all antique. It was something right out of French Aristocracy.

Russell drew the drapes on what I first thought to be a large bedroom window, but then he opened what turned out to be double doors that opened onto a balcony overlooking a small private garden where I got a glimpse of someone through the trees. They were naked down in the garden on an elaborate bench carved out of white marble that overlooked a beautiful softly lit Koi-pound.

"Beautiful isn't it?" Russell said to me, absent of any notice to what was obviously going on below.

"Yes it is."

The sounds of their passionate moan drew me closer to the balcony, where I peered over the side down in between the small trees. I could only see parts of them; their faces were obscured, because the soft glow of the Koi-pound's light and that of the full moons glow in the clear night's sky just wasn't enough to shine through the low growing trees to show me them. I could tell though that both were women; the one on the bottom had unblemished alabaster skin color. Of all the things there was something about her breast that struck me as familiar, as I watched them unmoving, unnatural, their pink nipples were obviously hard. The alabaster skin tone woman was toying with her own nipples, each being fingered between the index and thumb of each of her hands, as the other woman with skin of a lighter shade of brown that too was unblemished and beautiful, kissed her along her stomach.

I placed my hands on the balcony rail, as I felt Russell come up behind me; his hands were outside my dress slowly moving up and down my hips and outer thighs. The touch of Russell's hands, the feel of him grinding on my ass, his hardness crossing from one of my ass cheeks pass my crack to the other ass cheek, gave me a sense of arousal.

"I watched you tonight Miss Jones and I made it perfectly clear that no one was to have you tonight but me," he said between kisses on my neck and nibbles to my ear."

"I'm happy you reserved me for yourself, because I wanted you as soon as I saw the painting of you on the --," I suddenly lost my voice at his hand going up the front of my dress, and his finger finding its way up inside my pussy. I felt his other hand suddenly pushed between my shoulder blades. I leaned onto the balcony rail, resting my elbows on it when through the corner of my eye I saw Russell discard an empty condom packet.

For the first time I could see in between the trees below, and the face I was looking down onto that belong to the woman with the alabaster skin and perfect breast, was Deloach. She couldn't see me though.

Russell raised my dress up over my hips and went in me from behind. He held me by my waist in each of his hands, and I spread my legs widely apart to get all of him up inside of me. I rested my stomach on the balcony rail, and that's when I saw who the woman was with the beautiful skin complexion that was making love to Deloach; her head down in between Deloach's thighs. She turned and looked up past Deloach and wiped her mouth with the back of her hand. She was I.S.U Sergeant Suti Ali. I was at first startled; this was the woman who made me nervous, who always put me on guard. But at that moment I felt none of that about her, and her cold black eyes seemed at peace to me. She didn't see me though; neither of them had. She went back down on Deloach, and I just relaxed and looked towards the stars.

I needed to take control of this situation from Warden Russell Brennen, and I knew just how to do it. I had learned a new pussy trick from this video I brought. I was the boss of this pussy and he was about to find out; I closed my eyes and relaxed as he pushed inside of me, constricting the muscles deep inside of me every time he withdrew. The first time I squeezed down on him he groaned and tightened his grip on my waist as he thrust himself back inside of me, and slowly withdrew again, his groans more intense with every time.

He started murmuring in a foreign language with every slow withdrawal of himself from up inside and repeating my name as I squeezed even harder "Gaudeamus Igitur, Oh Juvenes dum sumus, Sessie Jones," he softly repeated.

I glanced back over my shoulder at him and his head was slumped onto his chest, his eyes closed, and tongue hanging out his mouth. He looked like he was in pain. I quickly looked ahead before he could see that I was looking at him, and rapidly tightened and loosened my grip on his dick with every stroke he made, and then I felt him go stiff. He pounded inside of me and collapsed bent over with his face resting on my back, and his arms wrapped around my waist. He could barely hold himself up, and I could feel his every breath. I wanted to know what he was saying, so I asked him.

"My dearest Sessie Jones; why I merely gave way to my moments passion, and asked the gods of passion and lust to 'let us live then and be glad, while young life is before us'," he answered.

"Can we go again?" I asked him.

•••

I ended up spending the whole weekend with Warden Brennen. His wife and two sons were out of the country on vacation in the South of France. He invited me to drive his new Porsche to the coast, and I went from wanting a Mercedes to wanting a Porsche as soon as I got behind the wheel.

We took the ferry out to Catalina Island, where we stayed in a motel and I fucked Warden Brennen's brains out over and over again. I used every trick I knew on him and he paid me five more times. By the time our little sexcapade on the island was over, he was smitten by my kitten, and I had made an additional twenty-five grand. I learned that Warden Brennen was involved in all kinds of criminal things going on with his prison, and several other prisons that were all pulling in millions for the state's top players. In our pillow talks of rest between my turning him out, he told me about scams he had going with the prison industry corporation, where they produced industrial products using prison labor who they paid pennies on the dollar, to manufacture goods that they eased into the consumer market at wholesale profits all across the country as well as onto the foreign markets. Warden Brennen was involved in all kinds of illegal contracting with outside businesses who paid him a kick back to do business on the states dollar, that sold prisoners everything from chicken dinners at gouged prices where a portion of the proceeds went to the officers local, and another portion went to some charity that made the Warden look good. And he did this with businesses of every kind who sold consumer goods to the prisoners, and everyone at the top was in on it.

Once he started talking to me about himself, he couldn't stop. He told me about his wife; how he wished I could teach her the art of making love. He told me about his two sons. He told me that he kept a black book that named all of the players; it was his protection against any of them ever crossing him.

Chapter 27

Back on the job, a kite had been dropped over the weekend that identified a threat made against staff on another wing. We were briefed that Monday morning that the threat had been made against the life of Officer Irvin Schwartz and the prison was placed on modified programs. The brass believed the threat was bogus; but our Union protocol demanded that every threat against an officer be investigated.

We were running controlled showers; Deb and Lucy Velasco's wing was up. Glenda Joy and I were running support custody for them. There was no tension on the wing. So that in itself was another tell-tell that the threat against staff was bogus, just as Warden Brennen had suspected. In-spite of all the slick shit going on at the prison, Brennen really did know how to warden it. Showers were full. Every time I looked at them, I thought of the showers back in school, only this was much larger in that there were about thirty showerheads on one side of the wall. There were no stalls or lockers. There was only a low waist high privacy wall. It was always loud, and very crowed most days. The steam mixed with soap, aftershave, cologne and the musk of men all sort of appealed to my sense of smell. It was a turn on; and then there were the muscles --very few men in prison were fat mostly all of them were toned.

Deb, Velasco, Joy and I were all watching the shower area from the front of the wing, when Deb asked Velasco, "The dude showering with his boxers on, what's his name?"

Velasco put the finger of one of her hands to the side of her chin, in thought.

"The one who's always looking at your pussy asking is the monkey on swole," Deb said.

"I know who you're talking about. If you ask him what he's talking about, he flips the script and will ask you something like, 'Are we allowed to use chokeholds now do you like cereal in a bowl —or something close to what he said," Joy said as she laughed.

"Exactly," Deb stated.

Velasco snapped her finger in recall! "Thomas, Carl Thomas," Velasco said.

"Why is he always showering in his boxers?" Deb asked Velasco.

"Most of these guys don't want another man peter gazing while others stay ready for the fight, so that they don't have to get ready when it jumps off, because they just never know when somebody might rush them," Velasco answered.

"Well he done made me curious about what's behind the linen with all that skinnin' and grinnin' he be doing. Put eyes on me girl, I'm going back there," Deb said and started towards the back of the wing to the shower area.

Velasco took several steps behind Deb and stopped, "What are you going to do Bovaise?" Velasco asked.

Deb paused and turned to us. "I won't know that until I get up in his airspace," she said and continued on her way.

"Hey, you got to be careful saying things to them while they shower. Some of them can't handle just for laughs and peter gazing. The religious ones will rat you out, if not outright disrespect you or worst," Velasco said with a note of concern in her voice.

"I'm off that dirty Eastside Low Bottom; Hell, all we know is to get it, whatever it is," Deb waved Velasco off and kept ahead. I got Mendez's attention back in the shower areas gunners cage with a jester of my hand, and then signaled her to keep eyes on Deb. Mendez, turned her cap around backwards, and slung her rifle from around behind her, to rest cradled in her arms.

"Mendez, got her Lucy, don't trip," I said.

Lucy Velasco relaxed immediately at the sight of Mendez, and directed her attention to the three of us.

"So where did you disappear to at the mansion Miss Thang?" Joy asked me.

"Yeah girl, you were missing in action the whole weekend. No one could reach you for Sunday's get together at Deloach's either," Velasco said.

"If I told you, I'd have to kill you both," I answered them with a playful look as if they would be dead if looks could kill.

They laughed as I walked off to keep a better eye on Deb. Deb posted up near the shower that inmate Thomas was in, and inmate Thomas turned his back to her.

Carl Thomas was twenty-five years old, six feet tall and lean, with a well-tone basketball player physique.

"Hey you, what's your name?" I heard Deb ask Thomas.

"Tommy Wang Thang," Thomas answered. The other men all softly laughed at Thomas tough guy tone.

I posted up far enough from Deb that I gave her space but close enough that I would be right at her side should any drama jump off.

"Mr. Thomas, would you please turn around and face me when I'm speaking to you. I mean, it's quite rude to make a person talk to the back of your head," Deb said.

Thomas slowly turned around and faced Deb.

"Sir, why are you showering with your boxers on?" Deb asked.

"It's my preference not to be exposed," he answered.

"You sho' it's not because you're in possession of contraband," Deb asked.

This statement served to insight more laughter from the inmates and one of them chimed in," Coach Snake alert."

"That all depends on what you find as contraband," Thomas said.

G-Fly is a twenty-six year old, handsome Black man with a light complexion. His suave rapid fired gift for gab and pimp's proclamation is tempered by a street tough suaveness and a well-read intelligence. "Brotha' me man; go on and dispense with the semantics, and let little Mama have at ya' contribution to human evolution," G-fly said with a chuckled, that silenced all the others.

"Yeah, strip out," Deb demanded.

"Is that a direct order?" Thomas asked.

"That's exactly what it is," Deb answered.

"In that case then," Thomas stated with a smile. Inmate Thomas abruptly bent at the waist simultaneously pulling his boxers all the way down around his ankles, then took his dick in hand. I walked over and stood beside Deb for a closer look.

"You got an audience now Young Fly; give 'em a glimpse at that penitentiary steel, do us proud homie" G-Fly stated.

Thomas soaped up his hands, took his more than average size limp dick in one hand, and begin stroking it while his other hand rested on his hip. His eyes glossed over as he gazed at Deb. He was giving her a show, and we both watched in amazement as his dick slowly grew. He took it in both hands stroking it like a black snake, and still it grew to no less than nine inches. It was as fat as my wrist, and the head reminded me of a fist with veins bulging out of it.

"Don't hurt her Tommy-Wang-Thang!" an inmate shouted to an eruption of laughter from all of them.

"Yeah dawg, put that monster up before it bite somebody!" another inmate shouted.

Inmate Thomas suddenly raised both of his arms and hands in surrender with a broad grin, and his dick stuck straight out like black iron. It was the largest hardest dick I had ever seen, and when I looked at Deb she was staring at it wide-eyed with her mouth open.

"Damn!" Deb said.

"Well, recognize tall black timber from a small twig then," Thomas said with pride.

The other inmates erupted in thunderous applause and whistles.

I looked up at Mendez in the gunners position to see if she could see what we were looking at. Mendez smiled, turned her hat back around forward on her head, and slung her rifle back to drop behind her again.

"Three more minutes gentlemen and the water is going off!" Joy yelled from the wing front.

Deb gave inmate Thomas a wink of approval, and we walked towards the front of the wing.

"Hey Jones," Deloach called from her office.

"Yeah Serge," I answered.

"Hite is calling about sweet cheeks again. Will you escort her over to the kitchen for me on your way out," Deloach asked.

"I'm on it."

"The rest of you let's get 'em locked down for shifts change."

...

I had finally gotten a chance to be alone with Katie. It was shift change and I was escorting he-she on the critical worker's list to the kitchen.

"How long have you been down Katie?" I asked.

"Seventeen years now," Katie replied.

"Wow! You look good girl to have been here seventeen years. What's your beauty secret?"

"Honey, staying stress free, keeping a man with some money on my line, and lots and lots of cum and bubble gum," Katie said with a soft laugh.

I couldn't help but laugh with him. His manner was more laid back than any real broad I had ever known. I got a real genuine feeling that he-she was trustworthy, and we could talk about anything. I just wasn't ready to let Katie know it yet.

"Where did you get your red lipstick and black eye shadow? I didn't know they let you buy makeup here."

"They don't, they don't let you buy it. Po' bitches make they own lipstick out of toothpaste and paint from the Colgate tube or some other toxic shit. They make the black eyeliner from the soot of burnt chest pieces; they just poisoning themselves. I buys my shit though. My eyeliner is Max Factor, my lipstick is Maybelline, my perfume is Channel and my panties are Victoria's Secret. I don't need no bra with titties like mine."

I laughed and asked, "So how do you get it?"

"Miss Jones, I know you are new here honey, but damn you're nosey."

"Shit, I can't help being curious. How much in dollars does it cost you," I asked.

"You just ain't gone stop with the twenty-one questions are you girl? I'm not gone give you my beauty tips, shit as I see it, you're my competition," Katie playfully said.

I couldn't believe that I was actually having a conversation with a man made up like a woman, about beauty tip, but what the hell, I found Katie fascinating and genuine. "Well excuse the hell out of me girlfriend," I playfully said to Katie as we arrived at the kitchen door.

Katie bucked her eyes in surprise once again at the way I addressed her and then she smiled at me. I wanted her to know that we didn't have to be on the police prisoner tip when it was just us but we had to keep it on the low, so that no one gets in our mix on the staff and inmate over familiar tip.

Katie went into the kitchen and I took several steps away from the door, and paused. Out of curiosity I leaned back and looked in through the kitchen door window, to see Officer Hite pat Katie on the ass before he disappeared in a storage room behind Katie. I walked off mentally making a note that I would holla at Katie when I came back to work.

•••

When I reached Central Control on my way out the main entrance, I caught up with Deb, Joy and M.T.A Sally Ramirez walking through the parking lot together. We could see Velasco and Frank standing alongside her car, and as we got closer to them it became apparent that they were arguing.

"Listen, I'm not your personal property. I could fuck who I want, when I want, for what I want!" Velasco angrily said to Frank.

Frank roughly grabbed Velasco by her collar, "Why you punk –".

"Hey, take your goddamn hands off of her!" Deb shouted as she dropped her igloo, and rushed towards Frank ready to fight.

Joy, Sally Ramirez and I were right on Deb's heels. Frank was no dummy; he released Velasco and stepped back off of her. Officer Erving Schwartz came up from behind Frank and pushed

Deb. M.T.A Ramirez moved in on Schwartz as Deloach, Tag and Sanchez came out of nowhere, and separated all of us from one another.

"What the hell is going on here?" Deloach demanded.

"Butch bitch, you and all of your whores know exactly what's going on," Frank roared on Deloach.

"Muthafucka if you wanta get in a dog fight with me, you better have bite to go with that bark," Deloach countered.

"Come on Frank, it ain't worth it man. Let's roll," Schwartz said as he pulled Frank away and off to their cars they went.

"What in the hell happened here?" Deloach asked us.

Velasco explained to us all that Frank had found out about our arrangements on Mount Olympus, and he was upset that I wouldn't be having free sex with him anymore. She told us that Frank had slapped her, and called us all whores. I watched Frank across the parking lot talking to Schwartz, and I knew that there was going to be some shit out of Frank or Schwartz before long. Deloach insurance us that she would take care of it, and for us not to worry about it.

Chapter 28

Time began to fly with all of the fun we were having, making lots of money. The days turned into weeks, and weeks into months. I had come to recognize prison life for the microcosm of society that it was. It had its own rules, its own laws and it basically ran itself. The public knew very little about what took place on a day-to-day in its prisons, nor did the public want to know, and in the state of California it paid generous taxes to not know what takes place in its prisons.

Warden Russell Brennen had taken my understanding into the State of California's prison system to a whole new level; I learned most of what I learned from him while sucking his dick. He and I would meet regularly in his office for what he called "desk duty", and while I was bent over his desk with my uniform and panties pulled down around my ankles, he would pound away inside of me while talking the system to me. He told me how California ran the largest state prison system in the world; that it was larger than Texas and Florida state prison systems put together, and that some of its thirty-three facilities were multi-complex systems. I had learned how to keep him hard and keep him talking. I had come to love listening to his lessons, and he always paid for the pleasure of listening to himself talk while he built on his climax.

Russell told me how he had read an article in the San Francisco Chronicle, where visiting Germans to our state had given California the title of Great Industrial Prison Complex of the World, and a model for rehabilitation failure to all sensible nations, due to the state's highest recidivism rates ever known. Russell told me that it cost eight point eight billion dollars a year of taxpayer's money to run the prison system, and that every year that cost was rising.

Russell would arrange for our whole clique to entertain his very important friends on weekend excursions to Napa Valley, California, on vineyards where we would ride horses drink the finest wines, eat cheese, dine on the finest meals and then have lots of sex. He never spent his time with anyone in our clique except me, and he would always talk the business while he fucked me. He put me up on why CDC reported that it only held a hundred and seventy people in prison; it was really closer to a hundred and ninety thousand men, women and children. He told me how the officer's union had quietly taken control of the juvenile facilities, and the state mental hospitals while also looking for ways to expand into community policing. They wanted to cut into the sheriff and police street action of to protect and serve.

Before I knew it the year had come to an end, and I had made so much money that Yorkie and I had come up with a plan for renting out our home on fifty-eight and Normandie, while the broker who initially hooked us up explained to us how the housing market was about to open up and he could swing a deal with my credit union that would put us in a new home in the suburbs.

The school system in Los Angeles seemed like it was falling apart to me; too many students and not enough teachers. And a better life for my brothers and sisters was what got me into the game to begin with, so Yorkie and I settled on a five bedroom, two and a half bathrooms with a pool in the backyard up in Fontana California. We were only the second Black family in our predominantly White neighborhood.

The person living in the contemporary home at the end of the cul-de-sac was now me and the hood was so far behind us that Yorkie really did have to commute to work. She loved the bumper to bumper traffic the long ride. To her this was the thing that said we had made it.

Shortly after we moved into the new home, I woke up for work one morning to the soft sound of Yorkie's crying. I found her looking out over our backyard. She had already turned it into a kind of tropical paradise. Our pool was even larger than Deloach's, it had a slide along with the diving board.

"Mama, what's wrong?" I asked her as I slipped my arm around her waist.

"I'm just happy is all. We've come a long ways from the projects in Brooklyn."

"What I like most about out here are the schools. Both of them damn near look like college campus."

"I know, I saw them," Yorkie said as she dried her eyes.

"No more crying now Mama. Oh shit, I'm late for work I got to go."

•••

Warden Russell Brennen took our whole clique along with his special guest to a cabin in the Tehachapi Mountains, where we skied, rode snowmobiles, and did some skeet shooting. We had a ball. Deloach told me that Russell was sprung on me and that I needed to make the most of it; that I needed to start playing him for special favors, because he could afford to give me whatever I wanted.

For the new year I had worked out a deal through our investment group with the GMC Chevrolet dealership, for our whole clique to drive off of their showroom floor in the year. Deloach went straight for a new Cadillac, and Deb flipped her old Camaro on a trade-in for a brand new Z28 Camaro convertible. Everyone was paying the lowest monthly note in a way that had been constructed to come directly out of their accounts. I didn't get a new car though, and that fact was missed on no one. None of them could see where my money was going except Deb who knew about the home in Fontana. Deb cried more than Yorkie when she first saw it. I asked her to keep it to herself because I was beginning to keep my family life and my business life separated. I had to protect my family. It was like Mac had drilled in me time and time again, "never let your right hand know what your left hand is doing, meaning keep your home life separate from your street life," and so I did.

Second week of the new year, Russell asked me to drive him to a Porsche dealership where he picked himself out a brand new canary yellow and black color Porsche Carrera. Yellow being my favorite color, it was everything that a car could be. I sat behind its wheel, dreaming about the day I'd get my own; and when the time came, the Porsche I'd get would be exactly like the one Russell was buying for himself. But for the moment, I would be happy if he just allowed me to break it in on our ride up the coast to the Napa Valley Vineyards that we were heading to. When Russell came out of the dealership, he slipped into the passenger side, handing me the keys along with the title of ownership, he had paid it off in full. Russell told me that it was his gift to me, and in return I made a gift of pussy to him anytime anyplace he wanted it free of charge. That weekend I fucked, sucked and jacked Russell off in every position I could think of. Before the weekend was up, I realized that Russell was not just having sex with me; he had been smitten by my kitten and was making love to me.

Russell told me that a scandal was about to break in the news out of Corcoran State Prison that would put the world spotlight on the States entire Prison system in a way that was really bad for business as usual. When I asked Russell about it, he told me that the Fed's had launched an investigation into the eighth amendment violation of prisoners' rights, brought on by a series of questionable deaths from gladiator-type fighting events held in the segregated housing units there, where big bets were being wagered in fights that had ended in some prisoners being shot to death.

•••

Once back home, I made arrangements to have my old car delivered to Fontana, where I posted a for sale ad for it in the Penny Saver. Russell had told me its best that I say I won the Porsche in a raffle at a Casino in Reno, Nevada that he had read about. But I'd have to keep it clean with our people though. I hadn't seen the news, and I made the mistake of leaving my cell phone in the car over the weekend, so when Deb finally tracked me down she had me to check the evening news where the Corcoran prison scandal had broken, just as Russell said it would.

When I arrived at work in my new Porsche, my crew was blown away. They played it cool in front of our fellow employees who weren't down with us in the business. But once we were inside and I broke the weekend down, they were all happy for me. They had checked a hundred grand on the Mount Olympus sexcapade that I had lined up for them before I took off on my trip with Russell; the money had been placed in our venture capitalist account.

After my security check that morning, I sat down with Deloach in her office where we talked about the Corcoran State Prison scandal, and then she congratulated me on getting a Porsche out of Russell's ass. "You know that Brennen is sprung on you. But you have to control the situation Jones because too much of a good thing will ruin a man, make the man possessive. Brennen's wife could be a problem for us all if you lose control of him, understand?" Deloach asked.

"Yes."

"You made us all a lot of money girl, and you did it in a little over a years' time. My kid's college is paid for, and my mortgage ain't gone ever be a problem. Hell, I could pay the whole thing off right now, if it wasn't for it raising a red flag with the government. If we could keep at it for another year, we can go or do damn near whatever we want until retirement," Deloach said to us. A call came through on Deloach's institutional phone, and she answered it. "This is she" Deloach said. She cupped her hand over the phones transceiver and looked at me, "I have to take this," she mouthed to me.

I stepped out of Deloach's office to find Deb seated at her desk waiting for a relief.

"Deb, where you going?" I asked.

"I got range time this morning. I forgot all about it. I waiting on my relief now," she said.

"Damn I forgot too," I said and checked my date planner.

"When is yours?" Joy asked.

"In two days," I answered.

"I think they have us all scheduled for every two days right after one another to target shoot with the new Heckler & Koch 9mm," Velasco said.

"That means they'll rotate a relief officer in here every day this week," Joy stated.

"I think they are sending that asshole Schwartz as the relief," Tag said from the Gunner's station.

"It's him, I heard the 10/21 go out from control, redirecting him to our hall," Mendez said from her Gunner's station.

Deloach poked her head from her office door, "Bovaise, did you know you had range time this morning?" Deloach asked.

"My fault Serge, shit just got past me," Deb answered.

"I can't get you out of this one, its mandatory. So, see you tomorrow," Deloach said.

Schwartz walked through the wing door like he owned the place. I didn't like this guy, he was trouble and I knew it. He seemed to immediately focus his attention on Velasco.

"Sessie, you know we gone race, don't you?" Deb said on her way out and everyone laughed.

Deb locked eyes with Schwartz as she past him on the way. Her animosity for him was obvious to everyone. Deloach stepped from her office as Deb exited the wing.

"Schwartz is there any reason why you think you may not be able to work with my people? Say so right now, and I can call in a favor and have you reassigned again," Deloach said.

"No problem **Serge,** I'm good," Schwartz said as he flopped down in Deb's seat, and kicked his feet atop her desk.

Chapter 29

Later that day during the first voluntary yard inline unlock, Joy and I made our way along the third tier in our rounds, I spotted Don with a couple of other Black inmates in front of Don's cell huddled in a conversation. I was happy to see him and I damn near forgot myself and yelled out his name, I quickly checked my composure, and dropped my head before anyone noticed how flushed from blushing that my cheeks had become. Don was in full control of his emotions. He was always at the top of his game; his composure was never faltering. He in no way acknowledged me, never turned his head from the two inmates that he was locked in conversation with. I recognized one of the inmates as G-Fly from the showers, the guy who had lightened the encounter between Deb and inmate Thomas. "Ford, get over here," I said to Don with a look that said he had done something wrong.

Ford looked to me with eyes that said get a grip, while speaking to me in the most respectful tone, "Beg your pardon?"

"What's going on?" I demanded.

"We're just talking, Officer Jones, as men do. Shouldn't you be about the business of performing your duties or something? I mean I'm sure that interrupting men in conversation is outside of your scope, you feel me?" Don stated condescendingly.

I was startled by how Don just spoke to me and how he had shown no sign of who I was to him. I knew that he was moving correct and that I was fucking up, but I couldn't check myself and before I could catch myself, I blurred out "I need to see you later. Same place, same time, be there," I said and walked off.

I walked down the tier and I couldn't help but feel angry and confused at how Don had treated me. I thought that he would have been happy to see me after the weekend, and then I heard G-Fly say, "Damn Don, you need to tighten the cork dawg. Wrong folks see that and the genie is out the bottle. The folks will have your ass jammed up state so far, that the sight of another Black face will be a novelty." As soon as I heard what he had said to Don, I knew that I had fucked up– that I had allowed the situation to control me, instead of me controlling it.

"Jones, that was really messy girlfriend and obvious to everybody who heard it, that your personal feelings are involved. You need to get a grip on yourself in a real way. You're slipping out of control right now," Joy scolded.

"He was ignoring me and I lost it."

"Isn't that what he's supposed to do– I mean the guy has to keep a low profile, or both your asses are out. You lost your smarts on that one. No way to know what rat caught wind of that. Tighten up your shit," Joy continuously scolded.

As we continued on in silence, I knew that everything that Joy had said was right, and I sort of just kept to my own thoughts of why I had acted that way. And then it hit me, I was beginning to feel guilty about my lifestyle, and it was because I had fallen in love with Don. But how could I have allowed my feelings to get me twisted in love. My thoughts turned to Deb. How would she react to my having committed the foremost mistake in hoe hustling: mixing business with pleasure and falling in love. I just had to keep it from her until I could figure out what I would do, how I would handle it.

●●●

I took my break early and I waited for Don in the little room off the diet-kitchen, but lovemaking was the furthest thing from my mind. I was still very angry at Don, but angrier at myself because I didn't want to be in love with anyone. Instead of sitting on the bed while I waited for Don as I normally would, I stood in the shadows out of sight, my arms folded in anger, my thoughts racing so fast that I couldn't keep up with them.

I heard Tubbs open the door and lock it. The two taps to the door sounded, that told me Don was in the room and making his way through the maze of boxes. The two taps on the door also told me that the coast beyond the door was clear. Don walked out of the shadows into the light, but couldn't see me watching him. He sat down on the bed and I knew that his eyes were adjusting to the lone light of day shining through the window above the bed, and once his eyes did adjust he would see me. So I waited, I had time to burn. I watched him for what had only been a matter of minutes and he took off his shirt and then his t-shirt. He really was a handsome man in every way. And then he noticed me; he grinned and stood to his feet.

"Why didn't you say something?" Don asked.

I walked over to him, and he aggressively grabbed me and began to passionately kiss me. The palm of his hand pressed to the back of my head, and his tongue stuck in my mouth. I was so upset with him that I bit his tongue, and he pulled away from me in pain.

"Ouch! Why in the hell did you bite me? What the fuck is wrong with you?" He angrily asked.

I wasn't aware that I was pointing my finger at him while I was going off, "Don't you ever disrespect me again like you did on the tier today," I scolded.

"Disrespect? Slow down now, Cadillac. I didn't disrespect you. I merely did what the fuck I was supposed to in that situation, so that it keeps people from peeping what it really is with us. You of all people should know that better than I do," Don blew back at me.

"You don't run this situation, I do. So when I tell you to jump, you check your ego and ask me nothing but how high. "And don't you ever speak to me like that again in front of anybody, or this shit we doing, will come to an end real quick."

Don took a step back, disbelief masked on his face. "Check it! I'm a man foremost and a prisoner second. If you think the later gives you cause to flex your authority to me, then you can miss me all together because I don't need the drama of you not being in control of yourself. Ain't too many broads that I can't fuck in this bitch after some conversation or some money or a bit of both, don't play yourself Officer Jones." Don sarcastically said then he left the room.

I sat on the bed for a moment and I felt my anger slowly turn to sadness tears welling up in my eyes and streaming down my cheeks. After a moment I snapped out of the shock of Don's just having left me there, and pulled myself together. It dawned on me that I mistook him for some desperate prisoner starved for female companionship.

After I shook the feeling off, I headed back to my wing, and as I walked down the Central corridor I contemplated how I would get Don back for hurting me, how I would teach him a lesson, instead of allowing him the thought of having taught me the lesson. I made up my mind in the time that it took me to walk the corridor that I was done with Don on the personal tip. It was all about the business of the contraband he was slanging for us, while he could spend his money fucking some of those other broads he spoke on.

As soon as I walked into the wing I saw Lucy Velasco and I knew something was wrong with her. Her face was red on one side, her mascara was out of place her hands were shaking. Joy was with her, and I could see the sudden relief on both their faces with the realization that I was there. I looked toward Deloach's office, the door was closed and I couldn't hear what she was saying to Schwartz, but she seemed really calm as she spoke from where she stood across the desk from where he sat.

"What's going on?" I asked.

Glenda Joy told me how Velasco had been solicited by Schwartz and she had got Joy to keep watch for her while she and Schwartz ducked off in the supply room to get down. Velasco picked up the story from there. She said that Schwartz had given her three-hundred bucks for what was supposed to be a quick blow job. Once in the room, Schwartz gave Velasco some sob story about being short a hundred bucks and he'd give her the rest later but Velasco told him no deal and that there wasn't nothing happening until he got the rest of the money. She said that she had only turned her back on him for a second when he must have judo chopped her across the back of her neck, and everything went black. Velasco said that she came too, to find her uniform was down around her ankles, and her panties were torn off, shoved in her mouth and held there by his hand. Schwartz had her bent over a utility cart, with her hands behind her neck as he sodomized her. She tried to scream, but she said she couldn't.

She told us how Schwartz laughed at her as he told her "don't no mixed black mutt bitch tell me to fuck off," She then turned her back on him. He called her a sinner and a whore, and told her that neither man's laws nor God's commandments will judge him guilty for punishing her mongrel ass. She said that when he was done, he kicked her in her behind, wiped himself off on her uniform and spat on her. He told her that if she told anyone what he had done, he'd make sure that his lawyers exposed her whole whore crew, then he took his two-hundred dollars back and left her laying there.

Joy went into the utility room when Velasco took too long to come out after Schwartz and she found her out of it. Joy had cleaned Velasco up and told Deloach what Schwartz had done. I looked to Schwartz who was watching me through the window of Deloach's office from where he sat across from her. He knew that in spite of whatever bullshit tale that he was spinning to Deloach, right now I knew the real.

He smirked at me. Deloach's words, whatever they were. Fell on his deaf ears. I smiled back at him, there was no need for words to be spoken between he and I. The smirk on his face slowly subsided, with a glance at me from Deloach. She stopped talking to him. There was an expression on her face as she looked at me that said to Schwartz what no words could say in that moment about payback's being the bitch who was looking back at Schwartz, but he was too damn smug to recognize it.

The remainder of the day, Joy worked with Schwartz and Velasco with me. After work my whole clique met at Deloach's home, except for Velasco who went to her doctor to be examined. We all sat around Deloach's living room. Deb was the last to arrive because she had dropped in on Velasco first before coming out to Deloach's.

"Well she had to get stitches in her butt and the disk along her third and fourth vertebra, were bruised where the bastard had judo chopped her across the back of her neck," Deb said.

"Schwartz knew exactly where to hit her; and he could have really hurt her," McCoy said.

"He did really hurt her; she's wearing a fucking neck brace. She told her doctor that she fell down while off the job and he told her that she's going to have to stay home and take it easy for the next two weeks," Deb went on to say.

"I didn't mean it like that. I didn't mean it like it sounded. My thoughts were on the fact that Schwartz is a black belt in Judo," McCoy said.

"I didn't know that," Deloach answered.

"Most people on the job don't. I know about it because my kid made it to the State Championship last year, when low and behold I look up to find Schwartz placing second in the Senior Masters Circle," McCoy stated.

"Fuck all that, Joy told me that he threatened to rat us out, so what I want to know is how we gone deal with him?" Deb asked.

I popped out my switchblade and said, "I could do it and make it look like one of the inmates did it."

Everyone laughed.

"I thought I told you to leave that thing at home. One of these days that thing is gone get you in trouble," Deloach said.

"Girl don't listen Serge.," Deb said.

Deloach told us that she was going to use her juice to keep Schwartz on the wing during Velasco's sick leave, and that will give us time to figure out how to deal with him. I, then gave everyone an accounting of their money and they were all very pleased, it was a reminder to us all of why we were in this, and what we had to lose if Schwartz wasn't reigned in.

As everyone left, Deloach held Mendez, Tag, Deb and I back. Once the others had all gone, Deloach told us that Schwartz was going to have an accident that he was not going to recover from. "Schwartz is dangerous, and it doesn't take a rocket scientist to know that. Pending on were Schwartz takes this, we could all end up without a pot to piss in and a window to throw it out of at the least; while at the most we could add prison time to go with that. This gets done my way and I mean it. And Jones you'll be working with Schwartz on B-Wing until it's done. I'll have a watch commander give me Tubbs to work with Joy, and have a redirect hold Tubbs spot down until Velasco is medically cleared or Schwartz is history whichever one comes first. So, shut down everything– well everything but your sessions with Brennen, Jones okay," Deloach said.

After we had left, on the ride home I wondered why Deloach chose the three of us to stay back, instead of saying what needed to be said in front of everyone, and then it hit me. Deloach was going to see Schwartz dead, and she knew that anyone of the four of us would volunteer to be the lone wolf to take Schwartz out for the greater good of the whole.

Deloach knew that when none of us said anything against taking Schwartz out, that we were all in. I looked around and Deb was driving along side of me. She powered down her window. "Hey bitch, did you think I was bullshittin'?" Deb yelled across to me.

"What the hell are you talkin' about?" I called back.

"I'm spending the night at your house tonight. Go!"

Deb took off like a bat out of hell and the race was on, in under a minute we were both racing through the late-night nearly deserted freeway traffic at over a hundred miles an hour.

We hadn't had that kind of fun since we were kids back in high school. I let her beat me.

•••

Deb never slept in the guest room when she spent nights at the Fontana house. She always slept in my room which was at the end of the hall, with the room balcony door open on the backyard pool, where we would lay in my king size bed talking until we fell asleep while listening to the slow jams.

"You know that Deloach is going to have Schwartz downed while you're working with him, don't you?" Deb asked.

"Yeah."

"Are you good with that?"

"If she don't get it done, then I will."

"So, tell me sis, what's really going on with you and inmate Ford-- I mean Don?"

"It's just business Deb."

"If you were feeling something more you would tell me right?"

I could see Deb's face mirrored in the glass of the balcony door as she watched me intently, waiting for an answer from me.

"Yes, I would tell you Deb," I lied.

"On our blood oath as sisters, you wouldn't put this dude over what we got going, over me?" that's what she really wanted to know.

"Never," I lied again.

I knew that my feelings were all over the place when it came to Don. I knew that I had never felt about anyone the way that I felt about him. I knew that I was in love.

I faked like I was falling asleep, but I lay awake late into the night thinking about the lie that I had just told Deb. I justified the lie by telling myself that I was through with Don on the physical tip, so there was no need to tell Deb that I had fallen in love. I would just stick to my guns and all together shake off that feeling; control it, fall in love when I was ready to, now that I knew what love was.

Chapter 30

The following day I worked the wing with Schwartz, at no time ever turning my back on him and he knew that my guards were raised the entire time. Deloach had met in her office with Big Buffalo, shot caller for the Whites. Deloach had usually left her dealings with him up to Deb, but not this time. The next time I checked Deloach's office, Buffalo was nowhere to be seen. He had ducked in and out of Deloach's office so fast, that no one had noticed him.

I took my break without a word to Schwartz, and when I got to the wing front, I found Deloach in her office talking to G-Fly, and it wasn't any coincidence that she had privately talked to two different shot-callers in a single morning. G-Fly, glanced over at me through Deloach's office window, and he gave me a slight nod of his head before turning his attention back to Deloach. I knew that something had just been said between the two of them about me, but whatever it was it couldn't have been bad because I didn't feel any negative vibe.

Joy and Velasco joined me at the wing front, and Velasco sat at my desk just as G-Fly walked out of Deloach's office on his way back to A-Wing when Schwartz walked off A-Wing. "Hello ladies," G-Fly said to us with a nod of his head just as he was about to pass.

"Ain't no ladies out here sport. Them is whores," Schwartz said to G-Fly.

"Oh then my bad, cause that makes them all noble ladies of value that know their worth," G-Fly said with a wink of his eye at us.

"You got to be shittin' me. Hit the wall sport," Schwartz said to G-Fly. G-Fly as assumed the position to be searched, his hands raised palms to the wall as Schwartz began searching him.

"I ain't ask you for no fancy lip service," Schwartz said as he became more aggressive with his pat search. "You hear me boy?" Schwartz said.

"Permission to speak, candidly while facing you Officer?" G-Fly asked.

"Yeah, turn around," Schwartz ordered him.

G-Fly slowly turned around and faced Schwartz. In the same moment Deloach walked out of her office, folded her arms across her chest as she stood in the doorway.

"The era of a Black man --," G-Fly begin to say.

"G-Fly," Deloach said.

"Yes Ma'am," He answered while never taking his gaze off Schwartz.

"As you were Mr. Fly," Deloach commanded. G-Fly continued on his way without a glance back at Schwartz, leaving him there to scratch his head, before he turned to look at Deloach who smiled at him.

"Officer Jones, I'll be holding your post until your return; the Warden wants to see you in his office," she said to me without looking from Schwartz to me.

I exited the wing. Walking the main corridor to the Warden's office, I played back in my mind everything that I had seen with Deloach that morning so far, to try and guess when and how whatever she was about to put down on Schwartz would go down, but Deloach was crafty and nothing she did really gave me insight into her move. She had met with Big Buffalo; shot caller for the wood pile – White boys. And I had peeped Mendez whispering something down to Bugsy-- shot caller for the big Southside Government Mexicans. The Pissas were talking Spanish so fast that I couldn't catch a word of it. I knew that Deloach had pow-wowed with the shot callers for the Damu's, the Kiwe's, Kumi's and Jama's, and that covered all of the major Black gangs. The only question was when, where and how it would jump. I thought back to when Deloach had the White dudes throat cut that first day Deb and I started and then I thought back to what Joy told me that first morning I worked her wing, of how if you rat Deloach out you was assed-out. And then my thoughts returned back to Schwartz.

I walked into Warden Brennen's office, and his secretary sent me straight in. soon as I saw Brennen seated behind his desk on the telephone, I forgot all about what I was thinking on the way there, and I felt a sense of relief. He was a distraction, a moments pleasure I was certain.

Brennen beckoned me into his office, and for me to close the door and sit down. He wrapped up his phone call with the Governor. "Of course Governor, it's in your account as we speak," he spoke into the phone.

Over time I had learned something new about Russell Brennen's get down as Warden with every sexual encounter and I was waiting to hear what secrets his dick was about to tell me today. I also learned that Russell was the kinkiest freak that I had ever encountered behind closed doors.

His call with the State Governor concluded, Russell leaned back in his large chair and swiveled in it from left to right like a little kid, obviously happy with what was said between the Governor and him.

"Miss Jones, come round here to my side of the desk darling."

I did as Russell requested.

"Look down in the bottom right-hand drawer, and pull that brown bag out of it for me."

As soon as I bent over in front of Russell, I intentionally tooted my ass up in his face as I opened the drawer. I felt Russell's hand reach between my legs, and caress my pussy in the palm of his hand. There was a bag in the drawer.

"Is this something for me honey?" I asked.

He suddenly pulled his hand out from between my legs and lovingly slapped my ass. I took the bag from the draw, set it atop the desk.

"Open it up sweetie then you tell me," he answered.

I opened the bag to see a pink jell strap-on dildo, some flavored jells, a small leather whip, fur covered hand cups and a small pink box.

"Don't open the box until we're done. Now you take those tools out the bag and excite me baby," Russell said.

I straddled him face to face, opened up one of the flavored jell packages, squeezed its jelly like contents onto the dildo. Russell's eyes were wide with anticipation for the unexpected.

"What, what are you going to do?" he stammered.

"Shut up and open your mouth wide for Mama honey," I commanded him.

He complied and I stuck the jelly covered dildo inside his mouth, and slowly moved it in and out as he mumbled in delight. After a moment I slowly began to kiss and lick around the sides of Russell's mouth, catching the flavored jelly that was running down the sides of his face.

He suddenly grabbed me by my hair. "Get up," He garbled through dildo shoved in his mouth. I pulled the dildo out of his mouth, and begin to suck it in that big stick ice cream kind of way that I had perfected. He released his grip on my hair, unfastened my utility belt, and we were both standing behind the desk with Russell unzipping my jumpsuit, and its falling off of my shoulders down below my waist.

"You know what I want," Russell hastily said.

I took off my uniform as Russell unbelted his pants, and they slipped down below his waist to reveal his boxer underwear. They were white cotton with little pink hearts all over them. I always found myself expecting to be brought to the verge of historical laughter and Russell never failed to disappoint me. I erupted into laughter, and he just loved it as usual.

"You know what I want," he again stated.

He stood in front of his desk and I handcuffed him in the furry cuffs. I laid the dildo down on his desk top.

"You've been a real naughty bitch Russell Brennen," I stated.

"I don't mean to be mean, Mama."

"Shut up!"

I shoved him down bent over the desk, and roughly pulled his boxers down to his knees. I picked up the leather whip as he watched me, the side of his face pressed flesh to the desktop, his eyes wide with fear.

"I think that you are long overdue for a spanking to set you right. It's for your own good," I said. I let the tassels of the whip tickle the crack of his ass, till he squirmed and whimpered. "Am I understood?"

Before he could answer I swung the whip and struck him on the ass with its tassels, and he squealed with delight. The more I whipped him, the more turned up he became. He was thoroughly enjoying himself, as was I. In a strange kind of way, I too enjoyed the pleasure I brought to Russell's world, it was like the kinky shit I did served as some release of the pressures he experienced from his job, but outside of that, along with the money Russell paid me, I felt no other attachment to him.

Russell had a deep rooted fantasy for role reversal that I just couldn't understand for the life of me, and I thought my psychology classes back in college had taught me everything.

"You know what to do baby, punish me," he whined.

I strapped on the dildo, and went up inside his butt with it. He cooed, oohd, groaned and called my name with every stroke. I turned my head to one side, so that he would not see my face twisting up in my every effort of self-control in keeping from laughing at him.

"You like that huh bitch? You, you want it deeper don't you? Tell me I'm your superior bitch. Tell me right now before I fuck your brains out all over this desk," I said in my best imitation of Russell.

"Why yes daddy, you are my superior, my King." "Oh yes beat me with the dick daddy," He whimpered.

I pulled his hair and he cried out in climax. I wondered what his secretary thought was going on. But whatever she knew, she would never volunteered to anyone that much I was sure of, because Russell Brennen paid everyone in his personal employ very well to keep his secrets; and his money was long enough that if you crossed him he could ruin your life, at the least for your betrayal of his confidence. I unstrapped the dildo, and then unhand cuffed him. He sat back in his chair, and took a silk hanky from one of his desk drawers, where I saw the small beautiful black leather bound journal that he often had with him while on our many trips. It was gold leaf embroidered, with a lock clasp made of gold. Russell often read the secrets to me that the book contained, whenever I sucked his dick.

"May I open my present now?" I asked.

"Not just yet," he answered.

After he had cleaned himself up with the silk hanky, he pulled the little black journal from his desk, along with the flavored condom so I knew what he wanted, and that meant that he was about to read secrets from the journal to me. Russell had told me that the journal was his insurance policy against some very powerful people that he was in business with, that the journal held secrets that some of those people would kill for. They were fascinating stories but it was all just Hollywood shit to me, but I enjoyed hearing them. Russell had long ago shown me the little secret compartment built into his elaborate desk, where he hid the journal whenever he was on prison grounds. He took the little golden key that he wore on a chain around his neck, and opened the journal with it.

He placed his balls inside of a small leather electro filled pouch, with a cord attached to it that was connected to a hand control at its other end. It wasn't the first time I had used it on Russell; it was just another one of his toys. He gave me the hand control, and when it was time, I pressed the button at intervals that will send a sharp electrical charge through Russell's balls that filled him with orgasmic delight as I blowed and jacked him off.

I slipped on the condom and took him in my mouth, stroking his dick with my freehand as he read the details of another intricate criminal enterprise from the black journal, about an elaborate credit card scheme that Lieutenant Mark Zimmerman and he had going, using the social security numbers of inmates who were serving life sentences. The prisoners were none the wiser to what was going on. Lieutenant Zimmerman had come up with the perfect scheme, in that no one paid much attention to a lifer's social security number; because they never needed it for anything as property of the state.

I pressed the electric shock button, and Brennen winced with a moan of pleasure. "oo baby" he said.

He read from the journal how Lieutenant Zimmerman and the head of prison industry Authorities joint-venture program, were producing airplane parts for penny wages on the dollar that they paid to the prisoners, that were then sold through a subcontractor to a private manufacturer for top dollar, who then resold the parts to the pentagon at highway robbery prices.

I pressed the electric shock button again, and Brennen's teeth chattered with a low whimper of pleasure. And I hummed on his dick as he read on with all of the skills merit of a Hollywood actor. I did love listening to him read. He read how it was all profit because the initial cost for the raw materials were underwrote in the prison's annual hundred and fifty million dollar operating budget, followed by a bogus income tax return filed on behalf of the prisoners without their ever knowing, that any of it had taken place. It was a hundred percent profit.

I pressed the electric shock button again, Brennen jumped, with a delightful squeal. He caught his breath and resumed to read.

Russell, read to me from the journal how the leftover scrap medal from the airplane parts, was also turned into profits in yet another deal that Lieutenant Zimmerman had with a gun manufacturer, who had probably made guns that ended up in the hands of the very criminals housed in the California prison system. At every reading of the journal revelations were given into the millions being made, as well as into the politicians and businessmen who were profiting. The journal was a ledger on everyone paid and on every dollar made.

I touched the electric shock button again and held it. Brennen arched his back, through his hands up in the air, his eyes rolling back into his head, as he gurgled and exploded in the condom. "Mercy, mercy me, mercy, mercy me oo wee," he said as he found his breath. "Gosh, I love you woman!"

"I know you do honey. I'm your relief daddy now be good to Mama and let me open my gift," I said as I gave him a box of Kleenex.

He gave me the small pink box and I opened it to a diamond bracelet set in gold. There was a small note inside that read, you keep my heart and you keep everything else.

"It means exactly what it reads darling," Russell said as he looked me directly in my eyes.

He took the bracelet from my hands and fastened it on to my wrist. With his toys now put away and his pants back on, it was as if our kinky encounter never took place.

"Now dig down in big dick daddy's trouser pockets here honey, and get the envelope out of there for yourself."

I did and I knew that the envelope was money. I shoved it down in my jumpsuits inner pocket, and started out the door.

"Same time, tomorrow now hear?" he said with an affectionate pat to my ass.

As soon as I walked out Russell's office and into that of his secretary's, I saw Lieutenant Zimmerman of the institutional security squad, and the black patch on his uniform seemed to stand out. He looked at me in a way that raised the hairs on the back of my neck because I had the strangest feeling that he knew exactly what Russell had just read me. No words needed to be spoken between he and I, I just wanted to get the hell away from him as fast as I could.

Chapter 31

I walked onto the wing at ten minutes before the first inline group going one way for the morning yard, where I relieved Deloach. I flashed my new bracelet on her; she smiled and shook her head naughtily at me.

"Where's ours at?" she slyly asked.

I unzipped my jumpsuit and showed her the very fat envelop, that I had took out of Brennen's pants pocket, and she whistled at it softly.

"Okay then." she said.

Walking amongst the inmates, I headed up to the third tier for A–Wing, where I found Schwartz waiting at the front of the tier with one of his feet resting back on the lowest of the three guardrails, his arms crossed over his chest, mean-mugging the inmates and obstructing their right-away down the tier to their cells in his normal provocative manner.

"What were you doing? Lap dancing for the Warden I'll bet," Schwartz sarcastically snapped off to me. He started down the tier unlocking cell doors as he went. I followed him three quarters of the way when I passed inmate G-Fly's cell, he sprung up out of his rack, and ran to the cell door.

"Officer Jones, I need a word with you," G-Fly said.

"Not doing inline G-Fly."

"Put breaks on that thang little Mama, this is a matter of life and death."

Momentarily distracted I stepped closer to his cell door, my sight on Schwartz lost.

"What did you say?" I asked.

"Look down the tier," he said.

I looked in Schwartz's direction to see an inmate they call Eddie-Fly walking towards Schwartz. As he passed Schwartz, he suddenly whirled around and struck Schwartz in the back of the head with what I knew was a lock in a sock. It was one of the weapons of choice that inmates preferred to use; twice Eddie-Fly struck Schwartz in the back of the head, I heard the bone of his skull fracture. Eddie-Fly kept walking towards me, when all of a sudden he tossed the sock with the lock in an unknown cell; dropped from view amongst the inmates moving on the tier. I could see Schwartz staggering in the opposite direction, and then Eddie-Fly slipped beneath the lowest of the three guardrails and dropped down from view.

It was as if everything began to move in slow motion, as big Buffalo emerged from one of the cells, and tossed Schwartz over the tier. The sound of his body slamming head first three tiers below, reminded me of the sound the guys made back in high school when they got hit on the varsity football team.

I was shocked. Big Buffalo was coming straight towards me, I grabbed for my panic button, when G-Fly suddenly reached through the cell bars, grabbed both my wrist and roughly pulled my hands into the cell bars and held them.

"Not yet," G-Fly calmly said to me.

Big Buffalo passed me by without even looking at me. I looked down the tier where it all begin, to see Bugsy pouring water from a mop bucket onto the tier where Schwartz went over as another Mexican inmate placed a wet floor marker beside the bucket.

"Now," G-Fly said as he released me.

I hit my alarm and before I could look over the guardrail, the tier was completely deserted. I ran down the stairs to where Schwartz lay. Deloach, Joy and Velasco were already standing around Schwartz when I got there. Deloach was barking commands to all the inmates to clear the tiers and lock it down, but she was talking to no one, because it was as though the lights had come on in a dark kitchen in the ghetto, and scattered all its cockroaches.

Tag and Sanchez was standing in both Gunner positions, their weapons at the ready, as Schwartz lay twisted on the floor in an unnatural position, the back of his head was cracked open and everything inside of it was spilling out onto the floor. His blood was so red that it looked burgundy. His eyes were wide open, and I could see that he was still breathing.

I thought that I would feel a since of joy, but I did not. Hating someone and planning to hurt them or even kill them was one thing, but to actually carry it out and witness it was entirely something else. It tugs at your soul if you have one, and inspite of myself, I have one.

Responding staff seemed to take forever, but it had only been a few minutes. Velasco looked away, and then she walked off. As I looked in Schwartz eyes I heard him draw his last breath and exhaled it, and then he was gone. I thought I saw his soul leave his body through the windows of his eyes. I flashed back in thought to the dead man on the toilet from the drug overdose. I saw the Jesus piece around his neck, the diamonds in its eyes sparkled. I again flashed back in thought to the dead man who got his throat slit my first day and then the image of the Jesus piece again returned, the diamonds of its eyes sparkled.

All of a sudden responding staff converged from everywhere at once, and then there was complete silence after realization that all were looking at another officer, and that officer was dead. It wasn't the same thing as the death of an inmate. Death became a reality looking at one of their own as the subject thereof. While a callous disregard for the life of an inmate was the norm, it was something altogether different to see the officer laying there.

I walked off as Lieutenant Zimmerman and the I.S.U. squad arrived on scene. This time Lieutenant Zimmerman looked at me intensely as we passed one another. And he paused and turned to me. "You were partnered with Schwartz, correct?" He asked me.

I stopped in my tracks; his voice was cold and calculating, insensitive and separate. I turned to face him, Sergeant Suti Ali was standing at his side and the black patches of rank identified on their fighter pilot flight-suit uniforms, always stood out in a menacing sort of way to me.

"Yes Sir. I was," I answered.

"Report to my office and wait there to be debriefed," Lieutenant Zimmerman ordered.

He and Sergeant Ali, walked off to where the rest of the team had begun photographing the crime-scene.

...

Deloach found me in the staff restroom. I was back playing the whole thing in my mind, she told me to forget whatever I saw, and to say that I saw him slip down the tier by a mop bucket, and he rolled in between the first guardrail and landed on the first tier. She told me to tell them that I hit my alarm and by the time I made it to the first tier Schwartz was dead. That was my story. During the debriefing in I.S.U, I held to the script that Deloach gave me and never deviated from it no matter how many different ways Lieutenant Zimmerman and Sergeant Ali put their questions to me. They drilled me for five hours after my shift, and I knew by the debriefing end that Lieutenant Zimmerman's interest in me transcendent the death of Schwartz. Hell he could care less about Schwartz, he was compiling information on me. He was studying me.

When I was done, I found Deb waiting for me in the employee's parking area. She was sitting in her car, and she jumped out as soon as she saw me. She met me halfway to my car. "Are you okay sis? I tried getting to you, but that Big Buddy Cox mutha fucka wouldn't let me near you," Deb said.

"I'm okay, I'm just tired Sis,"

"Look, we gone go to my house. Play shit cool, talk when we get there."

"Okay."

We each pushed through traffic like the night we first raced, but this time we were glued to our rearview mirrors to make sure we weren't being followed. For the first time in our lives we felt guilty of having committed a crime, and not just any crime but the murder of one of our own.

When we reached Deb's spot, Deb took a quick shower while I settled on a long hot bath. I was so tired that I dosed off while sitting in the bath until Deb woke me up for dinner. Over our meal I told her everything that had went down with Schwartz, how they killed him in less than a minute how I had seen the whole thing.

"I told you sis, Donna Deloach is one ruthless bitch. You threaten her, you cross her, she gets wind that you a snitch and she'll lay you to sleep in a permanent dirt nap," Deb said.

We sat in Deb's kitchen in silence for a little while before I finally spoke, and told her what I had went through with Lieutenant Zimmerman and his clique, but that I never lost my composure with them. I told Deb that I got the feeling Zimmerman was more interested in Russell and I, than in the death of Schwartz.

Deb told me that the prison had been placed on lockdown pending the outcome of an investigation, but so far Schwartz's death had been ruled an accidental slip and fall.

...

I got a week off work and I took the time to get some family things done. Sitting around the house I begin to rethink my priorities and for the first time the career in the California Department of Corruption, as the inmates called it, just didn't have the appeal it had had when I was broke. I had gotten into it for the money, for a better life for my family, for the benefits. I now had enough money to move in the direction of going into some legitimate business for myself.

I was also thinking a lot about Don. I missed him and things he had said to me were beginning to take on a new meaning. I had been on the job for nearly two years now, and Don had told me that he was on the grind because he needed to stack his paper and pay his legal fees for the Parole Board when his hearing comes up. I just needed to get away from everything and everyone for a few days, so before I had to report back to work, I drove to see the one person who always had time and answers for me.

When I walked into the store I instantly noticed the expansions that had taken place. Mac had purchased both buildings on either side of the Liquor Store and it was an entirely different set-up now. There were three registers with youngsters working behind each, and a new butchers counter full of meats, fish and poultry. Mac had even added a music section with all the latest hits where two teenage girls worked behind his counter.

"You need a job?" I heard Mac's familiar voice say. I turned and saw him standing in the doorway of his new office, a grin on his face wearing that penchant green grocer's smock with the right top pocket protector with its array of pens. He opened his arms out to me with all of the love of an adoring father, and I rushed right into them.

"Mac Daddy!"

"You should have called, Sassafras, I would have turned the store over to these kids, and we could have went out to dinner or something," Mac happily said.

"I wanted to surprise you."

"Well that you did. Come on back here so we can talk."

I glanced around the store, "You've done well Mac Daddy."

We went inside Mac's office and I talked to him about everything. I told him about the parties with all of the corrupted people who masqueraded on TV in the states Capitol spouting off all of their moral bullshit and the law. I told him all about Russell's kinky ass and most of what was going down inside the California Department of Corrections and Rehabilitations.

"Hell Sassafras, I got boys in all of the level four joints in this state, and half of the level threes. The guards are some of the biggest crooks in them stoops. The whole damn system is designed for a person to fail. Every one of the young men I got working the line on both shifts, have some kind of criminal past, but if I don't give 'em a shot, then they go back to the joint learning how to be more ruthless from the very folks who are charged with correcting 'em." Mac always could lay the raw out to me in a way that made me look at my options in life, and then make a choice based on the best one. "So, this brother Don you keep going on about; now we can't control who we love baby girl. Love is a fickle thang that you just gotta walk away from, should you find that you're somebody just ain't loving you back. But if yo' somebody is loving you back, well then you got to let go, let God and pray fo' the best possible outcome. But I tell you what, ask him what his plan is for touching down, and if it's feasible then you take it from there. Test the brother; use somebody close to him to fuck with his head, and that will tell you were his heart really is. If he loves you, he'll act out and if he don't, he won't."

Mac and I talked about everything no holds barred. He gamed me where I needed to be gamed, and checked me where my shit was raggedy. By the time Mac and I where done talking, I had formulated a whole new plan in the direction that I was taking my life. I was getting out of all the illicit business I was in and I was done with pursuing a career in Corrections. But I had to do it slowly. I had to pace myself, I had to bow out gracefully but most of all I had to figure out how I was going to tell Deb that I was done with it all.

The two year mark was my goal and it was just six months away. I had made everyone a little more than a hundred K', plus shares in various cooperation's that were worth another quarter million. I had done my part for the clique, and now it was time to get out while I was ahead; to get out before a good thang came to an end, as sometimes good things do.

Mac had put school on my mind and I made the decision to return for my Master's degree in business. I could afford to attend a University for fulltime now, because some of the Silicon Valley startups that I had invested in independent of anyone else had real potential.

I promised Mac that we would spend more family time together now that Yorkie wasn't working all of the over-time anymore. For the first time I told him about several investments that I had made for him, and he told me he had noticed the extra money showing up in his quarterly statements, but he wasn't going to say anything to his bank until the bank said something to him.

"I thought it was free money and I wasn't about to blow the whistle on my good thang. Hell, I figured they'd catch it before long and when they did I'd just work out a payment plan for payin' 'em back," Mac said as he laughed.

"I should have told you before now, but it just got pass me. I'm sorry for that."

"Sorry my ass. I ain't. I was wishing there was more where that came from," Mac stated.

Mac and I laughed as we had done all those times when I was a kid. And that night after I had left Mac's, I took the Porsche out on Mulholland Road and raced with a White woman pushing a Ferrari. I beat her and she gave me the thumbs up as we parted ways and I pushed on home.

Chapter 32

I returned to work with new insight into how I would move and a sense of relief from all the anxiety that had built up in me from witnessing Schwartz murder.

As I made my way through Central Control, I was feeling a bit anxious about seeing Don and feeling a need to fuck with him to test his feelings for me. Before I had even made it to my post, I learned that Schwartz's death had been ruled an accident and that the prison was now functioning on modified program but it would be back to normal program after Schwartz's funeral. We were all expected to attend; Deloach had even made it a direct order.

Once on the wing, I checked the daily movement sheet for the inmates to be released on seven a.m. ducats, and found that Don had a job change from working with me as my a.m. porter, to a morning kitchen job position. I knew that he had to have made the move through one of the inmate assignment clerks because this kind of move just didn't go down by chance.

Deb was back on the A-side wing with Lucy Velasco, and Tubbs was on redirect working B-side wing with me, while my girl Joy was logging her range time with the Heckler Koch 9.mm rifle, and when she was finished with it, it was going to be my turn.

Deloach popped her head out of her office. "Hey Jones, Hite is up my ass about Katie needing to be escorted over to the kitchen for work, but I can't get a hold of an S and E right now, so are you up for it?"

"Yes Serge. I got it."

I walked the first tier to Katie's cell and the pungent smell of marijuana they just smoked hit my nose so hard that I started coughing. Katie was laughing with her cellmate to the soft sound of Tina Marie's, "Sucker for Love" playing from the radio in Katie's cell. "Ain't you got no kinda air fresher you can spray?" I asked Katie as I stepped in front of the cell door.

Katie was dressed and ready to go to work, sitting at the foot of Clark's bed, who was stretched out on the bed reading a Jet magazine.

"My bad Officer Jones," Katie answered as he-she pumped lotion into his-her hands and rubbed them together. The overwhelming smell of strawberries filled the air, completely masking the marijuana smell.

"Oh God that smell so fresh. What is it?" I asked.

Katie and Clark both laughed at my reaction to the fragrance. "it's religious oil that we buy from the Muslims," Clark answered.

"Stop it!" Katie playful said to Clark. "You can't be putting Ms. Thang up on game," he went on to say.

"Oh, I can find out what it is. You forget I'm the police. Now bring your butt up out of there, they calling you for work."

As I escorted Katie to the kitchen, it gave us another chance to talk. I had read Katie's C-file and knew that he had never snitched on anyone; that he had been involved in stabbings at four other prisons, and each time he had gotten away with it. Katie first suspected stabbing was believed to have been because the guy tried to pressure Katie for sex and money. The other three stabbings had to do with drug- smuggling, gambling and some money scheme that Katie had going with a gangsta working in the prison industry. Katie had refused protective custody at each incident, as well as decline to transfer to the S.N.Y Sensitive Needs Yard program where most all homosexuals were housed as a result of just not being able to deal with the pressures of general population. "I ain't no punk-bitch fag-hag; I'm a bitch born with a genetic deformity. Shit, they put me in a man's prison instead of a woman's institution. So I'm hanging right here. Give a bitch 'liberty or death' is my philosophy," Katie stated with the most dramatic feminine antics.

Katie's juice around the prison was obvious to me. Black inmates were talking in code to him most every time they came in contact. Katie was in the game, gettin' money and making it happen. Hoeing was just one of Katie's hustles. He told me that I would be surprised at who was flipping and flopping staff on the down low, and gangsta's on the down-low. Katie just outright told me that he had been fucking Hite for years.

"So Hite's been going up in you for years?" I blurted out in amazement.

"Going up in me? Honey, hell naw, Hite's a switch hitter taking it straight in the hip. I think it's disgusting that he has to remind me of my genetic defect like that all the time, but hey he payin' for it so the customers always right." I couldn't help but laugh. I laughed so hard that other people in the corridor also begin to laugh as they passed us. Their expressions conveyed that they wished they knew what was so funny. "Hite likes for me to hold his ass cheeks and squeeze them together while I'm going up in him."

I laughed so hard tears rolled down my cheeks. Katie was the most flamboyant person I had ever encountered, and I genuinely liked him and so I decided to open up to him.

"Are you getting your paper out of your little sexcapade with Hite, or are you selling yourself short?"

"Honey please, it's a hundred dollars a holler every time I pop my collar, "Katie answered with a snap of his finger to one of his collar fronts.

"And what are you doing with your money?"

"I move it out of here when I can. I mean I got a little savings account setup at B of A where anyone can drop money in it, but no one can withdraw from it but me."

" I read your file and I know you wanta get your hustle on, so hypothetically speaking if you had access to whatever you need for a payday what would it be?"

That was the beginning of my get down with Katie, Katie the cleanup lady. Slinging powder was Katie's hustle, the bitch had plugs for moving dope on two other yards besides the one my clique was working and no one on my yard was any the wiser that Katie had a dope sack. The he-she's had their own network and before long, Katie was hitting me up for ounces of powder, crank, rock cocaine, heroin and weed. Katie was giving me no less than a couple of grand a week.

I was banking Katie's money for her and in a month, I hooked her up with a dividend reinvestment plan of her own. I learned that Katie owned several apartment complexes that he had inherited from his grandparents after they had died while Katie was half way into his sentence.

Katie trusted me so much that he gave me power of attorney to take control of the property and I restructured all of his shit in a way that a management company over saw the day to day operations of his rental properties and collected all of the rent. Katie turned out to be the slickest and the quickest of all of the inmates, he was smart and reliable.

...

I avoided Don the whole time I had returned to duty. I had my daily sessions with Russell, and I kept my mind on my money and my money on my mind. By that Thursday of the first week back, it was my turn to report to the range. The Heckler Koch 9.mm was a short, black colored rifle that had a plastic stock and a plastic butt it was surprisingly light weight with a sixteen round magazine. As a joke, the firing range Sergeant had designed all of the targets to look like inmates. And some of the jokes made about blowing off their limbs, their balls or out right killing them with a single shot to the heart or head, bothered me.

Whatever doubts I may have had about the job, I lost that first day on the firing range. I shot horribly, my scores were the worst anyone had seen and I knew that I would never be assigned to the gunners post and that was just fine with me. The guns were the one thing I had come to hate about the job. It was the whole shooting at another person who wasn't a threat to me, that didn't sit right. I understood that the guns were a necessary to keeping the inmates from taking over the prison or more so to prevent any of them from escaping but still, I didn't like the guns.

Firing round after round at the inmate targets, I hit everything but the targets and I couldn't wait to get away from the smell of the gun powder. It reminded me of rotten eggs. Everyone on the range was whispering things about not wanting to be on the floor while I was manning the gun, and I didn't want to shoot anyone who wasn't trying to hurt me, so that made it just fine that they felt that way about me.

I was so glad when the range time had passed and I was back working on my wing.

Chapter 33

Over the weekend I gave everyone an accounting of their finances in our meeting at Deloach's. Joy told me that Don had been bugging her about where I was, and when would I be back on the wing.

"I told him that I was not your keeper and that I had no idea when or if you were coming back at all. And that Negro must have worn out two pairs of state boots pacing the cell floor," Joy said with a laugh.

"It's always good to shake-up the consuming market; hell you do it right, and they'll spend more," I said.

Everyone laughed at that. "The girl is nonexpendable I'm telling you," Deloach remarked.

As I sat at the round table with the whole clique on Deloach's patio, inspite of the good food, and the festive mood everything was not all good for everyone. Deb knew that something had changed in me and business as usual was no longer the case with me. I never could put on airs with Deb. We were cut from the same cloth and she knew me all too well. She was biding her time for me to come to her with whatever it was that I had on my mind and I could see as much in her eyes every time she looked at me.

With everything that had happened we all had decided to forgo our regularly scheduled meeting at Deloach's, and came together on a Saturday. I told everyone about a big V.I.P get-down that I had arranged with our Mount Olympus clients that would take up the whole upcoming weekend out on a hundred and forty foot yacht that they had chartered.

I told everyone that the party had been dubbed the *'Freak fest at sea'*, and that there was going to be a number of foreign dignitary types on board. I told them that we were all to meet up at nine at night the following Friday, at slip thirty-three in Marina Del Rey to board the Vesta, where we would sail north with stops in Santa Barbara, Monterey and San Francisco where a private jet would fly us back down to Los Angeles by midnight Sunday.

"If it's a go, it's worth fifty-K a head," I said.

Everyone looked at me speechless, their expressions disbelieving what I just said to them. That was how I left them, when I drove over to the Brennen family's mansion in Altadena where it had all began between Russell and I that first night. The Victorian mansion seemed so much larger than I remembered as I pulled into the side entrance, that Russell had directed me to. I was met by the hired help, who had me park in one of the servants garage's, and then escorted me to one of the guest cottages, where I was instructed to wait for Russell.

I waited for nearly an hour before Russell came through the door, by then I was thoroughly agitated and wanted an explanation as to why I was taken to the back of the estate and made to wait in a guest house.

"My wife is in the mansion, and for obvious reasons I thought it best we meet back here," He said as he begin undressing.

"Ah-hell-naw. Are you crazy? This is just too close for comfort Russell. She could come back here and catch us together at any moment."

"Then I suggest you hurry and get naked, so that we can be done with this before she ever knows that I'm gone," Russell grinned as he stood there in his stars and stripes polka-dot boxers.

My expression conveyed all that I couldn't find within myself to say out of my mouth, as I stood there staring at him. It finely dawned on me that what Russell and I were doing had gone way past a business relationship. Russell had convinced himself that I was his property, and I was his to have as he chose when and wherever he chose, and I had no say in it.

I had lost control and I knew it but what I didn't know was how I was going to take it back. I knew that Russell's wife could be dangerous because I had been told by Deloach that she had shot a woman whom she caught in an affair with Russell and she was acquitted for the crime when her high powered legal team convinced a jury that she had stumbled in on an intruder and it was ruled an accident.

"I'm not going to play your wife this close. Now, we can go someplace else if you want, or we can just save it for the office," I said.

"You let me worry about my wife."

"No, this isn't about you. It's about me."

"Why Miss Jones, are you seeing someone else?"

Something was wrong. It wasn't what Russell said to me, but the way in which he said it, that raised my suspicion. He was becoming agitated in a way that I had never seen him. "Russell, this is just not the place and time for this, baby."

Standing there in his silly underwear, Russell's small stature struck me as that of a child who was on the brink of a tantrum. "You don't fucking tell me about the time and the place, I tell you! Now you get out of your fuckin' clothes, and I mean like yesterday," Russell yelled with clinched fist and spittle coming from his mouth.

He reminded me of Adolf Hitler, in those old black and white film footages that I had seen in school. I lost any sense of intimidation that he had impressed upon me by his wealth and authority as his words registered on me, and I began to get angry while mentally measuring how I would kick his ass if he made me. I politely picked up my purse from the bed, and started towards the bedroom door to leave.

"What are you doing? What did I tell you?" he screamed.

"I'm leaving Russell."

"You'll leave when I say so got dam it, now get out of them clothes, you little ungrateful bitch!"

Ignoring him, I walked towards the bedroom door to leave when just as I was about to pass him, he grabbed my arm.

"You think you're smarter than me you little neighborhood rat, don't cha? You think you can make me play second fiddle in a trio? Answer me?" Russell screamed. I felt his spittle spray in my face, I saw the anger in his eyes, and then I replayed his words in my "Now you do as I say and I say, for the last time, get naked bitch," Russell whispered.

I snapped, my academy training kicked in, and absent of any thought I grabbed Russell's hand, wrenched his grip free, knocked him down on his ass, and walked out.

On the freeway heading home, Russell's words continued to play over in my head, "you thank you can make me play second fiddle in a trio." What in the hell did he mean by that, I thought.

Chapter 34

When I got home, I closed the deal on the cruise and our Mount Olympus clients and then I notified everyone that it was a done deal. I turned off my phone, and just hung out at home for the remainder of the weekend with Yorkie and my siblings.

Yorkie never was for certain about my moves, but she knew that I was into something more than a simple civil servant's job of guarding prisoners. I had always kept my hustles clear of where I laid my head because a player in the game just never brought any part of it into her home.

The time and the opportunity had come for me to put Yorkie up on everything that I was into. I told her about all of the criminal shit that I was aware of, that was happening in the prison with the clique, Warden Brennen and how I had charged him; but he had lost his mind making the mistake of thinking he owned me. I also told her that we outright owned our house free and clear, and about all the money I had invested and hidden in the names of everyone in our home.

After she knew all of what I had to tell her, we sat there on our patio each lost in our individual thoughts, as we watched the kids and their friends playing in the back yard. I hadn't noticed until that very moment, that the kids playing in my backyard with my brothers and sisters were of all colors. Yorkie slid one of her hands across the table top without looking at me, took mines in hers with an affectionate squeeze as she looked over at me.

"So where do we go from here baby-girl?" she asked.

"I'm going to resign Mama. Go back to school, and get my Masters in Business. I got a good feeling that this internet stuff is going to blow up, and I've got some wholesale, retail ideas for buying and selling consumer goods to the public on a level like you wouldn't belief Mama." Yorkie laughed. I told her that I was going to finish out the next three months and that would give me two years of civil services. I told her that I had to break the news to Deb that I was through with all of it, and that I was going to advise Deb to get out of it as well.

I felt a since of relief like I hadn't in a long time after coming clean with Yorkie. There was just one more thing that I had to do; I had to work out my situation with Don. I would have my answer where he was concern, before I sailed up the coast with the Mount Olympus clients.

That evening Yorkie and I cooked a big dinner and Mac joined us. Mac just naturally fell in place at the head of the table. Seeing him there while listening to the conversation was the household that I had dreamed about as a kid. I forgot about all of what had to be done in the week ahead and for me there was only the night of family.

•••

When I arrived at work that Monday morning I had a clear plan of approach on how I would test Don and as I headed down the Central corridor to my wing, I ran it through my mind once again.

The day progressed uneventful. Everyone in the clique was secretly hyped about the upcoming cruise with our Mount Olympus clients and I mostly hung out at Katie's cell killing time until the moment arose for me to make my move on Don. Katie had slipped me another two grand, and we chopped up the game. I told Katie between him and I that he should try and stack all of the paper that he could, because I was moving on to better things at the years end.

"Well load me up bitch, course now cause I'm out of here before long."

"I read your file Katie and your dates still ten years down the road."

Katie reached back on her desk, and handed me an envelope that was from the 9th Circuit Court of Appeals.

"Game changer babygirl. The Fed's just cleared the lane for me to push through the paint for the sentence modification. I got that legal mail last night."

"No shit," I said as I read the letter.

"I paid them damn lawyers enough. Hell, I got on the phone last night and they told me that I'm out of here in six months. But keep that between us, cause you know how hating is in here."

I handed Katie's letter back and he whooped and danced in delight. I kicked it with Katie about our hooking up in the free world together and getting into some legitimate business. I told Katie about the internet boom, and Katie agreed with me about it having the potential to make crazy money. Katie and I talked until it was time for me to bust my move on Don.

I had avoided and ignored Don that whole morning, so when I popped up in front of his cell, Don rolled out of his rack fully dressed and ready to go. He just knew that I was there for him. "Yes, Officer Jones."

"Hello Ford," I said.

He smiled broadly and responded, "Hello yourself stranger."

"Could you please step back off of the cell door," I directed him as I keyed open the cell door. "Mr. Wriden," I said to Don's cellie.

Arthur Wriden, was a tall lean, handsome brother with a low-key disposition, who for the most stayed clear of all the prison drama. He didn't hustle because he had a rich brother on the street who gave him everything he asked for, so his focus was on nothing except making his parole date in the next six months. "Wriden, I need you to step out of the cell and come with me," I said. "Come with you? Why? Where?" Wriden asked as he stepped from the cell. I keyed the cell door locked behind him. "I need you to go to the diet kitchen with me. I have something that I need you to do."

Wriden started walking towards the wing front, and I glanced at Don and caught his angry expression.

Once we reached the diet kitchen Tubbs unlocked the door to the little room, and I turned to Wriden. "I need you to stay in here until I come back. I have to check something out first, and if the coast is clear I'll be right back but if not I need you to just hang tough until I or Officer Tubbs comes to get you, and I'll make it worth your while."

Wriden hurried in the room as if freedom was waiting for him on its other side. With Wriden secured in the room, I went to the snack bar and picked up Tubb's and Yizar's lunch for them. I brought Wriden back a double chili cheese burger, fries, a slice of sweet potato pie and a strawberry soda. It took every bit of forty-five minutes for me to let Wriden out. He was grateful for the meal, but he wanted to know what he had done to deserve it. I told him that it was just a little something in the way of my appreciation to him for keeping his mouth shut, about different things that I was sure he was up on.

As I walked him back to the cell block, I told him that I needed him to keep his mouth closed about what I had done for him and if it didn't get back to me, I would reach out and touch him more often. Wriden gave me his word that he would never speak on our little get-down, and I felt a little guilty at having used him. So, I made a mental note that I really would bless him with snack bar food from time to time because I knew how the inmates love to get their hands on anything to eat from the free world.

I un-keyed Wriden's cell door and he stepped inside the cell with me keying it locked behind him. I could see that Don was seething with anger; so much of it that he wouldn't even look in my direction.

"Thank you so much Wriden, it was a pleasure doing business with you. You're alright with me, and its okay to holla at me on the under, okay?"

"Cool," Wriden answered with a grin.

Don finally looked at me and then at his cellmate; his eye-brow raised in curiosity that was killing him. As soon as I knew I had his attention, I smiled at Wriden and walked off. I knew that Don was going to quiz Wriden about what went down and I was hoping that he told Don about the little room in the diet kitchen and Don's imagination would do the rest.

I made my rounds and then sat at my desk to make my notations in the wing log when I glanced over at Deloach's office and caught her eye. She gestured for me to step in her office and I got up, walked over to the door and poked my head inside.

"The Warden called for you several times in the past forty-five minutes" Deloach said.

"The next time he calls, just tell him I'm busy Serge."

"If I do that he's just going to order you to his office. What's up?" she asked inquisitively.

"He ripped his ass with me. Let him think about it." Without another word I turned to my desk and finished logging in my rounds. I heard the phone ring, and then I heard Deloach say that I was on the wing, and she would give me the message. I looked over at her and waved her off. She smiled at me, and resumed doing whatever it was at her desk.

On my return to Don and Wriden's cell, I held my keys so that they wouldn't jingle as I creped down the tier. Most of the inmates were out at yard or at their work and school assignments, so the few of them who were in their cells hardly paid me any mind. Five cells before Don and Wriden's, were all empty and with no one to tip them off to my creeping, I posted up in front of the cell next to theirs. I could hear Don's and Wriden's conversation over the music unfolding from their cell, it was Bone Thugs and Harmony's "War and Peace". I thoughtfully keyed open the empty cell that I was standing in front of, and ducked inside of it.

"What the fuck did I do man?" I heard Wriden angrily ask.

"Did you fuck Jones?" Don angrily asked.

"Hell naw and why would you think that? And if I did go up in her, what the hell does that got to do with you? Are you fucking her?

"Naw, naw ain't nothin' like that. I just thought that if you had touched it you run the risk of making the cell hot. You know I can't have 'em up in my mix, with what I'm doing." Don said in an apologetic tone of voice.

I listened to how Don cleaned it up and I had to admit that I was impressed at his forty-two fake. But I also knew that Arthur Wriden was no dummy, he was just staying out of the way. And I felt a little bad about having played him like a pawn in the game. I really have to look out for him, make it up to him.

"You didn't have to steal on me first, you could have just asked me. I ain't feeling her like that anyway man."

"Hey, I apologize, I just lost it that's all, now let the shit go." There were several moments of silence, and I started to ease out of the cell, when Wriden spoke again and I stopped.

"Apology accepted; but you don't get to just steal on me. I need that." No sooner than Wriden spoke, he and Don were fighting. I stepped from the cell to stand in front of their cell and found them in mutual combat. The sound of men fighting in prison always reminded me of the sound that gorillas made when they beat their chest in anger. There were no words, just the squeaking sounds of their tennis shoes on the concrete cell floor, and the pounding of their fist striking one another.

"Hey! Hey! Hey! Knock it off!" I shouted.

Tag was down the gun tier in a flash; his riffle at the ready. Don and Wriden had separated in the moment that it took me to see Tag standing behind me.

"I got this," I told Tag, who acknowledged me with a nod of his head.

Don got on his rack off of the cell floor, while Wriden moved over to the sink and begin washing blood from his mouth.

"Am I gone have to go code one?" I asked them.

"Naw we straight," they each simultaneously said.

I un-keyed the cell door, "Ford, I want you to take it to the front of the wing and wait for me there."

Don exited the cell, and walked down the tier to the wing front.

"Come here, Wriden let me look at your mouth man."

"I'm good Officer Jones." He said.

"Yeah I know you are. Come here anyway though and let me check you out," I ordered.

Reluctantly Wriden let me look in his mouth. "Aw shit Wriden, I know you're not going to tell me what jumped off and so I'll tell you where it goes now, you need stitches. Go over to the M.T.A's and see Ramirez. Tell her that I sent you, okay?"

"Yes Ma'am." Wriden walked out the cell.

"Tag, do me a favor and 1020 Sally. Tell her that inmate Arthur Wriden is in route, e.t.a in ten minutes."

"Got it," Tag said and walked off.

I met Don at the wing front where he was waiting. I told Joy what had happened. I got her to cover for me and I ordered Don to the diet kitchen. As I escorted Don through the Central corridor, it was mostly empty of inmates. I was walking two paces behind; but close enough that what I said to him was out of earshot to anyone else that might be listening.

"You're a fucking prick you know that?" I softly said to him.

"And you're a fucking bitch," he softly snapped back over his shoulder to me.

It was all clear when we entered the diet kitchen, and Tubbs hurried un-keyed the little room door, with Don filing straight into its darkness.

"You got twenty minutes girl," Tubbs said to me as I filed past her into the room with the door locking closed behind me.

I made my way through the maze of boxes in the darkness, back to where the bed was. I was right on Don's heels, and as soon as we reached the little clearing, into the rays of sunlight that shined through the frosted window above the bed.

Don turned around without any warning and grabbed me around my throat, pushing me back against the wall. Starring into my eyes the grip of his hands around my throat relaxed, as he began to softly kiss my mouth while I unbuckled his pants. I lost all track of time, and our movements became one and then we were both completely naked standing in the dark.

I already had the condom in my hand when I reached down and grabbed his stiff dick, and began to put the condom on it when he suddenly pulled away.

"No," he said.

"But it's for your protection and mines," I told him.

"I'm safe. I haven't had unprotected sex in ten years what about you?"

"I've only done it once, back when I was a teenager in high school." He took the condom from my hand and threw it to the floor.

"But what if I get pregnant?"

"Then lucky me!"

He again stepped close to me and took my face in his hands as he lovingly kissed me, while looking into my eyes. I caressed his dick in one hand and his balls in my other as he begin to first suck on my bottom lip, then my top lip, and finally my tongue. His hands moved down the sides of my face, to find each of my breasts. I threw my arms around his neck and wrapped my legs around his waist to find him effortlessly up inside of me. My back pressed to the wall, he held my ass cheeks in his hands while slowly stroking me. He sucked on my neck his rhythm unbroken as he told me he loved me, and that he didn't want to share me with any other man, He sat me down on a stack of boxes and I leaned back on my hands as he slipped his arms beneath the backs of my knees, and held my thighs apart with his hand around my waist. I watched him sliding in and out of me, the rays of the sunlight glistening off of my feminine juices on his dick with every stroke. I felt him penetrating me deeper than any man had ever before him, and I threw back my head, closed my eyes and let myself go.

I felt one of his hands rubbing my lower back, while his fingers dipped between my butt crack, as I found the nipple on one of my breast in his mouth. My pussy begin constricting on his dick and he begin to moan my name, as I felt my climax slowly build from deep within me at a place that I had never known, and I heard myself moaning, "Oh God" over and over again.

I felt Don lean back and spread my thighs wider apart, as he raised my legs higher and thrust himself even deeper inside of me till my pussy jumped like never before. It was the sweetest pain that I had ever felt, I thought the head of his dick was banging against the bottom of my pussy, and I didn't want it to ever stop!

And then I saw the first flash of light, and I knew what was going to happen next. I never heard the door to the little room open just before the blinding white light closed in on me from all sides out of nowhere.

My senses slowly returned to the feel of Don leaned over me, his arms wrapped around my waist and his face pressed against my breast. I could feel his every exhaled breath against my skin as his breathing slowly returned to normal. And then I saw her; Deb was standing there in the shadows with her arms folded across her chest.

At first I couldn't believe what I was seeing until she stepped into the light and walked off without a word. And for the first time in my life, how someone else thought of me didn't matter.

As Don and I got dressed, he told me that he acted in the foul way that he had because he was jealous.

"Being denied you just gave me a whole new appreciation for you. I know you got to do you in pursuit of your riches; but I want something more from you than what we have Sessie."

That was the first time he had ever called me by my first name and I had told it to him a long time ago, I thought "and what more is it that you exactly want from me Don?"

"In all candidness I want you to be my queen if my standing is good enough to be crowned your king... I got my paper partially right; I'm about to go before the Parole Board with my own privately retained attorney. I mean fucking with you the game has been really good to me and its un-denied suitability before the Parole Board this time. I got a solid foundation to stand on a Writ of Habeas Corpus."

"All that sounds good; but the reality of this is, to have something more than sexual relations with you would call for my walking away from this whole prison life and living as normal civilians do."

"And what's so wrong with that?"

"What's wrong with that is this? Nothing is wrong with that. I know that you're pushing for me to get out of the game, but on the real how would we survive once you got out of here? You ain't been doing nothing except prison hustling for over a decade."

"True that. But my time hasn't been wasted on the rehabilitation tip, I've learned several vocations and I'm certified in all of them and getting bonded at any one of them is a guaranteed Federal protection. Is that good enough?"

I faintly heard the page over the PA system for me to 1021 Cypress Hall, and I had a feeling that it was nothing more than Russell looking for me. Russell had become a situation; a fatal attraction and I was going to have to try and bow out of his bullshit gracefully, I had given that old adage in the game of all money not being good money, a whole new meaning. And I was cool on him. That page over the PA system had become the final factor in my decision to get out of the game, to get out of everything.

Now both dressed, I located the condom that Don had discarded and I saw him watching me through the corner of my eyes as I saved it to one of my pockets.

Don took me gently in his arms and just hugged me for a moment, before looking into my eyes. "I'd like you to give us a chance Baby; I fell in love with you the first time I saw you. I know where I can see myself in ten years from today, and that's with you as my wife, the mother of my kids, my best friend in a life together, up against all odds blessed by the grace of God... so where do you see yourself?" he asked me in earnest.

For the first time I saw the gold chain around Don's neck; and noticed the small gold piece crafted into the face of Jesus with its crown of thorns, and diamond stone set eyes that was draped from his neck. I took it in one of my hands, and its eyes shimmered by the sun's rays shining through the window, with a twinkle of life.

"I'm going to be handing in my resignation at year's end; that's another three months from today. You have till then to lock your foundation down; to amass all the paper you can get your hands on before then. I've been pulling the adverse documentation from your C-File bit by bit over the past several months, and loading it up with positive chrono's to give you the best chance at the Parole Board... I've got you."

He just stood there watching me; his expression one of disbelief, as I walked off.

"Shake that dumb-found look off your face, and bring your ass on out of here man; their looking for me," I told him.

Don laughed as he hurried up behind me, grabbing me about my waist and kissing the back of my neck. I heard myself giggling with an ease that I hadn't known.

•••

Escorting Don through the corridor on our way back to the Wing, as we passed Central control, we came upon the I.S.U squad in their full intimidating presence. Lieutenant Zimmerman, Sergeant Ali, C.O's Big Buddy Cox and Antony Solece, with their new Timber Sheppard dope sniffing dog. The muzzle that the dog was wearing made it appear as menacing as their black patch insignia.

I never looked at Zimmerman as I passed him, but I could sense that he was staring at both Don and I as we passed. I couldn't help but make eye contact with Sergeant Ali; and every time I had done so, I got the same feeling that her oil black eyes were windows into her absent soul. But this time she slightly smiled at me in a way that no one else could have noticed, and I glimpsed something very warm about her, something that was strangely friendly to me.

Back on the Wing, Deloach told me that Russell had been blowing up her office phone looking for me, and each time she had shook him off of me with an explanation that she had me running some errand or another.

I found Deb, Velasco and Joy on peter gaze control down by the showers as was expected. Measuring dicks at shower time had become our most prized secret past time, as most of the men had come to enjoy it as well. Lucy Velasco had changed after her experience with Schwartz; she didn't really hustle on the job anymore, and she only rose to her full Ho' hustle potential in geddowns away from the prison. For the most she no longer had conversation for other Officers outside of those of our clique, and no one except me knew that the money she was now pulling down, had fell way off from her position of number one go-getter, to a mere drop in the bucket; but I wasn't telling.

"Lucy, look to the showers down at Long dong silver, I think he's the winner by a dick-head for the day, what do you think?" Deb softly said for all of the women to hear.

Lucy ducked the question for the most; her body language said to me, that she wasn't really into it anymore, where before her ordeal with Schwartz, she was the most vocal of us all. She and Deb use to always compare Black and White dick sizes, and Lucy was always pumping the once you go Black you never go back old saying, after having been introduced to Black sex by the clique.

On more than one occasion I caught Deb looking at me in a way that was brand new to me, and I got a funny feeling that she was avoiding me. I had made up my mind to tell her while we were on the trip that I would be resigning from the department and returning to school.

"Hey Sis," I said to Deb out of ear shot of anyone else.

"Hey yourself."

"Are you okay; I mean, you seem distant?" I inquired.

"I'm straight –just keeping my priorities in perspective," Deb answered in that tone of voice she got whenever she had something on her mind.

Before I could get in her head, she walked off and avoided me the rest of the day, which turned into the rest of the week.

Chapter 35

The weekend came, and I packed lightly for the trip at sea aboard the Vesta. I had found myself looking forward to it. Russell had blown up every phone number he had on me and I just needed the distraction of the cruise to get away from him, if nothing else.

I had arrived at Marina Del Rey and boarded the Vesta before any of the other members in our clique. My first impression of the Yacht was that it came from money longer than Russell's. The thing that stood out most about it, was it had a helipad aboard it for landing helicopters. It carried jet skis and four lifeboats. It was a lifestyle of the rich and famous ship for real.

Our host, the big shot record executive came to my quarters and personally greeted me. The party's theme was "Pajamas or nothing", so he was already wearing his PJ's and a smoking jacket. I let him watch me change into my extra short nightie with matching G-string and stiletto heels. His smile told me everything that I needed to know, about my choice of outfit for now.

Ivon was a really nice guy who lived life to the fullest as the ultimate playboy. He had amassed a billion dollar fortune in the music industry, and it always amazed me how a White guy knew so much about Black music. Rhythm and Blues, hip hop, jazz; he knew it all and he taught me that there was no such thing as Black music, White music or Latin music, but that all music was just music, because it was an universal thing that belongs to everyone in the world.

Ivon, was a really handsome White man with intelligent eyes that was so blue they shined like polished glass. His teeth were white as porcelain, and you would never believe him a sixty-year-old. He smoked the sweetest tobacco from a beautiful pipe and he loved listening to women talk; he valued their opinions, and didn't have a prejudiced bone in his body. It was Ivon who pointed me in the direction of some of the clique's most profitable investments and told me I could come and work for his company if ever I wanted a change in careers.

"The Helicopter will be arriving and departing the whole trip through, ferrying guest to and from the Yacht, and I want you to enjoy yourself. Everyone will be allowed shore time to get in some shopping and what not, all along the coast," Ivon told me, just before he kissed me and ducked out of my cabin.

In thirty minutes we were under way, and as soon as we were out on the open ocean, I ventured above deck to find none other than the Isley Brothers performing their classic ballet "The Voyage to Atlantis' for all of their, pajama garbed fans. My whole clique was there among the rich and the famous, and I couldn't help but think how crazy this would go down in the tabloids.

Ivon took Deb, Lucy and I on a tour of the Vesta; it was his way of telling us we were his for the trip, which was how it always went whenever we attended one of his events. The Yacht was a virtual floating palace that was built for an Arabian King, whom Ivon had purchased it from.

The yacht had twenty-five state rooms, crew quarters and two master suites. Ivon had Deb, Lucy and I move into one of the master suites with him where we listened to brand new never before released music from some of the hottest artist in music. Ivon had us give him opinions on what we thought would be a hit record or not. We made love to Ivon over and over again and I was amazed at his stamina, at his sexual appetite. Ivon genuinely enjoyed us and he always kept us to himself whenever we partied.

We dropped anchor in Santa Barbara California, and Ivon splurged on a shopping spree for our whole clique, that he placed me in charge of. Every time I looked at his American Express Card I couldn't believe that the damn little piece of plastic was worth a half a million dollars.

There were about twenty other women who went to shore, but we only knew some of them from other parties held by Ivon, are they were the actual clientele of love for sale. The men were all off doing whatever the men were doing.

"Girl, that phoon-tang of yours is a whole new meaning of a gold mind." Deloach joked as we shopped in one of the Santa Barber boutiques.

"I don't think we be this well off, if it wasn't for you," Yizar chimed in.

"Who you tellin'; hell every night I pray Sessie's pussy stays tight," Tubbs clowned.

Laughter unfolded from our group. Except for Deb; who was quiet and distant. She hadn't said much to me since I saw her standing in the shadows of the little room in the diet kitchen, watching Don and I. But I was going to get at her before the trips ended.

"I wish I knew your secret, so that I could package it and sell it to women all over the world," Mendez said with a nudge of her elbow to Velasco.

"Oh, I can tell you what it is, it's that nasty walk that girl got," Ramirez said.

More laughter followed from everyone with Joy saying, "Yeah, she walk like her phoo-nanny so good, that she wants some of it for herself.

The joking continued all the while we shopped, and it just served to make things all the more festive. I could see that Lucy was having a good time, but still she was different; not distant like Deb, but reserved with her outgoing personality and I made a mental note that I was going to speak to her as well.

•••

Back aboard the yacht Deb, Lucy and I were having Lunch topside along with several other groups, who were all taking in the sights of the watercraft as we moved out into the open ocean. We weren't twenty minutes out to sea, when a helicopter flew from out of the horizon and landed on board the Yacht.

Ivon lite up with the helicopter's arrival, and I knew there was someone aboard very important to him. Ivon, excused himself from Deb and Lucy then requested of me to join him in greeting the new arrivals.

We walked on to the stern as the new arrivals disembarked from the helicopter. He was an Arab dress in traditional Caftan of white silk, piped in gold. He wore a head dressed of white silk, wound by a band of the same gold piping. A golden sash about his waist supported a jewel and ivory handle dagger fashioned from gold. And his feet were covered in fashionably chic, golden threaded slippers.

His skin was the tone of polished copper; his features sharp and hawkish, with eyes as dark as night, yet filled with life and a smile as bright as sunlight. He was everything that romantic movies portrayed of Arabian royalty.

Two massive bodyguards accompanied him; each dressed in expensive European cut suits. One of them carried an attaché case. I could immediately tell that Ivon and this man had a genuine affection for one another, and they were very happy to see each other.

"Your highness, so glad you could join us," Ivon said to the man as he extended him his hand.

"Ivon, pleasures all mines my brother," the Arab responded in an Oxford educated accent as he affectingly embraced Ivon, with a mock kiss to each of Ivon's cheeks.

The Arab gesture to the bodyguard carrying the attaché case, who in turn opened it, and extended it out to him. The Arab removed the diamond covered Rolex watch that he fastened onto Ivon's wrist, and I figured it to be worth every bit a hundred K. As Ivon marveled at the watch, sunlight hit it and its diamonds flickered like fire burning on Ivon's wrist.

"I picked it up from a Swiss jeweler on my way through Bruni, and its supposed to be a one of a kind piece so let me know if you see another, and I'll have my men behead the scoundrel." The Arab said with a grin.

"I'm afraid I have nothing of equal value for a man who has everything," Ivon replied.

"Oh but you do," The Arab stated and then looked in my direction.

Ivon caught the Arabs gaze, and then looked to me with a smile. "Miss Sessie Jones, may I present to you Prince Afayat Bindar of Atari."

"Hello," I said as I extended my hand out to the Prince.

Prince Afayat took my hand in his, and kissed the back of it as he slowly looked me up and down. "Thank you my brother," the Prince said to Ivon, and then offered me his arm in a chivalrous gesture and a bright smile.

I slipped my arm in his, and that was my introduction to one of the richest, most educated and wealthiest men in the world. Prince Afayat was just forty years old and in excellent physical shape. I found him to be the ultimate conversationalist as he taught me about Atari; a little know monarchy in the Arabian Peninsula that couldn't be located on most world maps.

Prince Afayat Bindar had put his Oxford education to use, in improving the living conditions of his countrymen. He used his degree in geology to locate the eighth largest reserve of natural gas in the world, and then used his degree in business marketing to sell it. With the blessing of his father the King, he created a free healthcare system for all of his countrymen, clean public transportation, and a free educational system that allowed everyone an opportunity at an Ivy League University.

Prince Afayat Bindar, had over saw the modernization of his nation with equal rights for women, religious freedom and a complete absences of poverty. He worked hard and played even harder as an international ladies man of leisure, that perfect gentlemen would enjoy discussing world political affairs and finances.

I loved his zest for life, and he loved my performances of the latest dances to all of his favorite Michael Jackson tunes. And after all that dancing, we showered together before ending up in bed where we lied naked alongside one another.

"What would you say your highness if I told you that the best thing in life is its coincidences?"

"I would say that there are no coincidences; only divine destiny and here is where ours intertwine," he answered.

With that said, I slipped the condom on his hard dick and then I straddled him, taking his dick in my hand, guiding it inside of me and slowly sliding down on him until he filled my pussy.

"I need you to just relax your Highness, and allow me to do all the work." I told him as I rested the palms of my hands flat on his chest, and leaned forward closer to him.

"Ivon phoned me all the way in Atari, and told me all about how a man could feel you literally tug at his soul," he said with a broad grin.

"Oh he did, did he?"

I tightened my pussy muscles as I slowly rose on his dick, and then relaxed the muscles as I slid down on him again. "Close your eyes; rest your arms outstretched at your sides and listen to my voice," I commanded him.

I told him to slowly inhale as I tighten my pussy muscles while rising on his dick, until nothing of his dick remained in me accepted its head and then I again relaxed the muscles as I slid down on him with his exhaling. Our rhythms together was immediate; his breathing in time with my strokes and squeezes.

I began emptying my thoughts to him in none stop whispered conversation, in ways that proceeds his country made from the sales of their natural gas, could be invested in other diversified consumer goods that his people could manufacture, that would insure his countries financial future.

The more I talked while riding him, the more ecstatic he became; I felt his dick spasm inside of me and I knew that it was the approach of his orgasm. I paused, the motion of my hips with him deep inside of me, while the flow of my conversation continued none stop as I rubbed his face in my hands and let his climax subside.

I resumed the motion in my hips in a new left to right direction, as I slid my hands back down to rest flat on his chest, while I continued the squeeze of my pussy. I followed the lessons that I had learned in the sex education encyclopedia's I studied. And I controlled the sex for three hours, when Prince Ayafat Bindar cried out in orgasms so loud his body guards kicked in the master's suite door with their guns drawn, right in the middle of my milking his nuts under the squeeze of my pussy.

"I'm okay, I'm okay," Prince Bindar yelled out to his bodyguards.

Flushed with embarrassment, the bodyguards gracefully bowed out of the room, as I collapsed on top of him; both of us laughing. His arms wrapped around me, as we lay like that for several hours of sleep together.

...

The Prince and I had sex several times-- never really leaving the suite and we had forgone the anchor in Monterey Bay electing to stay aboard the Vesta and have more sex. Prince Bindar was so impressed with my insight into business, that he had offered me a job in his country as an Investment Advisor at an annual salary of a million American dollars starting. If it wasn't for Don, I would have take the job and left with him. But Prince Bindar told me that the job would be there for me, if ever I wanted it.

I awoke to discover that a feast had been laid out but the Prince had departed for business abroad during the night. There was a note on the bedside nightstand of gratitude from the Prince, along with his private phone number. A small Tiffany store gift bag sat on the nightstand; I picked it up, and it was immediately heavy to me for such a small bag. I opened it to find a woman's version of the watch that the Prince had made a gift of for Ivon, along with a banded stack of brand new hundred dollar bills that read a hundred-K.

I sprang from the bed and hurriedly secured the watch and cash. I sat there naked and drifted off in thoughts about nothing in particular, as I dined on the spread that the Prince had prepared for me.

I then showered, freshened up and dressed in a white Chanel pantsuit. I was done. There would be no more sex for me on this trip. I took a stroll onto the second tier of the stern and stood under the first deck facing the sun, looking out onto the open ocean. I thought about my future under the silent power of the yachts engine, when I looked up to find Lucy Velasco joining me. At first we both just admired the beauty of the ocean view, until I turned to Lucy and tightened the belt of her robe about her waist.

"Sessie."

"Yes."

"I won't be going back to the prison."

"What do you mean Lucy?"

"I quit. I submitted my resignation papers Friday before we left, and I sold my condo two weeks before that."

"But why?"

"I bought a restaurant in Arizona, and tomorrow when we get off of that private jet I'm driving away and never looking back."

She hugged me goodbye with a kiss to my cheek, then turned and walked away without another word. I stood there looking towards the lights along the distant shoreline. As the fullness of what Lucy just told me registered, I knew that she was going through it after that whole episode with Schwartz and I took her move to be just another sign that it was time for me to push off into better things for myself.

Lucy hadn't been gone ten minutes; I turned and looked to find Deb setting at a table on the sterns first tier. She had heard the whole exchange between Lucy and me, this I was certain of.

"How long have you been setting down there in the dark?" I called over the guardrail to Deb.

"Long enough." Deb replied.

I descended the spiral staircase down to the sterns first tier, and sat at the patio table with Deb. At first she wouldn't even look at me.

"What's wrong Deb?"

"You tell me Sis."

"Okay then. I know this may come as some surprise to you, but I decided to walk away from the business let you take over the bookings." I waited for her to respond but she didn't, so I continued. "I can still oversee the investments for everyone, but I'm done with the dating, the drug trafficking, and come the year's end I'm resigning from this whole prison thing all together."

"You too, huh?"

I didn't answer her.

"What the fucks wrong with you? Are you serious? we're getting far too much paper right now to get out of the game. Why would you even want to give up a good thing like what we got going here, Sessie?"

"Don and I are going to get married."

Deb angrily leaned back in her seat, folded her arms across her chest and looked at me long and hard.

"Don and you."

"I've retained an attorney to represent Don in his next parole hearing and if he's not outright found suitable for parole, then we're going back to court on a Habeas Corpus... I'm going back to school; I'm going to work a regular job, a job like normal people. And I'd like you to come with me Sis."

"You are out of your fucking mind. What do you mean work a regular job like normal people? Take a look around you; normal people don't live like this, so fuck normal. What's gotten into you Sessie? or let me rephrase that; this trick ass Don has gotten in to you with some bullshit ass fairytale about running off to never, never land with Peter Pan and living happily ever after."

"I've taken us as far as we could go in this criminal thang, and if we're in it to win it, then we have to get out of it while we're ahead Deb."

Deb sat in silence for what seemed the longest stretch of time, but in actuality it had only been a matter of a few minutes. And when she broke her silence; her voice cracked as she spoke.

"I tried my best not to interfere with your relationship with him, but if you step out on us, the whole operation will shut down and you know this. It's not fair to me nor the other girls, so it's now come down to this Sis, it's us or Don. And I don't think Deloach is going to take this lightly. If she knows that Don has gotten in the way of her income, you know what I mean." Deb's eyes whaled up with tears that overflowed, and streamed down her cheeks.

"Now hold on Deb, don't fucking go there with the bullshit. You could get somebody hurt if you put this out there like that," I angrily whispered.

"Somebody's already hurt Sessie, hurt that you put a loser before our sisterhood," Deb said as she wiped her eyes.

I reached across the table for Deb's hand; but she pulled it away from me, then got up and walked away. My first instinct was to go after her, and tell her that I would never forsake her; but I figured it best that I just let her cool off first.

Chapter 36

Deb obviously had told no one about the conversation that she overheard between Lucy Velasco and I, because Lucy's abrupt resignation without an explanation had stumped everyone in our clique except Deb and I, while it had created rumors of every kind by other Officers and inmates alike.

While back at work, I was still ignoring Russell's repeated request to see me, and now Deloach was beginning to quiz me about him. I hadn't figured out just how I was going to wean Russell off of my pussy, and gracefully bow out of the business with Deloach. My own dilemma was beginning to give me an appreciation for how Lucy just upped and shook the spot, but then she didn't have Don to be concerned with. Deb was completely avoiding me at work, while working all the overtime that she could. And when she was off duty, she wouldn't answer her phone. She was thoroughly pissed off with me like never before, and I was beginning to find myself wondering if she was angry enough to feed Don to Deloach in the preservation of the game.

The next morning I arrived at work to find Lucy Velasco standing out in front of the prison near the prisoner's release area beside a chauffeured limousine. She was dressed in a black, cashmere military style business suit adorned by gold, braided ropes and other decorations. She wore a beret style hat of black leather that was broke down low over one eye-brow; with black leather gloves tucked down the belt front of her uniform. She held a riders crop in hand, and the pant legs of her uniform were tucked in thigh high leather horsemen riding boots.

As I sat in my car watching Lucy, no sooner than I wondered what could have brought her back to the prison, from out of the prisoners release area walked G-Fly dressed in a beautiful, blue doubled breasted business suit. The two waved at one another, and then he turned around looked at the prison and flipped them off. She opened the limo's rear door, as he started walking towards her and jumped into G-Fly's arms, planting kisses all over his face; her legs wrapped around his waist, as he walked to the limo and got into the back seat with her.

"You go then bitch, with cha bad ass," I thought as I watched the limo pull off.

I could feel the charge of whispers generated by Lucy's curtain call on the game, as it coursed through the whole prison. The bitch done that; she did it her way, and it was so fly that anything negative said about it, wasn't nothing but hate.

When I made my way to Don and Wriden's cell, they were sparked about the talk with G-Fly and Lucy, the whole Wing was. I released Wriden from the cell to report to his job assignment, and then I told Don that Deb hadn't took it well about my checking out of the game.

"I love you for standing by me; and just know I got you baby. We gone be alright," Don said resting his hands on the cell door bars.

"Please, don't ever make me regret this. I love Deb; she's my sister, and someday I have to make up to her because I'm all she has that's real in this life. But right now, she knows that I've been keeping my relationship with you from her."

"You –we got to live our lives for us baby. I mean I know Deb's your girl –that you got the whole sisterhood pact thang going, but that don't give her power over who you can and can't love, or what choices you can make based on our love."

"I know that your right and I'm good with it; but can we talk about something else?" I said.

"Yeah baby. Peep, the strangest shit happened to me last night."

The expression on his face made me forget all about the issues with Deb.

"What was it?"

"I woke up to find the Warden and his Goners just standing in front of the cell door watching me," Don said as he looked off in thought.

"What did they say?" I nervously asked.

"That's just it, they didn't say anything. They just walked off."

Without another spoken word, I left Don standing there and went over to B-Wing where I found Deb supervising a couple of inmates whose toilet had over-flooded and they were mopping and disinfecting.

Deb's expression conveyed her surprise at seeing me walking towards her so fast.

"Deb, I need to holla at you."

Deb took several steps back, until she was out of ear-shot of the inmates cleaning the cell, and I got close enough in her face where only she could hear me.

"What the fuck you need to holla at me about? you made your mind up to cut off our bloodline on that boat so whatever you're selling, hell I'm not buying nor am I even interested in it at the least," Deb said in a dismissive tone.

"I know that you're mad at me Deb; but I just wanted to know, did you speak on me and Don to anyone?"

Deb face masked into a frown.

"Miss me with that bullshit, get the fuck on Sessie. You and that broke ass nigga don't mean that much to me, that I would take any time out of my grind to speak on either one of your names."

"Deb, stop acting like you don't care about me, when we both know you –"

Deb interrupted me before I could finish, "excuse you Miss lady, don't talk about me acting like I don't care when it was you who were the one that showed just how much you cared about –uh – bitch, and that's fuck me. And to add insult to injury, you want to insinuate that I'm some kind of snitch. Bitch get off my line with that shit."

"Deb, I didn't mean it like that. I'm just asking because the Warden is on me right now, and I need to know what's going on, so I know what to do. Please Deb, don't trip on me right now I need you," I pleaded with her.

Deb angrily reared back with her hands poised on her hips. "Don't trip on you? Oh you need me? What about when I tried to express that the team and me needed you Sessie? All I got out of you was fuck us, I'm rolling with Don. Well roll on Sessie, I got nothing for you."

Without another word, I walked up the tier and paused for a moment turning around to look at Deb and mouthed "I love you." But Deb just waved me off.

When I got to the Wing front, I found Russell accompanied by all four members of the I.S.U squad as they escorted a small tour of four women and six men; that were down at the prison from corrections headquarters up in Sacramento. With the tours moving down the first tier of my Wing, Russell eased over to where I was standing.

"Officer Jones, why hello," he said in a cheerful voice.

"Hello Warden."

"I've some documents in my office that require your signature. And that being the case, I'll need to see you come your mid-shift break, uh hu,"

Russell stated as he walked off to catch up with the tour.

I trailed behind the tour, part ways of the tier and stopped in front of Katie's cell as I watched them continue on about their way out of view around onto Deb's side of the Wing. I looked up and caught sight of Joy standing on the second tier talking across to Tag in the Gunners cage.

"Hey Miss Thang, what's on your mind girlfriend," Katie asked.

My thoughts were racing with wonder as to what kind of paperwork that Russell could have for me to sign. I shook my head in a gesture of not having anything on my mind to Katie.

"Well honey, I know that I got man problems look, and you got it; you shouldn't but you do," Katie said.

I could see that Katie's cellie was gone; but I needed to be sure before I started talking.

"Where's your cellie?"

"Officer Joy released him on a ducat to see the eye doctor; he's getting tested for glasses, and that shit takes all day. So, what's on your mind girlfriend?"

I got Joy's attention still upon the second tier talking to Tag in the Gun gage.

"What's up?" Joy called down.

"I'm going to be in one-twenty-three doing a cell search."

"You need me to help you?" Joy asked.

"No, I'm good."

I gave Joy our hand sign for keeping watch for me, and she knew what to do if anyone came on the Wing that shouldn't be. With that I un-keyed Katie's cell door, and stepped inside. Shutting the cell door behind me I sat on the lower bunk beside Katie. I really needed someone to talk to and it was always easy for me to talk to Katie.

"I fucked up Katie; I lost my sister and best friend, all because I decided to step down from the game and put this prison life behind me. But that's just what Deb –Officer Bovaise wants me to think she's tripping about," I told Katie as tears begin to well-up in my eyes, and stream down my face.

"I could sense the tension between you and your girl. Maybe you should just let a little time pass, and see if the situation rectifies itself –heals itself, you know?... what do you think your girl is really tripping on?" Katie asked me in earnest.

"It's about Don –you know, Don Ford upon the third tier."

"Damn, I knew Miss Velasco was knocking down G-Fly on the under; but you and Don too, I didn't see that one."

I looked at Katie inquiringly.

"I mean ain't nothing wrong with dude; he's straight. Like G-Fly and a couple more Africans up in this piece, they got real street potential and I don't think that certain dudes will ever get caught up again when they get out of here. I heard Officer Joy call your boy Don out for an attorney visit earlier; I've been --."

"You did," I cut Katie off.

"Yeah girl."

I looked at my watch; it was time for my break.

"I got to go see what's up with that" I told Katie.

Don wasn't scheduled for an attorney visit; they were by appointment only, I knew because the daily movement sheet always reflected that in the ducat section and I checked the D.M.S. first thing every morning when I arrived on the Wing. It was my job to know who moved where, and when they moved. I stepped from Katie's cell, gave Joy and Tag the all clear sign and hurried off to the Wing front.

No sooner than I got to the Wing front, and sat at my desk to check the D.M.S. to see if Don was listed for having a scheduled attorney visit, Deloach stepped from her office and ordered me to the Warden's office.

"This is not an order you can ignore Jones. What's going on?" She asked me in a concern tone.

"Same as always Sarg ... Sarg, did you know if inmate Ford was called to an attorney visit?"

"Yeah, I got a phone call about thirty minutes ago from the visiting Sergeant, and I had Joy release him."

"Thank you Sarg." I said to her on my way out the Wing.

I reached the visiting room and found no sign of Don. I checked the visiting room log, and the Sergeant had logged the time of Don's arrival and departure. So I just assumed that he had ducked out to the yard and I would catch up with him later to learn the details of his surprise attorney visit.

I made my way to Russell's office all the while hoping that he was not calling me to have sex with his ass, because I was done with that and there would be no going back. I knew early on going into the Ho' game, that one of its major draw-backs was that married clients could get so into you, they sometimes would fall into crazy delusions of mistaking you for their woman. They'd get pussy for sale twisted with some weird sense of ownership.

As soon as I arrived at Russell's office, I saw no sign of anyone except for his secretary, who directed me to go straight in where I found Russell seated at his desk with his hands folded together resting atop it. He was wearing his prescription reading glasses, peering over the top of them as he slowly looked me up and down.

"Close the door Officer Jones, thank you please," he commanded.

As soon as I closed the door I could sense that something was very wrong. He was sweating profusely. And then I caught glimpse of movement to the left of me where I looked over to find Don beyond the open door of another room. He was lying face down on the floor bleeding. The I.S.U. Officers Big Buddy Cox and Antony Solece was standing to either side of him; both wearing their black leather gloves.

Don had obviously been badly beaten; his face and lip were swollen like a seriously botched Botox job. And his eyes were beaten closed to a point where he couldn't see, but I was sure he recognized my voice. Looking at the two Goners, I knew that they hadn't beat Don because he would have been in far worst condition than what he was. I figured they must have just held Don while Russell beat him; sense Russell was the only one sweating. That was my academy training talking to me again.

Another door off to my opposite side opened and out walked Lieutenant Zimmerman and Sergeant Ali. I could tell by her black shifting eyes, that this was all new to her as it was to me. Sergeant Ali posted up near me while Lieutenant Zimmerman walked over and stood behind Russell's desk beside him.

It took every bit of self-control that I had in me, not to go over and comfort Don. I could hear his moans of agony and I wanted to hold him in my arms and call for help. But my training had come all the way into play, and I was now looking for a way to take control of the situation. The Goners were poised over Don like a pair of pit-bulls, ready to attack on command.

Russell stood up from his chair; a shit eaten-grin unfolding on his face, as he walked over and stopped in my face. He suddenly grabbed me roughly by the chin in the palm of one of his hands and squeezed my cheeks really hard.

"So what the hell were you thinking? Did you honestly believed that you and that clique of whores you congregate with, could come up in my house and operate your own fucking brothel, without giving me my entitled thirty-three and a third of every dollar? You fuckin' slut," he angrily stated through clenched teeth.

He waited for me to speak; but I said nothing. I was lost in thought, evaluating the situation for my best option on how to proceed in gaining the upper hand.

"Nothing moves in here without my say so. The only reason why I allowed you –all to last this long, was because I had taken a fancy to the way you suck me off," he said, and then pushed my face back so hard until my neck jerked.

The rage had now gotten the best of me. "As much as I took a fancy to butt fucking you with your little strap on rubber dickey," I said.

The tension immediately relaxes in the room, as the Goners all kind of snickered at my retort. Russell hadn't expected that to be my come back and it was very possibly a window into my upper hand on the situation. I had the Goner's attention now, and I had to keep it while I thought of a way out of this for both Don and I.

"You were a business arrangement, just like all of the other business arrangements that you write down in that secret black book of yours," I said.

I could tell by Lieutenant Zimmerman's reaction to my mention of the journal, that I had bought myself an audience with them; that the game had just change. The looks from big Buddy Cox and Antony Solece at Lieutenant Zimmerman told me that I had their attention as well. But Sergeant Ali was altogether an entirely different matter; I couldn't read her, or the journal just had no meaning to her one way or another.

"You sit in that big chair of yours, and the further I ran my finger up your asshole while I was sucking you off, the more you told me about helicopter part deals and tax schemes between you and who, read right from that little black book."

I spoke with so much rage in my voice that Russell stepped back in disbelief.

"Well the shit is over with you bitch. As for this low-life criminal that you forsook me for –your man, well I've been known to break lesser men," Russell said.

He walked over to Don, and kicks him in the rib cage with such force, that the blow rolled Don over onto his back and caused him to cough up blood. Russell placed his foot on Don's throat, slowly applying pressure till Don began to gasp for air.

I felt a sudden sense of desperation; my mind was racing, and I could hear the pound of my own heartbeat, the blood coursing through my veins causing my temporal to throb under the pressure. My throat was suddenly dry and it was hard for me to swallow.

In one swift motion I freed the switch blade from beneath my protective vest; the same switch-blade that I had carried for protection since high school, and I heard the click as it popped open, as I lunged for Russell. I saw the fear in Russell's eyes before I reached him.

Chapter 37

A non-stop ringing filled my ears and grew louder inside of a strange, pitch darkness that made no sense to me. I could smell the strong aroma of fresh roasted almonds. I was dreaming, and then came a sharp sense of pain, mixed with several voices all heard speaking at once. What they were saying was at first unclear to me and then I saw it. A distant point of light coming for me out of the darkness; it was quickly closing in on me, and it was that light which carried the voices. I opened my eyes and with every blink of my eye lids, my situation became clearer. I had been knocked unconsciousness and the voices I heard were those of the Goon squad, as I laid with one side of my face pressed to the shag carpet floor in Russell's office. I was on my stomach and I could feel my hands cuffed behind me.

My vision cleared to reveal Don lying on the floor across from me, and I could see that he was still breathing. I sighed in relief that he was okay, and I was thankful to God. Antony Solece, rolled Don onto his stomach and as Solece cuffed Don, I heard the mechanical clicks of the metal tighten around his wrist.

"Ten twenty-one Ad/Seg, with one in route," I heard Zimmerman say. It was Big Buddy Cox who radioed in Lieutenant Zimmerman's directive.

"Get this piece of shit out of here," Zimmerman said. I watched Big Buddy Cox and Antony Solece each take hold on one of Don's arms; effortlessly lifting him up between them. He was too weak to stand, so the two giants carried him from the room, his feet dragging across the floor between them.

Lieutenant Zimmerman bent down in my face. "Nap time is over; wake up in there," Zimmerman said to me with a clap of his hands in my face.

Zimmerman grabbed me roughly by the back of my collar with one hand and by the back of my utility belt with his other, and suddenly snatched me up from the floor to land on my feet. He then sturdy me by the grip he had on the back of my uniform collar and lightly slapped both sides of my face with his freehand, allowing me to shake off the wooziness I felt coming on.

"Jones, you're in serious trouble here. But we can fix it; tell me where this tender dick flat foot, bourgeoisie asshole here keeps that journal, and we pawn all your troubles off on the convict," Zimmerman said.

My head began to throb and I felt something crawling down one side of my face, followed by the thump of drips onto my chest. I looked over to see that it was my own blood, as I realized for the first time that I was seriously injured.

"Let me help you out in your decision making," Zimmerman said. He suddenly and roughly whirled me around to see Russell lying on his back along the carpet with my knife stuck in his chest. There was a circle of blood around the knife and he was obviously dead; his eyes agape in deaths stare everything went pitch dark again.

I next regained consciousness cuffed to a gurney in inmate Central Health, being treated by McCoy, who was stabilizing me for transport to an outside hospital by an awaiting ambulance.

"Sessie if you can hear me, just move your right finger," McCoy softly instructed me. He was nervous; his eyes shifting about the room at the unseen. I could hear indistinguishable conversations, and I recognized Lieutenant Zimmerman voice, but not those of several others. My situation had changed; I no longer felt the immediate threat to my life that I had earlier, but I knew that Don could very much still be in danger or dead.

My head begin to throb like I had been hit by a freight train. I tried to move it but I could feel that my neck and head were in some kind of brace that was tied down to a wooden board between the gurney and I. I moved my right finger to the relief of McCoy, who got down really low and close to my face as he worked on me.

"Don't try to speak," McCoy whispered. "Just listen, I need you to act as incoherent as you possibly can, to anyone but your own lawyer... some foul shit is at play here, and black patch has dropped you right in the middle of it. Stay cool; I'm going to call your mother."

I wiggled my right finger, and closed my eyes to rest. I could hear McCoy barking off orders, and I felt the gurney moving as I began to playback in my mind, what happened in Russell's office. I wasn't sure if I had stabbed him or not; but it didn't feel like I had. I momentarily blacked out again.

I awoke in the ambulance, and I saw McCoy riding along while the Paramedic was attending to me, as he called off my vitals into a phone.

"I have an African American female with head trauma, loss of blood, in and out of consciousness with no response to voice commands. BP is one hundred over fifty; pulse is ninety-eight, respiration is sixteen, age early twenties. The patient is a Chino State Prison employee where injury occurred. Approximate injury time reported to be fifteen hundred hours. I'm starting an I.V drip 5w 5000cc's. Our E.T.A is nine minutes out."

Then the Paramedic spoke to me, "hold on Miss Jones we will have you at Chino Valley Medical Center here shortly."

"Sessie, I.S.U. is right behind us; who else can I call besides your mother?" McCoy asked.

I don't know why; but I thought of Dickerson. "You can call James Dickerson at the Sheriff's Testing Center and tell him what my situation is," I said to McCoy.

"I got it; but what the hell happened?"

"I'm not sure, all I know is I was summons to Brennen's office where I found inmate Ford –"

McCoy cut me off, "Ford is okay; I secured him on a one fourteen D lock up psych eval, that keeps black patch at bay for the next seventy-two hours. After that, I'll have medical so far in Ford's mix that Black Patch won't be able to get near him without medical being present."

I was relieved that McCoy had secured Don, and now I was free to concentrate on my next move. And so, I told McCoy some of what I could in front of the Paramedic, hoping that would jar my memory or help me figure out what next to do. One thing was for sure, so long as I was the only person who knew where Russell's journal was hidden, I was safe from Lieutenant Zimmerman and his Goons.

"I found inmate Ford with the hell beat out of him, and Warden Brennen was trying to crush Fords throat – with his foot man. He was standing on his throat. I pulled my knife out on him, and all I remembered after that is waking up on the floor in handcuffs."

"Well their saying you murder Brennen."

As soon as the ambulance arrived at the hospital, the emergency medical team took over, and the Goon squad had no access what so ever to me. By the time the medical staff had done their thing, it was lights out all over again.

I was dreaming about pushing my Porsche at full speed along PCH in a race with a Lamborghini Diablo that was kicking my ass when I awoke in a private hospital room, with both my hands cuffed at my sides to the guardrails of a bed. My vision cleared to the sight of Zimmerman and Sergeant Ali, both seated at my bed side. My head felt large as a beach ball, and the pain was so bad it made my eyes water.

Zimmerman glanced over the top of his newspaper at me, and folded the paper as he got up from his seat without a word. His expression told me that I looked as bad as I felt. The smell of almonds was gone; now there was only the smell of antiseptic and disinfectant, that hospital smell that people complained about. For the first time in my life, I knew exactly what they disliked.

Under the cold stare of Sergeant Ali, Zimmerman leaned close to me before he spoke in a soft, menacing tone.

"For two days you've been off in La La land, while I've had to fend off every son of a bitch and your whining ass Mama, to get this wrong right that you've gotten your ass ensnared in girl. Now, I'm gone say this again; tell me where that fucking book is and this all goes away for you. The boyfriend gets the murder; hell, I'll even put you on my team, should you decide to stay on the job. What's it gone be?"

"Boss, it's her Mama again," Antony Solece said.

I cut my eyes to see him and Big Buddy Cox both guarding the room door.

"Arrest the bitch for impeding a Peace Officer in the performance of the Officer's duty then," Zimmerman snarled.

"She ain't by herself this time," Big Buddy Cox said.

"Well arrest who she's with as well," Zimmerman snapped back. And then I heard it; that familiar smug tone of voice that I knew all too well, and I smiled to Zimmerman.

"Captain, James Dickerson of the Los Angeles County Sheriff's Department Special Investigation Unit."

Zimmerman angrily walked over to the room door.

"If you know where the journal is hidden; do not tell Zimmerman what you know. If you don't know, then keep pretending like you do," Sergeant Ali whispered to me and then she walked away to the door.

It took every ounce of strength that I had in me, to turn my head so I could see the door. Past Sergeant Ali, Lieutenant Zimmerman, Buddy Cox and Solece, I could see Dickerson, he was wearing one of his penchant expensive European suits, holding his gold star outstretched in front of him for all to see. He was with three other conservative dressed White men, who were obviously Officers of the law as well. And then there was my mother, Mac and a tall Black man wearing a purple suit.

"Captain whoever of the Los Angeles Sheriff's you're a little out of your jurisdiction here, and I'd really appreciated it if you give me some operating space. Now get lost," Zimmerman said in a demeaning tone.

"Didn't I speak to you over the phone?" Dickerson asked Zimmerman.

"That you did."

"Well sir; my jurisdiction has been expanded," Dickerson countered.

"Yeah, by who?" Zimmerman asked.

The youngest of the three other White men with Dickerson removed his credentials from his inner suit coat, and extended them out to Zimmerman followed by the remaining two White men.

"That would be Federal Agent George Hardimen, with the Department of Justice. And these are agents Cooper and Smith.

"By the powers vested in me from these guys; I'm ordering you and your people to vacate this room, before you find yourself in a pissing contest with the Feds," Dickerson arrogantly stated.

"Agents are waiting for you downstairs to take your statements; but you first get those goddamn irons off of her, unless you are arresting and charging Miss Jones with a crime," Agent Hardiman said.

Zimmerman stormed out the room, while Big Buddy Cox and Antony Solece waited for Sergeant Ali who was removing the handcuffs from my wrist.

"Mr. and Mrs. Jones both you and your Attorney can visit your daughter now; we'll be waiting outside, until council grants us access to his client," Dickerson said.

Sergeant Ali walked out the room, and continued with Cox and Solece behind Zimmerman, as Yorkie, Mac and the Attorney all moved into the room. Dickerson winked at me as he closed the door for privacy.

The tears began to flow from Yorkie's eyes before she had gotten into the room good, and the sight of Mac's hugging her for comfort seemed as natural as if he really was my father. I could tell by their expressions that I looked horrible. Dickerson referencing them as Mr. and Mrs. was not missed on me.

"How are you Baby?" Yorkie asked.

"I'm ok Mama," came my raspy reply.

My throat was so dry that I could hardly find my voice.

"Sessie girl, this here is Mr. Richard W. Brown; he's an attorney, and a personal friend of mine. Now, I done took care of every thang; and you can trust him like you trust me. I've been around some hairpin turns with this here old-boy, that we both came out of on the other side thicker than thieves," Mac said.

"I need to know everything from the top down, through to the finest detail," Mr. Brown said to me.

Mac poured me some water in a cup with a straw, and held it for me while I drank as I told Mr. Brown, everything about what was going on in the prison, and Mr. Brown kept looking from me to Yorkie as if maybe she shouldn't be hearing what was being said. I told Mr. Brown that I didn't keep secrets from my Mama and Mac. I went on to convey to Mr. Brown, how I was Warden Brennen's mistress and how he showered me with expensive gifts but he wanted more from me than I was willing to give him. By the time I had finished telling Mr. Brown my story; he sat there in silence, with a dumbfound expression.

"Man, that's simply the most fascinating shit I ever heard," Mr. Brown said.

I couldn't help but laugh at Mr. Brown's response; but the sudden pain that erupted in my head, had shot through my whole body killed all that.

"Okay this is what we gone do; you tell the Fed's about the affair with the Warden; all of the things he told you, the beating of the boyfriend Don, and about the journal, but you don't tell them where it's hid, because that's my trump card," Mr. Brown directed me.

In that moment the doctor and his aide entered the room, and I learned the extent of my injuries along with everyone else. I insisted that the doctor also allow Dickerson and the Feds into the room to hear what he had to say. "You suffered several fractured ribs as a result of blunt trauma; most likely from being kicked. You sustained a major blow to the head that fractured your skull, and caused swelling of the brain that created some cranial pressure that caused you to suffer blackouts. So we had to perform emergency surgery on your arrival to release that pressure which resulted in your lapsing into a mild comma for the past two days.

Of course we had to shave off your hair; but it will grow back, there are twenty-three sutures that will leave you a life-long reminder of this, but it won't even be noticeable once the hair grows back. You'll need to remain here for a week in the recovery process; so you'll be fine Miss Jones.

You're very lucky. Whoever beat you, very well could have killed you."

The doctor was suddenly paged on emergency, and he excused himself. By this time Yorkie was so overwhelmed by what I had endured, that Mac had to take her out of the room and comfort her leaving me to speak with the Feds.

I told the Feds exactly what Mr. Brown had instructed me on, and as I spoke their whole focus became the journal; it was what they were after all along, and they told me that they had an agent deep enough inside of the prison that their agent could retrieve the journal if only I would tell them where it was.

"Miss Jones, as you well know, that journal names, some very powerful officials and describes in details their involvement in various criminal enterprises and you knowing exactly where it's hidden, places you in a very unique position with the U.S. Government," agent Hardimen said.

"Are we speaking in terms of a position so unique that prosecutorial immunity from all charges is on the table?" Mr. Brown asked.

The room was quiet for several minutes. I could see agent Hardimen's mind was racing. And then Dickerson smiled at me, dropping his head and shaking it in amazement. I liked Mr. Brown. He was confident, but then his black ass had to be, to be caught dead in that purple suit. But more than that, I knew he was very good.

"Yes Mr. Brown. Unofficially at this point, prosecutorial immunity from all charges is open for discussion at the most, a reduction of charges in the least," Agent Hardimen says.

"So that we're clear here I'm talking about the death of Warden Russell Brennen, correct?" Mr. Brown asked.

"All things are negotiable if she could put this journal in my hands," Agent Hardimen answered.

I closed my eyes and rested while they went on talking and I allowed the sleep to come as my mind healed itself.

Coming soon Book 2...

" *Hearts of Steel*"
(The impossible Fight)

Acknowledgments

This book was inspired by my **childhood sweet-heart;** who is presently incarcerated in one of California's State Prisons. If he had given up his search for loving me; I would never have come to know myself on this level of life. And that is, knowing all things can be achieved *'if you let go and let God"* His encouragement and support will always be cherished.

Thanks to **Johnel Langerston and Val Lara at Phatefx** for the bookcover design, my flyers and for extended your location for the release party. Much love to you fellas.

Big Thanks to **Elexis W. from Model Chicks**, I look forward to you gracing the next book cover with your beauty. Good luck and big ups to your company Model Chicks...

Big Thanks to **LaShai C**. for being such a great model and extending your time and beauty on the cover of this book. May God bless your career as he has your voice; we all look forward to getting your album when your time comes to shine.

Big Thanks to **Adriene B. (A.K.A) AB** for being such a great model on the cover of this book and extending your beauty and support to this project. You are a genuine friend and I could not have pulled this off successfully without your added support. May God grant you everything you need in this life, because you are always so giving of yourself to others... Much love to you.

To My Big Homie **Big Daff...** Thanks for the support; your big heart will continue to take you far. I'm so bless to have you as a friend; they just don't make them like you... much Love.

I'd like to thank my dear sister **Gloria VanVactor** who put up with my being frustrated during this book process. She has given monetary and motherly support my whole life. I could not have completed this whole project without her. Thank you Glo for everything, Love you for life, your baby sister/daughter☺

Thanks to my sister**, Sister Rose (The Cake Lady)** for gracing me with loving support, her cakes and for being the first to purchase a book. I love you for believing in me.

Thanks to my big brother **William (Crow),** your support sure blessed this project and I want to thank you for allowing me to have been able to depend on you.

Thanks to my sister *Patricia* for helping out with this project, your support meant a lot to me and I thank you for the time you put into it.

Big Thanks **to all ten of my sisters and brothers**. Mom told you guys to take care of your baby sister and you have all done just that, I'm sure she's proud of you all. Much love for ever...

Thank you to my best friend *Yvonne,* God brought us together many years ago to be friends. Through all the ups and downs we both went through in life, we have been there to show each other, that Sister Love is strong and anointing between us. I thank God that he has covered us both. Love you.

To my oldest son *LaVance (A.K.A) G- Fly*; you've stood by me and supported this book and party the whole nine, I could not have asked for a better son. Thanks for gracing the cover of this book with your fly swag. May God bless your Rap career; you are so talented and such a hustler that you are bless to be rich, so go for it all, the world is yours ☺ My life I owe to you forever… Love Mom

My second oldest son, *Jeffrey (A.K.A) Yung Fly;* I am so thankful for the good son that you are, no matter what! You have always come to my rescue and never once complained even when I had another child that took your title as the baby ☺ don't worry, You will still be treated as the baby. My life I owe to you forever… Love Mom

To my youngest son, *Brenden (A.K.A Young Tsunami),* Life has many bumpy roads that can cause you to be side tracked from the things that are important. You are so young and yet so intelligent that those bumps in the road should never detour you from reaching your highest heights; You must stay focus for God, for me and for yourself. My life I owe you forever…Love Mom

To my only daughter *Rickie Jae* and oldest child, God has blessed me with one daughter and because he gave me one, I was able to give you the world I'd only dreamed of having when I was a little girl. You are so beautiful and intelligent, yet spoiled but disciplined. I never could complain about the way you've carry yourself throughout your life, I can only brag about how classy of a woman you are… Always know your worth and embrace the fact that God has blessed you with so many richest in life. Find yourself and you find the key to open more of you. My life I owe to you forever... Love Mom

To my *grand-daughter Naomi (A.K.A No-No)* who is the love of my life. God has poured many blessings upon me in my life time, and you are the cream of the crop. I never thought I would ever embrace begin called grandma until you spoke those very words. And now I wouldn't have it any other way. I'm Grandma' and proud of it... I owe my life to you too... Love Your Gam-ma

To *Tim M*, there's not much I need to ask from God for you, because of your God fearing and strong believing in him, encourages me to want to be as spiritual as you are. Thank you so much for your support. May God continue to keep you in his good grace... Much Love

To My Best Friend *Carnellia L.* who believed in me day one and showed support the whole nine... I'm thankful that God has put you in my life to remind me how good friendships could be.

www.ingramcontent.com/pod-product-compliance
Lightning Source LLC
Chambersburg PA
CBHW071230250626

47163CB00001B/122